Black Widow

Written By:

D. D. Hairston

Black Widow
Copyright ©2021
DD Hairston
Love Lee Unlimitedbeinglovelee@gmail.com
ALL RIGHTS RESERVED

☐ No part of this book may be used or reproduced in any manner whatsoever, electronic, or mechanical including photocopying, recording, or by any information storage without the prior written consent of the publisher and author, except in the case of brief quotations embodied in critical articles and reviews.☐

☐ This is an original work of fiction. Any reference or similarities to actual events, real people, living or dead, or to real locales are either products of the author's imagination or intended to give the novel a sense of reality. Any similarity in other names, characters, places, and incidents is entirely coincidental.

Contains explicit language and adult themes suitable for ages 16+

DEDICATION

This has been a long year, and it would have been impossible to get through it without several people. I wrote this book over a year ago and was not ready to release it because tragedy kept entertaining my world. I am so appreciative to Queen Jean for keeping me grounded, G-Lew for giving me a reason to keep moving forward, Eric for giving me a reason, the boys just for being my heart, mind, and soul. Most of all, All Praise To The Most High for not giving up on me.

SYNOPSIS

In Melech's mind, he had an amazing life. He married his college girlfriend, started a Hookah Lounge with his best friend from high school, lived a comfortable life, and had a fairly decent relationship with his parents. What more could a Black man in Los Angeles want? Roses don't grow from concrete, and spiders creep up on you.

A "DEAR MELECH LETTER" turns his world upside. The woman he never thought he'd have to share spins a web of deceit that ensnares everyone Melech loves. Melech quickly leans no one in his life can be trusted, not even his best friend! The once beautiful, supportive, loving wife veers into a mastermind of hypocrisy and revenge. Until Leana feels gratified, everyone's life is in peril.

CHAPTER ONE

Melech walked into the house and threw his keys and phone on the table that sat in the home's foyer he shared with his wife Leana. He was sweaty and in desperate need of a shower. Melech started every morning with a protein shake and a run at Kenneth Hahn Park. If he missed either one, it set his whole day off. Melech was a creature of habit, consistently doing the same things daily. You could set your watch by Melech's routine. Rarely did he cross over the line. It was the one thing Leana found attractive about Melech when she first met him. She knew what Melech was going to do at all times and where he would be. Most men she met in college were ready for a good time but had no direction in life, nor did they have a major by their sophomore year. Not her Leek. He was at UCLA for a business degree, and he wanted to invest in his own business once he graduated.

"Le," Melech called out to her as he entered the kitchen. Usually, Leana was waiting on him-starting breakfast before they headed out for work or started their day. He opened the refrigerator, grabbed a cold water. "Baby," he attempted to get her attention again. She did not respond to his calls. Melech drank his water as he headed up the stairs. Their room was empty as well. He sat the nearly empty water bottle on the dresser and went into the bathroom the two shared. It was unusual for his wife not to be home after his morning run. Melech turned on the shower and undressed. He decided to call his wife once he washed the morning's jog off of his body. Melech let the warm water take over his sore, muscular physique. This was the most soothing part of his day, clearing his mind and preparing himself for the days' pressures. Running a business was not as easy as he made it look. Melech kept a smile on his face, a positive attitude, and spoke kind words on most occasions. The first year he opened his Hookah Lounge with his best friend Levi, money came fast and furious. But, keeping the cash coming in took hard work. Word of mouth was not enough to keep the doors open. Continually bringing in customers was essential. Levi loved being on the floor and entertaining everyone, he was a showman. Melech had to deal with the books, orders, and advertising.

Melech turned off the shower, stepped out, grabbed his towel from the rack, and dried himself. He wrapped the towel around his waist and went back into his room. He was headed back downstairs to retrieve his phone to call his wife before dressing, Melech's mind was still on her absence. This was out of character for Leana. For the first time, he noticed a letter sitting on his side of the bed, propped up on his pillow. Melech sat down and opened it, thinking it would explain that his dear wife ran out to the store or something trivial.

The once confident, masculine, well-put together man crumbled as he read the letter written by the woman he loved deeply. His chiseled face grew weary, and tears fell from his deep-set slanted eyes. Melech clinched his strong jawline, while his full flat nose flared. He sat the letter down in disbelief. Melech could not comprehend the words that had just entered his soul. Lying back on his king-size bed, covering his eyes with his hands, the words ran through his mind.

My Dearest Leek,

I don't know how to explain my actions to you. The pain that I am about to

cause you was never my intentions. I hope that you can forgive me someday.

As much as I love you, I must leave. I find myself in love with someone else.

It is nothing that you've done. You're the greatest person I've ever known. This is probably the biggest mistake of my life, but I just want to be selfish. Do something for me. Step over the line. Do something bad and exciting. If I had to tell you this in person, I would've changed my mind because I love you so much. I know that you will hate me forever, and I understand. You are a good man.

Good-Bye, Le

Melech was filled with so many different emotions. Which one he was supposed to hold on to, he was unsure of. Pain, hurt, anger, and rage were all consuming him. The woman he gave his life to for almost ten years just ripped his heart out and sucked him void of anything positive. Melech felt a sense of emptiness. He suddenly wanted a stiff drink. Being that he rarely drank, there was no alcohol in his house. Leana kept wine to drink with her dinner. Although, Melech knew that would do nothing but give him a headache, instead of the comfort he was looking for, he took a hard pass. The urge to call Leana was beating him like a drum. Melech could not move one sculpted muscle on his body. He just lay on the bed, speculating where it all went wrong.

When did Leana have the opportunity to fall in love with another man? What was he lacking that sent her into the arms of someone new? To his knowledge, they had a great sex life. The two did not go more than three days without being intimate. Disgust flushed over Melech, realizing he had been sharing his wife with another man. A man he knew nothing about. Where did Leana meet this person? Did she even protect herself? Melech had so many unanswered questions. Leana's letter did nothing but tell him she was leaving him for another man because she wanted something new and exciting. Melech had ample opportunities to be with other women, yet never gave it a second thought. He was devoted to her. Leana was all Melech needed in a woman, so he thought. All these years, Melech thought he was considerate to his wife and her feelings. He thought they were happy. Up to this point, Melech was comfortable in his marriage and truly in love with his wife. Melech knew he wanted to be with Leana for the rest of his life until he read the letter. Now Melech was lost in his thoughts, trying to figure out where his future was headed. Leana was not the person he believed she was.

Leana was no longer the young girl Melech met in his junior year of college. Or maybe she's the same, and he did not look deep enough inside of her to see it. Melech was attracted to Leana's fire and the survival skills that she sustained. Leana lost her mother while she was still in elementary school and worked hard to get a full scholarship to UCLA. She had a way of helping Melech let his guard down. Leana was playful and spontaneous, keeping him lighthearted when Melech was getting stressed over life's endeavors. To him, Leana was his better half. She was what balanced him. Now Melech was shattered and broken by the woman he loved with every ounce of his being.

The day Melech met Leana, she disrupted his life. Melech started his day as he normally would with his morning run around UCLA's campus. He wanted to get back to his small apartment and shower when he was almost run down by a tiny woman on a bicycle. Melech was upset at her carelessness, but when she yelled at him for being in her way, Melech was stunned yet slightly amused. He tilted his head to the side, baffled at the anger she was displaying.

"You cannot be serious right now." Melech glared at her.

"Umm, yes, I'm very serious!" she exclaimed. Leana pulled her helmet off, allowing her hair to fall down her shoulders. "Pedestrians don't always have the right of way, you know?" She put her hand on her hip. Melech had to smile at the way Leana was challenging him.

"You are aware you're riding a bike on the sidewalk?" he sarcastically asked her.

"Well." Leana tossed her hair back. "You were still in my way, and I'm late for class," she huffed.

"You're telling me that your tardiness is my problem?" Melech teased her. Leana's soft brown eyes softened, and a smile came over her face.

"Are you being a smart ass?"

"Hey, you damn near ran me over then told me off." Melech put his hands up in the air.

"My bad." She shyly told him. "I overslept and haven't had my coffee yet. This girl lives for her caffeine," she conceded.

"Tell you what…" he fished for her name.

"Leana."

"Melech." He reached his hand out to her. Leana just looked at it.

"When your class is over, Leana." He flashed her a smile. "How 'bout I take you for that coffee you desperately need?" She pulled her phone out of her back pocket, checking the time.

"Why not now?" Leana offered. "By the time I get to class, I'm going to miss more than half of it. I'll get the notes from one of my friends."

"I need to shower." Melech looked down at himself. He was still drenched from his run.

"You're fine." Leana rolled her eyes at him. "By the time we walk over to get our coffee, you'll be dried up." She giggled.

"And funky!" he added.

"Then you can only go up from here." Leana gave him a flirtatious smile.

"You going to run me over with your car next time?"

"That's cute. You're a funny guy." She halfheartedly joked.

Melech kept Leana in his life from that day on. It was the first time he deviated from his routine. Leana took him out of his comfort zone. Deep down inside, Melech loved that about her. His dad was a straight shooter, influential, resilient in everything he touched. Kaden was Melech's role model. Disappointing his father was not an option for Melech. A clear plan was set in motion for Melech at a young age, and he followed it to his father's expectations. His mother, on the other hand, was a famous soap opera star. She, too, worked hard and was very disciplined. Leana brought a lighter side into Melech's life. She would stop studying and tell him, *'Let's go to the movies,'* or *'Wanna go for a walk,'* best of all, Leana would move Melech's books and do a little dance for him. His inner self wanted to protest Leana's need to be adventurous. Melech just could not deny her wants. From the beginning, Melech wanted to see her smile. It gave him a warm feeling that soothed his soul.

Levi was worried about his friend. He had not heard from Melech all day, and he had not shown up for work. He called Melech several times to no avail. After closing their Hookah Lounge for the night, Levi went straight to his house. Melech's car was parked in the driveway. That gave him a sense of relief. Levi walked into the unlocked front door. He was family and never knocked. Levi even had a key to the house. Melech, Leana, and Levi were the three musketeers. They did everything together. Levi was overjoyed when Melech decided to stay home and attend college. He dreaded to think about what he would do if Melech decided to leave the state. They had been friends since high school. Levi did not have the luxury of living in Baldwin Hills, but they both attended Crenshaw High School. The two lived entirely different lives. His mother raised Levi while his father spent most of his time in prison. Levi never felt less than Melech because his mother gave him everything that he needed, and Levi hustled for anything he wanted. Unlike Melech, Levi was known in the streets from a young age. His father was a well-known member of the Rolling 60s street gang. It was only natural for the big homies to look out for him.

"Yo, Leek," Levi shouted as he searched the kitchen and family room. He did not see anyone. "Leek?" He popped his head into Melech's office. Now the feeling of worry set back in. He rushed up the stairs, taking two at a time. Levi saw his friend lying on the bed, wrapped in a towel. "Leek!" he shouted at him. Melech turned only his head to see Levi standing over him. "What da fuck, man?"

"What are you doing here?" Melech asked in a haze. He did not know he had fallen asleep.

"Nigga, it's damn near three o'clock in the morning. Yo' ass never showed up to work, and you ain't been answering yo' phone."

"It's what?" Melech sat up, looking around his room, startled.

"Three…o'clock, my nigga. What the hell is going on? This shit ain't like you." Melech rubbed his eyes to find clarity of what was going on. The last thing Melech remembered was reading the letter Leana left him. He looked over to the side and saw her devilish words staring up at him. It all shook his soul again.

"I lost track of time." He admitted.

"You did what?" Levi was confused. This was not like the man he had known for so long. Melech was a well-oiled machine. He noticed Melech looking down at a piece of paper sitting on the bed. He went over and grabbed it. Melech tried to snatch it back, with no luck. Levi stood and read the letter that Leana left for her husband. Levi's heart raced. His mocha skin turned flushed, and his green eyes became dark. Levi sat on the bed next to his friend, stroking his goatee. The right words did not come to his mind. "Fuck!" Was all Levi could muster. The two sat in silence for what seemed like a lifetime.

"Yeah," Melech finally said.

"Have you talked to her? Do you know where she is?"

"Nope."

"She just left this?" Levi held the letter in the air.

"Yup." Melech had no answers to offer Levi. He felt so embarrassed over the whole thing. After only dating Leana for three weeks, Melech introduced her to Levi. He warned him that Melech was moving too fast with a girl that nearly ran him over, then blamed him for the entire ordeal. However, Levi accepted Leana into the fold, nonetheless. That was the only warning Levi ever gave Melech. Leana just clicked with both of them. She became a best friend to Levi soon after. When Levi came up to the school, she hung out with them, and when Melech went back to the neighborhood to hang out with Levi, Leana was shotgun. They always had a good time around one another. Leana also gave them their guy time without complaining that they spent too much together. She understood that they were like brothers. Neither one of them had any siblings of their own and had forged a bound like no other. Levi had his own place, his bachelor pad he liked to entertain at. He still spent a lot of time at the house with Melech and Leana. When they decided to open the Hookah Lounge together, Leana was on full board. Melech was a little skeptical about telling her. He was sure Leana would want to be his partner. It was a relief for Melech that she did not interfere with their childhood dreams to go into business together.

Levi had been his own businessman since Melech met him. He was a small-time weed dealer. Never getting too *big time* fearing he'd end up in prison. Levi made an oath to Melech not to go to prison or get a record the way his father had. Melech knew he had ties to his hood and would say, *"cuh"*, from time to time. You could lead Levi into a life of entrepreneurship, but you could not take the neighborhood out of his heart. Melech had hung out in the streets with Levi now and again while they were in high school, and he understood the excitement of it all. It was always a good time hanging around Levi and his homeboys. Melech never forgot about Levi's father doing a twenty-five to life prison bid. That was the downside, and Melech could not see giving up his freedom for a night of fun and laughs. He was going to make sure Levi did not do the same thing with his life.

At Crenshaw High, they made a vow to start their own business and answer to no one. Once Melech graduated from UCLA, the two started the Hookah Lounge, catering to mostly the college scene. It took Melech's fathers to help get the liquor license, but they were up and running, doing well.

"I don't know what to say," Levi solemnly told his friend.

"What can be said?" Melech felt the whole ordeal was unfair. He never thought he'd ever have to share the woman who was supposed to belong only to him with another man.

"Put some fuckin' clothes on, Cuh yo' shit is hangin' all out staring at me and shit. A nigga ain't feeling safe sitting here with yo' ass." Levi needed to lighten the tension in the room. Melech gave a half-hearted laugh.

"Your ass is stupid, man." Melech went to his closet and put on a pair of shorts and a white T-shirt. When he emerged, he noticed Levi rereading the letter again. Melech had replayed the words over and over in his mind, and he still could not understand it.

"I still can't believe she's gone and for another man."

"I...I..." Levi stuttered over his words. "Never thought she'd leave you."

"Neither did I, brother. Neither did I." Melech sat down on the bed. "I thought we were happy." Levi wanted to give his friend some type of advice. Say anything to make all of this go away, he just could not. Levi wanted to slip away, but he knew the one person who always believed in him and stood by his side no matter what was suffering. Levi knew that his best friend would have his back faster than his own hood would. But being next to Melech, was causing him a great deal of anxiety.

"It's not you, bruh."

"Yeah." Melech found that hard to believe when his wife fell in love with another man, she left him for. Somehow, he fell short. Melech could not figure out where it all went wrong.

"You gonna be okay?" Levi asked, still looking at the letter.

"Eventually. I just wish I saw this coming. Had some type of warning, you know?"

"You gonna call her?"

"Nah, I don't ever want to see her again. I'm going to have what she left packed up and moved to her father's place."

"You're done just like that, man?" Levi was surprised at Melech's response.

"She fucked someone else while she was married to me. If Leana just kept it to herself." Melech stroked his beard, shaking his head. "I'll be fine. My wife fell in love with another man. I'm done."

"You can cut the girl off just like that?" Levi finally looked over at his friend.

"Whatever, Levi. Fuck her and everything I thought we had. You know, I have always been faithful to that woman. You just don't walk away from a man who gave you everything because you found some random dick. So, yeah. Fuck her!" his voice elevated. Levi was not convinced of what Melech was telling him. He knew Melech was angry and hurt at the moment there had to be some love left for Leana.

"If you say so."

"Would you take her back?" Melech looked at Levi.

"Don't ask me that, man. I'm not in yo' place." Levi shook his head. "I can't tell you nothin'."

"Cause she's your friend now also." Melech was trying not to feel betrayed.

"Come on, bro. You all up in yo' feelings right now." Levi tried defending himself. There was so much more to the story than Melech really knew, and Levi wanted out of the conversation. "You know that girl loves you."

"No, Levi. She fell in love with someone else and left me for him. You read the fucking letter!" Melech yelled at him.

"You right." Levi did not want to argue with Melech. This was not the time. He just wanted to keep his friend at all costs. "Just remember it has nothing to do with you. You, the greatest dude I know. No matter what happens with all this. Leek, you a good man."

"Just not good enough for my own damn wife," he smirked. Melech gave Leana everything, his love and a ring. She left him wanting to lie down and die, but Melech's pride would not allow him to cry. He knew somehow, he needed to get over Leana's betrayal.

"Nah, man. Leana ain't good enough for you." Levi hung his head low. "Ain't no one quite like you, bro." He got up and walked to the door of Melech's bedroom. "This ain't about the type of man you are, Leek, you straight, man. Always remember that." He walked out, leaving Melech with his thoughts and the *'Dear Melech,'* letter.

CHAPTER TWO

Levi could not wait to get to his car after visiting Melech. First, he was worried about his friend, then the whole thing sickened him. As soon as he turned the corner onto La Brea, he pulled his phone out of his pocket and called Leana, putting her on speaker. She picked up on the third ring.

"Hello," she groggily answered the phone.

"What the hell, Leana?" Levi yelled at his phone.

"Well, hello to you too, Levi."

"I just left, Melech."

"Oh, he told you?" Leana did not like the way she left things with her husband. She knew if she had to face him, she wouldn't have had the nerve to walk out on him. Try as she might, Leana could not say one bad thing about Melech. He was so good to her. Melech gave her the direction in life she needed. He put the drive in Leana's heart to be the best person she could possibly be. Leana's selfish desire to taste, touch, and feel Levi drove her insane from the day she met him. He had an undeniable sex appeal about him, living on the edge at all times, with a powerful aroma of danger. Melech satisfied her in every way, but she knew that Levi was the unattainable fruit that she wanted to taste. Leana held her desire for him for as long as she could. One night they went too far. Levi always made inappropriate comments to Leana about stealing her from Melech and how he could make her scream his name more times than she could imagine. On that note, Levi was not wrong. Melech made sweet love to her, and she loved how attentive he was to her every need. Levi manhandled her, and she craved the way he took control of her body.

"What the fuck do you think?" He barked at her.

"I had to, Levi. I could not live this lie any longer," Leana's voice was soft and tender. She was trying to melt away his anger.

"Yes, Leana, you could. Why would you hurt, Leek, like this? He loves you! Melech lives for you!" The fury resurfaced.

"You should have thought about that before you fucked me, Levi. I cannot get your touch out of my mind," she cooed.

"I told you that was a mistake," guilt filled his tone.

"The first time was a mistake, baby. What about the second and third time, Levi? Can you explain that? We belong together."

"No…no, we don't…" Levi hung up the phone. He hit the steering wheel of his 2017 Dodge Challenger SXT Plus. Melech always laughed when Levi called it his little snow bunny. It was the closest thing he ever came to a white girl. Levi was so disappointed in his actions. How did he allow himself to sleep with his best friend's wife? Not just once, but almost a dozen times. She was just so beautiful, sensual, and giving. They often teased each other, saying that he was going to steal her one-day. For Levi, it was a joke. Melech was so in love with Leana from day one he talked about her, maybe a little too much. Levi was envious of what they had, not jealous. He was happy that Melech found the love of his life and settled down.

Levi did not realize just how special Leana was until he felt her touch. He quickly realized why Melech loved her so much. She was persuasively sensual. Leana catered to your every need and want. Levi did not know how he allowed himself to slide down that slippery slope between friendship to lovers. Leana had a way about her that hypnotized you. A simple touch to his check sent a warm shiver down Levi's spine to his manhood. He avoided his feelings for years until one faithful day Levi came over before Melech got home, Leana was cooking dinner. She was drinking her wine and being her usual flirtatious self. It was the norm, and at first, Levi thought nothing of it. He loved his weed and smoked like a Snoop Dogg protégée. Melech was not a drinker, but for some reason, Leana had a bottle of Maker's Mark. She poured him a glass as they talked and drank while she cooked dinner. Between the weed and the alcohol, all of Levi's inhibitions had flown away like the wind. Before he realized what he was doing, Levi was knee-deep inside of his best friend's wife. As good as she made him feel at the time, Levi was filled with guilt and rushed out of their house before Melech made it home.

He wished he could say that was the only time it happened. But, Leana made him feel so good Levi dibbled and dabbled a few more times. Each and every time Levi told Leana this could never happen again, it did. The last thing he ever wanted was for Leana to leave Melech for him. No matter how much he would love to make this goddess his woman. She belonged to his best friend, his brother. Levi was torn. Should he tell his long-time friend that Leana was the most manipulative woman he knew and ruin what they had built over a decade? Or throw his friendship away and be with the woman who captured his soul? Was Leana worth losing the one person who stood by his side through thick and thin? Women were the root of all evil. Her name was no longer Eve, it was Leana.

Levi pulled a blunt from his glove box, fished through his pockets for a lighter, and blazed his blunt for some well-needed relaxation. He programmed his music to MC Eiht. The last thing Levi needed was to listen to some romantic love song. Neo had the right idea when he sang, he was so sick of love songs. Levi wanted some hardcore West Coast head banging music to clear his mind of everything, Leana. She single-handedly destroyed any small part of good in him. As much as Levi wanted to be with her, he did not want to cause his best friend and brother, the pain he was enduring. Any other time he would have stayed right by Melech's side. The guilt was eating away at him. He was the cause of torment his fallen friend was going through.

Levi turned up his music and inhaled his blunt, driving down La Brea, trying to make it back to Crenshaw. He shut his thoughts off and listened to the lyrics of Eiht's new song, *'How U Do That.'* It reminded him of a simpler time. His pop used to tell him stories when they were all young, running through the streets and chasing their dreams. Levi wished he could rewind time and appreciate the little time he had with his dad. He would have taken the time to listen to some of the things his father had told him.

The streets were his father's life, and now that life took him. Melech was the one person he truly trusted, and Levi had betrayed him. *His friend knew his residential spot*, as Eiht would say. It was too easy for Melech to come for that payback. Being this careless was not usually Levi's character. Disloyalty was not a word Levi was familiar with. It was leaving a foul taste in his mouth and an ache in his heart he did not like. *'No Reason'* came on while Levi was in his thoughts. *'OG's back, Nigga fuck yo shit. Whole-body lean from the hollows that spit,'* rang in his ears. Melech was no OG but had every right to put a hot one to Levi's head or chest. He deserved it. Levi could not smoke his blunt fast enough. He wanted to clear his mind of every sense of guilt he was feeling. The overwhelming shame overtook his whole being.

♥ ♥ ♥

Leana stared at her phone after Levi hung up on her. She was staying at the Ritz Carlton in Downtown LA. Leaving Melech was the hardest thing Leana ever had to do. It wasn't that Leana was not still in love with her husband, because she was. Her life had just become so typical, the one thing she once admired about Melech had now made life mundane for her. Each and every day was like the next. Melech woke up and went for a run, came in, took a shower, then they ate breakfast together. After, Leana left for work while Melech cleaned the morning dishes. He called her every day for lunch to make sure Leana did not need anything before he headed to his Lounge. At times Leana would have him bring her something to her office when she was seeing patients and would fall behind.

While Melech and Levi were starting a business, Leana continued with her education to get her Ph.D. in clinical psychology. She was finishing up her Internship at the Mental Health Advocacy on Wilshire Blvd. Melech came home almost every night around seven p.m. to have dinner with his wife, then headed back to the Lounge for the night rush. Leana heard him try to quietly come in at nearly three a.m. nightly, except Sundays, when they closed early. Some nights Melech would wake her up to fulfill his needs, other times he slid next to her, falling asleep quickly. The next day it was like rewinding a tape and starting it over.

Leana began to feel like her life was Groundhog's day. This should have made her a happy woman. What woman would not want a husband like Melech? He was the most giving man she had ever met. Leana lived in a beautiful home in Baldwin Hills and drove a Mercedes E-class she received as a graduation present from her husband. Melech did not neglect her and was an excellent lover. Levi was just better at everything else; it seemed to Leana. They say the grass was not greener on the other side, but for Leana, it was.

Levi was adventurous, lived his life day by day, made her laugh, and the things he did to her body made Leana need a long soak in a hot tub. It felt so good while he manipulated her into any position his mind could think of. He fatigued her, and Leana could not get enough of him. Leana found her fingers touching herself just at the thought of Levi while soaking even after having several orgasms. Levi kept telling her how wrong they were for enjoying the time they spent together, but Leana did not care. Any and every chance she got, Leana took advantage of getting Levi inside of her. He became so weak after their first time. All Leana had to do was get close enough to Levi to put her mouth close to his ear, whisper how much she needed him, or gently touch his face. Levi would grow instantly. Once Leana stroked him, Levi had her out of her clothes in no time.

Leana started fantasizing about what it would be like to live with Levi full time. She watched several women come in and out of his life, and Melech talked about the women he would pick up at their Lounge. It was starting to make her jealous. Levi had missed dinner on three occasions with them, and it all came to a head for Leana. She wanted to show Levi that she was serious about being with him. He claimed to be loyal to his best friend, someone he considered a brother. In Leana's opinion, if this were true, Levi never would have slept with her and kept it a secret from Melech. He should have told Melech immediately, and they both should have thrown her out, but he did not. Therefore, Levi had some type of feelings for her.

Hurting Melech pained Leana. They had been inseparable ever since their first coffee date. Leana saw Melech around campus a few times. Everyone knew who the athletes were. Melech strutted around with such confidence, with or without his teammates surrounding him. Even with his popularity, Leana did not see Melech at too many parties or socializing with one particular group. When she almost ran him over, Leana was surprised to see it was him. Although she was irritated at the whole situation, once he invited her to coffee, Leana knew not to let the opportunity pass her by. She never seen Melech with another girl, and the way that he dealt with her anger, Leana knew right then he was someone she needed to keep close. Any time Melech got too serious with life and his studies, Leana liked to find the lighter side Melech had in him. He could be fun and have a good time, Leana just had to draw it out of him.

She also saw it when Melech was with Levi. You could not help but have a good time while you were with Levi. She did not know how the two became such good friends. Not only did they have two different lifestyles, they were complete opposites. Melech rarely drank, and she had never seen him use a drug in her life. While Levi, on the other hand, not only sold weed when she met him, but he was his biggest customer.

On top of that, Levi chased his chronic with shots of almost anything. Leana smoked with Levi occasionally. Melech would give her a disapproving look; he would never comment on it, though. The one thing Melech did not do was try to change Leana from who she was from the day he met her. The free spirit he fell in love with was the woman he wanted to spend his life with. Sadly, Leana realized she was more suited for a man like Levi. Her Leek was the one getting hurt through it all, and that was never Leana's intention. If Levi thought he could pull away from her now after she blew up her happy home, he was sadly mistaken. Leana would give him a day to rethink his decision. If she could not have him, Levi could not keep his friendship with Melech. They would all be losers in this torrid love triangle.

CHAPTER THREE

Melech woke up and decided not to change from his normal routine. He would not allow Leana to break him. He had already spent one day grieving the loss of his beautiful, sexy, and loving wife. Melech did not know the woman she had become. He was not going to dwell on her poor decisions in life. If Leana thought there was another man that could love her the way he did, she deserved him. Melech put on his Nike joggers and Dri-FIT performance T-shirt and headed out to Kenneth Hahn Park. He made up his mind that life was not going to stop for him. It was business as usual for Melech.

After his run, Melech took a shower, made breakfast, and cleaned up his mess. He stood in the closet and eyed Leana's clothes. Melech wanted them out of his presence. He wanted anything that had to do with Leana gone. Melech did not want to admit to his parents he failed at his marriage, disappointing them was always a sore subject for Melech, but he did not trust anyone else in his home. Melech knew his mother would dispose of all of Leana's belongings for him, and he would not have to deal with any of it himself. He felt as if the space Leana once had in his heart had died. The only difference was Melech did not want to mourn his loss. He wanted no reminders of Leana whatsoever. After lengthy deliberations with his conscious, Melech made the call to his mother.

"Hello, mother. How are you doing today?" Melech did his best to sound as if life was the norm.

"I'm fine, boy. What's going on with you?"

"I need a big favor."

"I knew you weren't calling to just check on me. I'm not giving you any more money for that little smoke shop you got going on."

"Mother, I call you almost every day, so you need to stop with the dramatics," Melech chuckled to himself. His mother loved to be theatrical on set or at home. She always acted like a camera was focused on her.

"Boy, what is it that you need?"

"Don't ask me a thousand questions. Promise me!" Melech demanded. His mother was beyond nosey.

"What...what, Melech. I have things to get to."

"Do you have to be on set?" Melech knew that his mother did not film often. Her role got cut back the older she had gotten.

"Are you being a smart ass?"

"No, mother. You know that I love you." He did not want to make her angry when he was the one who needed a favor. "Will you help me out?"

"Melech, you already know I'm going to give you anything that you need. Just don't tell your father," she shyly told him.

"I don't need any money, mother!" he demanded. "I need you to come and pack up all of Leana's things so I can have a mover take them to her father's house."

"Baby, what happened? I know you two can work through anything. Marriage is a job, Melech. You have to give and take, not give up at the first sign of trouble."

"Oh, she has taken enough, mother," he sarcastically said. "Now I want her things gone. Leana walked out, and she cannot come back."

"Maybe she just needed some time to regroup, Melech. All women are temperamental. You know Leana's been through a lot with this internship. She's almost finished. Give it a minute to let her cool off. You know you can be difficult at times." Melech looked at his phone in confusion.

"Are you my mother or hers?" he asked, a tad bit angry. "If I tell you that Leana walked out on me, you should be just as angry as I am."

"I am always on your side, baby. I'm just a woman also, and I know that we can be irrational at times."

"That she is, and I don't want to see her or anything that belongs to her. So, if you don't come and pack it up, I'm going to send it all to the Salvation Army!" Melech demanded.

"Okay…okay, Melech. Calm down. When do you want this done?" she asked him.

"Before I get off of work. I will have the movers here in the morning."

"Son, I think that you are moving way too fast, but I'll be there in about an hour."

"Okay. I won't turn on the alarm. The key will be in the backyard under the cushion of the lounge chair."

"Melech, I have a key to your house. Your father and I bought it for you."

"Isn't that just great?" He rubbed the back of his head.

"Love you," she said, quickly releasing the line.

Melech made it work in record time. He parked his Escalade in his personal parking spot. He noticed that Levi had beaten him in, which was rare. Levi did not anoint them with his presence until close to opening. Melech could not deny that Levi was the face of their establishment. He just had a way with their customers. Melech really did not like to socialize too much with their clientele. The background suited him just fine.

First and foremost, he did not smoke. Levi could tell the customer about every flavor they carried because he had smoked them all. Melech felt like a hypocrite at times for making the money he did on a product he did not indulge in. He had no problems opening the Hookah Lounge. It was the *'in thing,'* and Melech did not mind capitalizing on it. College students filled the place as well as millennials. Melech's body was a temple, and he did not want to destroy it with foreign substances. He played sports throughout his youth and enjoyed every minute of it. Football was his favorite. Melech wanted a scholarship on his athletic abilities, and it served his purpose. UCLA was impressed with him and offered Melech a full ride. The problem was he got injured in his sophomore year. After surgery and rehab, Melech was never the same. His days of being the greatest running back were over and he lost his scholarship. Melech was grateful his family had the means to pay for his education. Most kids from Los Angeles would have been lost if they had been in his situation.

Melech was not born with a silver spoon in his mouth by any means. His family was what is known as hood rich. They lived in the Beverly Hills of the inner city. He was never ungrateful for what he was blessed with. Being friends with Levi showed him just how fortunate he really was. Two people from totally different backgrounds ending up at the same high school was an eye-opener for Melech. They became friend's freshman year when Melech got into a fight with one of his teammates. The thing Melech did not know is that his teammate was from Levi's hood. Melech was fearless, and the ass whooping he put on his teammate did not go down as a boyhood tussle. Melech was walking to his car after practice, and the 60s greeted him, ready for a showdown.

Levi sat back and watched as Melech dropped his bag, preparing himself to take them all on. There was no way Melech could win this fight. He was physically fit, but no match for a five on one combat. This was not a made for TV high school musical. Melech impressed Levi. Anyone willing to take a beat down like a man deserved to be saved. He tossed the Black & Mild he was puffing on and walked over to the mayhem. Why Levi felt the need to rescue Melech, he was not sure. He didn't like his style; Levi was not really a fan of jocks, and Melech fit right into that category. Everyone knew who Levi was, so it only took his word to make the homeboys back off. Melech tried telling Levi that he did not need his help.

"So, I was supposed to sit back and let them niggas beat yo' ass?" Levi asked him.

"You really think them pussies could beat my ass?"

"You a funny dude. If they can't beat you, they'll kill you, my nigga." Levi tried to enlighten him. "You ain't from 'round here, is you?" he asked Melech.

"I've lived here all my life," he protested.

"Where you from?"

"Baldwin Hills." Melech had no clue Levi was referring to which hood Melech banged.

"Like I said, you ain't from round here. You don't know shit 'bout these here streets." he chuckled. "Why you ain't in private school or some shit?"

"Why would I be?" Melech was confused.

"You rich kids don't usually intermingle wit' us poor folk," Levi joked.

"Yeah, I don't know what you're talking about. I've never gone to a private school."

"So yo' peeps tryna *'keep it real'*?" Levi used air quotes.

"I don't even know what that means."

"They rich, but they don't want yo' ass to know privilege."

"Dude, what planet are you from? I'm not rich."

"Nigga, you live in Baldwin Hills and you pushin' yo' own whip. You ain't poor!" Levi snapped back. Melech thought about the comment. No one ever told him he was rich, and he did not feel that way. He felt like a normal kid.

"Nah, I ain't poor. I'm just like anyone else." Melech shrugged.

"I have a lot to teach you, bro."

"Teach me?" Melech had to laugh. How could a kid his own age *teach* him anything? He learned soon enough; Levi would open his eyes to a while new world. The one, his parents kept him sheltered from. They quickly became best friends. Melech's mind was opened to a totally different city less than a mile away from his home.

"Why you just standing out here?" Levi interrupted Melech's thoughts. He did not even notice Levi walk up on him.

"Yeah…I'm on my way in. Gathering my thoughts. Don't want to bring my troubles into the workplace."

"I feel you, bro. You can go home. I got you on this."

"Nah, I'm good. Sitting at home will do me no good."

"Rylee is here if you don't trust me."

"Really?" Melech glared at Levi.

"It will give you time to get your shit together." It may have been the guilt talking for Levi, but he did not think Melech was ready to come back to work so soon. He could pretend that he was unbothered by Leana's betrayal, Levi knew better. They had been friend's way too long for Melech to try and fool him, but Leana leaving Melech was breaking him. He had never known Melech to love any girl he dated the way he loved her. Levi was so angry with himself for causing his friend this kind of misery. It was never his intention. The first time was honestly a mistake. The other time he slept with his best friend's wife was a real weakness on his part. Leana allowed him to take control of her body with no protest. He could see why Melech gave her everything she asked for. Her golden palace made him betray the one person he was most loyal to besides his mother.

"I need this. It will keep me busy. If I stay home, I'm just going to think about ways to kill my wife and beat the shit out of this man she fell in love with."

"C'mon man. That shit ain't even worth it. Besides, there has to be an explanation for all of this. At the end of the day, that girl loves you. I know she did some foul shit, but Le loves you. Maybe she just wanted a little change. She can be self-absorbed at times, but Leana knows there is no better man than you."

"None of that matters to me, Levi. My mother is coming to pack up all her shit, and we're done. I will never take Le back. She betrayed my trust. Let her find her bliss with whoever fucked her better than I did!" The more he spoke, the angrier Melech became.

"Who said that?" If Melech ever found out it was Levi that Leana left him for, he did not want Melech to think it was because of sex.

"She did!"

"Nah, bro. I read that letter. Leana said she fell in love with someone else, and she wanted to be selfish. Don't start adding shit to make yo' self feel better or angrier at the situation."

"Why does it feel like you're on her side in all of this?" Melech was questioning his friend's loyalty.

"Whoa, nigga. I'm always on yo' side, first and foremost. Don't eva forget that shit. I'm just tryna spit a little knowledge to yo' ass."

"Whateva, man. I got shit I need to handle." Melech pushed passed Levi walking into their Lounge. He did not want to hear anything else Levi had to say. He stopped behind the bar and grabbed a bottle of Tequila and a glass. They carried top-shelf alcohol in full view, yet rarely served it. There would have to be a scheduled event for that. Most of these young patrons were not willing to pay the price for it. The off brand would have to do for now. Melech understood why people wanted to drink their sorrows away. He had not dealt with any until now.

His heart was broken, and Melech did not know how to mend it. He did not want to hear anything Levi was talking about. When you love someone, you just don't treat them bad, make them feel this sad. Leana was not supposed to share what was his with anyone else in the world. They took vows, which, he was realizing, meant absolutely nothing to her. If Leana needed to spread her wings, then go butterfly go. Melech knew the shelf life of butterflies was short-lived. When Leana was at the tail end of this freedom life cycle, she could not come running back to him. You could burn Melech once, and that was fine. She had already gotten her pass.

When he met Leana, Melech was unaware of the boyfriend she had at NYU. She broke it off with him once she realized Melech was the man for her. That was strike one. Sleeping with another man and leaving him was strike two. Melech was not going to allow Leana to hit him with that third strike. He was liable to take Leana's life. No matter how much love Melech had for Leana before he read the letter, it was not worth giving up his freedom. Even if a jury of someone else's peers would completely understand why he choked her until the life went out in her eyes.

Levi knew that he should have followed Melech inside to ensure he was okay. His words could say anything to convince others that he was fine. Levi could see the truth in his face. The more time he spent with Melech, Levi knew he should come clean. Losing his friend was not worth it to him. Leana tried calling him first thing in the morning, but he let it go to his voicemail. He was not ready to talk to her. Levi was livid that Leana would hurt Melech this way. It was strange to look at the situation when they both destroyed everything, once they tasted that forbidden fruit. He decided it was time to make that call. Levi sat in his car, pulled out a blunt from his glove box, and lit it up. Inhaling several puffs, calming his nerves before making the call to Leana. She picked up on the first ring.

"Levi," she quickly said into her phone.

"Take yo' ass back home and make this shit right with Leek!" he demanded.

"No, pleasantries?" she asked him.

"Fuck, nah! This some shady shit, you just pulled on my boy."

Sooo, while you had your hands all over my body…weren't you being shady? When you had me bent over slapping my ass…were you being loyal?" she sarcastically asked. Levi socked his steering wheel. He hated that Leana was right.

"If you weren't such a whore, the shit would of never happened!" The words came out before Levi could stop them.

"Really, Levi?" The words stung like satan's bath water. "I wasn't in this alone," Leana tried to keep the pain out of her voice.

"No, Le you weren't, but I kept trying to end it, and I would never, ever try to purposely hurt Leek. You did that! Your selfish ass walked out and told him yo' ass slept with someone else. No fuckin' man wants to hear that shit!" Levi tried explaining the obvious to her.

"Levi, we belong with each other. I know you are feeling the same thing I am," she tried pleading her case. "I didn't want to hurt, Melech, Levi, really I didn't, but I can't keep living this lie, and neither can you."

"Go home, Le. You and I will never be. Do you think that I could ever be with you? You, my man's wife? What part of that don't you understand? We made a horrible mistake, and Melech is paying the price for it all. I'm not 'bout to break that man any more than you already have. How could you even think that shit is cool? Who are you?" The sweet, devoted, adoring person Levi was attracted to, he was not seeing any of that in Leana. You could not hurt a man like Melech then want to rub his face in your disloyalties. She was asking for pure bad karma. Levi was not willing to dance with the devil's daughter any longer.

"Tell me you don't love me, Levi." Leana knew in her heart of hearts that Levi felt the same way about her. She could feel in in his touch, that's why she needed it so much. If she threw her life away for Levi, Leana wanted him to do the same for her.

"I don't. I love, my boy way more than I could ever love you. Go home!" Levi disconnected the call. He sat his phone on his lap, leaned back in his seat, and lit his blunt again. Leana was right. Levi had love for Leana. The three had spent so much time together somewhere before the lines got crossed. Yet, the one thing Levi knew for sure was Melech meant more to him than Leana. He made a terrible mistake, and Levi did not know how to fix his wrongs. There was no way he could take it back now that his actions had caused the meltdown of Melech's marriage. Levi wished Leana would have just stayed home with her husband. He knew sleeping with Leana was a colossal mistake, but Levi was willing to take the secret to his grave. Leana wanted to expose their dirty deeds. How she thought they could have a happily ever after baffled him. Melech would never allow that to happen. This was a man willing to get jumped for his pride. There was no way Melech would have a night of restful sleep with his best friend and wife moving on in life without him.

♥♥♥

Leana looked down at her phone, realizing that Levi had hung up on her once again. She knew Levi had feelings for her, though he would not admit it out of loyalty to Melech. Levi claimed that he was devoted to Melech, but if he was, Leana did not understand why he started the affair with her in the first place. She could not go home now, Leana had confessed to the worse sin imaginable. She knew her husband would never forgive her transgressions, Leana was rethinking her decision now. There was no way Levi was going to walk away from her. The connection they shared was real he could not deny it to himself. Leana understood Levi's devotion to Melech, but sometimes you had to think about your own happiness. Levi needed to step out of Melech's shadow and think of himself on this one. If the two were really friends, Melech would forgive Levi. They claimed to be brothers, so Leana felt they could work through anything. She knew that Melech would never forgive her, and she was okay with that.

Leana still loved Melech. If she had never felt Levi's touch, Leana would still be in her comfortable lifestyle. She was content with Melech. He was exactly what Leana wanted in a man; strong, supportive, giving, loving, compassionate, sexy, and always put her needs first. Her father loved Melech from the day he met him. Leana knew that he would be the perfect husband. Melech came from a good family, had goals and ambitions in life. Chester, Leana's father, only wanted what was best for his daughter. He did his best in raising her after her mother died so suddenly.

After a police officer hit Leana's mother car during a high-speed chase, Chester changed his entire life to cater to his daughters' needs. He worked as a butcher but made sure he was home every day when Leana got home from school. He made sure her schoolwork was done, she ate dinner, and was off to sleep before he went to work. Allowing Leana to live on campus was one of the hardest things Chester had to face. She was his little girl. Finding Melech was the best thing that could have happened to her. Chester was glad Leana decided to stay in California to attend college. Melech afforded Leana the ability to finish her education with no debt. He doted on her every whim. Chester gave Melech his approval immediately for them to get married. If anything were to happen to him, Chester knew that his daughter would be taken care of.

Leana laid back on the bed, completely confused with life. She wanted to call her husband, but Leana did not know what to say to him. There were not enough apologies in the world to make Melech forgive her. Leana was not sure if she should go home and make things right as Levi suggested or try harder to make him see that they were the ones who belonged together. She felt it in her soul. Levi was the man who could give her that something she was missing in her life. Levi's not the kind of man Melech is. Still he moved something deep inside of her. She honestly wanted to be in his arms more than she did Melech's.

♥ ♥ ♥

Melech sat at his desk, looking at the mounds of paperwork that needed his attention. The bottle of tequila seemed to gaze at him. He figured one glass would not hurt. It would most likely bring him some relief. He reached over, grabbed the bottle, and poured the magical liquid into the glass. Melech sat scrutinizing the glass for some time before he finally took a sip. The burning sensation took over his throat. He opened his mouth wide and took a deep breath, shaking his head. Melech took another sip. He leaned back in his chair. His cheeks tingled. Melech finished the glass, sitting the empty glass down. So many things were running through his mind. How did he not see the signs? Was he that preoccupied that he missed his own wife stepping out on him and falling in love with another man? She only went to work and home. Rarely did Leana spend time with her friends since she started her internship. Melech sat back up. It had to be someone in her office; he thought to himself.

Melech checked on her daily to make sure his wife had eaten or needed anything before he came into the lounge. Leana always met him outside. Her reasoning was that she did not want him to have to park or waste his time walking up. Now Melech thought there was someone in Leana's office she did not want him to see. He grabbed the bottle again. *'Why am I so trusting?'* he asked himself. He took this shot a lot faster. *'Everyone's not your mother.'* He held his glass into the air. That was a loyal woman. His mother had an acting career and still stayed faithful to his father. Melech thought he had found that same quality in Leana. This completely blindsided him. He hated that Leana told him she was a cheater; he would rather not know. Keeping him in the dark for life would have suited Melech just fine. What he did not know could not hurt him. Knowing that Leana fell in love with this person hurt Melech more than the cheating. Melech picked up his phone when he saw his mother's picture pop up. Now he regretted calling her. He should have just called a moving company and left her out of his business.

"Yes, mother," Melech said into his speakerphone.

"Why do you sound like that?" she asked.

"Like what?" He reached for the bottle once again.

"Boy!" she fussed. Melech poured the drink, ignoring his mother's tone. "I'm at your house. Are you sure you want me to do this? I still think this is a mistake. You and Leana need to try to work this out. Sit down and talk about things. Marriage takes a lot of work, baby."

"She slept with someone else, now pack up all her shit, mother, and leave it alone!" Melech snapped. This was entirely out of his character. He had a few disagreements with his father, but he had never been disrespectful to his mom. He immediately wanted to apologize, but she did not give him a chance.

"Young man, you need to watch your mouth!" she demanded. "I see now that you are hurting over this, baby," her pitch motherly. "I will get Leana's things together."

"Thank you, mother." Melech hung up the phone. He did not want to keep the conversation going on. He did not want to think about any of it any longer. The entire ordeal was driving him insane, Melech needed to get some air. It was all too much for him. He picked up his keys and walked out of the office as the alcohol was beginning to settle in. He could feel it in his head and legs. Melech was not much of a drinker. Trying to open up his truck, Melech dropped his keys.

"Yo, man! What's goin' on wit' cha?" Levi came up behind Melech. He was still sitting in the parking lot smoking a Black and Mild before going into the lounge.

"I...I...need to take a drive."

"Nigga, what's wrong wit' you?" Levi looked at him sideways.

"I'm good." Melech finally got his door open.

"You been drinking?" Levi could smell the tequila on his breath.

"Just a little."

"That's all it takes for yo' weak ass. Shit, a wine cooler, will have you drunk off yo' ass." Levi stood between Melech and the inside of the driver's seat. "I'm not 'bout to let you drive."

"Do I look like a child?" Melech asked in a threatening manner. Levi laughed at his friend. Melech was always willing to take on a fight.

"C'mon now, man." He rubbed his goatee. "You know we not gonna travel down this road. Give me yo' key, loc." Levi was not playing with him. They had a few tussles in their lifetime. Melech was jock cock strong, but Levi always found a way to get the best of him. Being an athlete was one thing, surviving on the streets of Los Angeles was a whole different way of life.

"I'm not your bitch, Levi. You plan on taking them from me?" He pushed Levi to the side. Without haste Levi pinned Melech up against the side of his truck.

"If I have to!" They were now face to face. "I'm not letting you drive. If you need to go somewhere, nigga, I'll take you!"

"Get the fuck off me!" Melech pushed him, then adjusted his clothes. "I barely had two shots."

"Leek, it don't matter. You don't drink, and you just did. Yo' ass is angry, and yo' mind ain't right. Let's go get something to eat. Chill and talk."

"I need to be alone." Melech tried pleading his case.

"Nah, man. I'm not leaving you alone."

"Fuck, Levi!" Melech pushed him again. If Levi wanted to fight, then they were going to come to blows right there in front of their business. Melech did not want a babysitter.

"Go ahead, push me, hit me, do what you need to do. I am here for you always, man."

"That's what she said," Melech gave a sinister laugh.

"You know that's not funny." Levi shook his head.

"Well, she did." Melech shrugged. "She lied."

"Yeah, she did, bruh. I don't like to see you like this. Leana made a mistake, and I know that you're hurting. I know you still love that girl, though."

"Not anymore." Melech rubbed the top of his head. "Nope, not at all. Fuck her, Levi. I hate that bitch."

"No…no…no, Leek. Don't do that. Don't do this. All this is foul, bro, and I know it's all fucked up. You're a good dude. Don't let this change you."

"It already has."

"You ain't neva turned yo' back on me. Shit, when you find out I've failed you, is you gonna just toss my ass out too?"

"Levi, you're my brother. You've never let me down."

"But I have, Leek. I'm not perfect."

"We can get through anything." Melech put his hand on Levi's shoulder. This is where Levi was supposed to tell his friend the truth, but the words would not come to him. Fear of sending Melech over the edge took over, and he just could not find it in himself to add more to his best friend's misery.

"Let's get out of here and have some fun. You wanna get some alcohol in you, let's do this. Get in. I'm driving yo' shit for a change. We 'bout to get into some shit tonight!" Levi exclaimed.

"Don't take me to no strip club." Melech protested.

"Now we goin' to the strip club. You shoulda kept yo' mouth shut." Levi got excited. That was the one thing they had never done before. "I might even get yo' ass laid tonight. Shit, you ain't had no otha pussy in years. Take this time to see what's out there before you get back wit' yo' wife."

"I'm not taking that bitch back."

"Yes, you are, just not tonight," Levi told him. "Y'all belong together. You just deserve a good time right now."

"Just cause your ass will hit and miss just about anything doesn't mean I will."

"Only flawless bitches, my nigga. You know I only hit the best."

"A big ass and a cute face are all you need," Melech teased him.

"And they can't live wit' they momma or have a kid." Levi elbowed Melech. He backed the truck out of the parking space. "You ready to do dis shit like we used to?" He gave out a big laugh. "We used to do dis, boy. Kinda miss this shit!"

"Yeah, me too." Melech put on his seat belt. If they weren't playing a pickup basketball game or at work, Leana was always around them. They rarely went out and had a boy's night since he got married.

CHAPTER FOUR

Melech woke up in his bed in just his underwear. He did not know how he got home or undressed. His esophagus felt like he swallowed a cotton ball. He sat up and scratched his head; it was pounding like Sheila E on the percussions. Now Melech realized why he did not drink. It felt good in the moment, but the aftermath was not worth it. He stumbled to the bathroom and scrambled through the medicine cabinet for some Motrin. Melech popped three into his mouth, turned the water on in the sink, cupped his hand under the flowing water, and swallowed the much-needed medicine. He needed relief, and soon. As much as Melech wanted a nice hot shower, his stomach was screaming for food. He headed down to the kitchen to find Levi cooking breakfast.

"How are you functioning right now?" he asked Levi.

"I'm used to partying all night. You are a tadpole, brother."

"What the hell did we do last night?" Melech stroked his beard.

"Well, yo' ass was trying to go to Vegas," Levi chuckled.

"You're lying." Melech shook his head.

"Dude, you was on one last night." Levi cracked eggs into the frying pan. "I had to stop you from bringing a stripper home." Melech burst out laughing.

"Now I know you're lying. There is no way I'd ever sleep with a stripper!"

"Don't knock strippers," Levi protested. "I've had meaningful relationships with some of them."

"Levi, you've had one-night stands with them," Melech corrected him.

"Not true! I have dealt with them for months on end."

"I'm gonna leave this one alone." Melech grabbed a bottle of water out of the fridge.

"I'm trying to cook up this weird ass bacon. Why this shit don't shrink or add no grease to the pan?"

"It's not that pork shit yo' ass eats. It's turkey, clean up your body, my man."

"I don't trust shit that don't create its own oil."

"That's not oil, its fat. The shit that clogs your arteries."

"Should I put your eggs in a glass?" Levi teased him. "Keep everything in its raw form not to fuck up that steroid temple of yours."

"You got too many jokes this morning. It's too early and my damn head hurts too bad for your sarcastic ass rhetoric." Melech retorted. "Besides, I don't put that garbage in my body."

"And…what is creatine?" Levi pointed the spatula at Melech. "You got more protein shakes than Wal-Mart got four shirts for ten-dollar deals."

"Here you go…"

"Do you shop at Wal-Mart?" Levi had to cut Melech off.

"Me, not personally," Melech admitted. "Leana got all of our cleaning supplies there."

"You're telling me, the ice princess, walked up into a Wal-Mart with one of them raggedy shopping carts and went shopping for some got damn tide?"

"Not exactly." Melech put his head down. She ordered online and they brought it out to the car." He drank from the *Essentia* water bottle. "Not because she wouldn't, Le just didn't have time in her schedule for that."

"Nah, bro, you spoiled her ass and those things are beneath her these days."

"That's not true. Leana was a good wife that why I scooped her ass up."

"If you say so, bruh. I think Leana was looking for the next best thing, and that was you. That Luca dude had a lot to offer the Leanas standing on the ritzy ass part of this city. You, my friend, have just a little more. Having a Buckley as a husband pulls a whole lot of weight in our community. Yo' pops made a lot of black folks wealthy men. He don't discriminate either. He helped some average muthafucca's earn that paper too. Mr. NYU wasn't eva, neva gonna give her what you could. Damn, yo' pops got us that liquor license with no problem. They wasn't handing that shit out like free cheese to some random ass twenty-five-year olds." Levi wanted Melech to look at the big picture.

"I see your point. On paper, I was the better choice. But, riddle me this Batman? What man do you know that is going to treat her the way I did knowing she cheated on me for him? Leana won't be able to breathe with this dude. That man will wonder what she is doing every time Le's not around him."

"True…" Levi did not want to reveal in his heart he felt Leana left Melech for the excitement she thought Levi was going to offer her. He would never possess the capital Melech had. Still, Levi was blessed with something a little different- charisma, and charm. All the money in the world could not buy you that.

"If you say so," Levi wanted to change the subject. "Hey check this out, we need to do a special event at the lounge make a few changes. You know...Start bringing in a special host for the night, Thursdays, or Saturday nights."

"Like who? I don't want no gang activities popping off in there." Melech built a reputation for the lounge and the demographic it served.

"Don't start judging the homies, my nig."

"Never that. I have much respect for their music and their gangsta'. You know good, and damn well, I rep all the West Coast old school shit. This new mess, I'm not feeling. It's all bubble gum shit. Instagram gangstas, with a how much money, fast cars and video vixens you can put in your video mentality."

"Well, we need to bring in some of those Instagram artists, because that's what they be looking for. Also, some famous OG's, stars, and local talent tryin' to get noticed."

"You want to have concerts?" Melech was curious. He was not really feeling this brainchild of Levi's.

"Nah, we ain't got the room for all that. We can spotlight different people. If they have music, we just play they shit over the loudspeakers while playing their videos on the big screens. If they just well known, they can host for the night. Take selfies and get they name out there. It gives them exposure and brings us some new business."

"It actually sounds pretty good." Melech had to admit.

"I sat and talked to Apple Watts last night while you were getting that personal lap dance, showering strippers like you were a rapper. She's game, but for a price. You know that she's hot as hell right now." Levi flipped the eggs he was frying. "I don't know if you remember those twins that were poppin' a few years ago on IG. One of them got killed."

"Yeah, yeah…that mess was sad. Le used to follow them. You know my shit is for business only."

"Yeah…yeah, nigga, I know you don't follow nobody. Anyways, the other one came back on with her daughter, named after her sister. She has a huge following, and she's promoting products. It might be nice to get her on board as well. Plus, you know, Eiht, he gotta new album out. He may want to come and promote his new joint. My boy, Misfit is really close to the Ramsey's, and you know Rommel is hot as shit playing with the Rams. That's another crowd drawer.",

"Apple Watts?" Melech asked. She was the only name he was unfamiliar with. "But, with Rommel you're on point. LA superstar who made it to the top. I still think they were robbed out of that Super Bowl."

"Yeah, she used to be a stripper, she's working on music now with YoYo. She's on one of those reality shows, but she from Watts and has a huge following. She's hot."

"So, once a month, you want to have a special guest sponsor?"

"Hell yeah, add a new element to what we got going on. We got a whole lotta regulars, but we need to upgrade what we got going." Levi was enthusiastic about his new adventure.

"I can get on board with that. It's going to take a shit load of social media promotions. Not just on our parts, but whoever is going to be hosting for the night and extra security also."

"I'll handle the social media; you handle the security." Levi offered up his assistance.

"And we have to agree on whoever is going to be hosting. You know I don't always see eye to eye with your type of clientele."

"Nigga, really?" Levi handed Melech a plate of fried eggs, turkey bacon, and wheat toast.

"Really. Your ass will have some ratchets come through, and we'll be closed down faster than we opened."

"You so foul for that one." He sat next to Melech at the kitchen island. "Foul, but honest," Levi conceded.

"Now tell me about this private dance I had." Melech started eating his food. He didn't even have a private dance at his bachelor party. Melech was not really interested in a woman taking off her clothes, and he could not sleep with her. Levi covered his mouth with his fist, barreling out a big laugh.

"My dude, I've never in my life seen you so carefree. Slappin' ass and making it rain, wit' yo' cheap ass."

"I am not cheap," Melech protested. "I'm frugal with my money. It doesn't grow on trees."

"The way you was showering them broads last night, it sure wasn't sprinkling up in that bitch." Levi bit into his toast, gloating. "You dropped a good grand."

"Don't play with me!" Melech stared blankly at his long-time friend. "Do you know what I could have done with that kind of money?"

"Ha…ha…ha, well, it's too late now, nigga. You can't get that shit back!" Levi laughed uncontrollably.

"Why the fuck would you let me drop cash like that?" Melech was furious.

"I'm just fuckin' wit' yo' ass." Levi could not help messing with Melech. He was so tight when it came to his money. The last thing he would ever do was waste it on a stripper.

"Man, that's not even funny!" Melech pushed his half-eaten food away from him.

"No…man…it really is." Levi kept eating his food.

"I'm going for a run." Melech started heading to the stairs.

"You did try to go to Vegas!" he yelled after him. "I didn't let you do that either."

"You're a dick, bro!" Melech screamed back at him. Levi's jokes were not funny at times. Having Melech think that he had wasted that type of money was no laughing matter to him. Wasteful was not in Melech's DNA.

"You don't need some steroids or something before you head out?" Levi teased Melech as he was walking out the door.

"Shut up, man." Melech slammed the door behind him. He usually made himself a protein shake before his run. But, Melech was not in the mood for any more of Levi's jokes. He just wanted to clear his head for a moment. Levi had good intentions in trying to take Melech's mind off his woes. His jokes missed the mark though.

Levi cleaned up the morning dishes. He knew that Melech was upset with him, but Levi could not help pulling his strings. It was just too easy. Anything to get Melech's mind off of Leana. She had been calling Levi on the hour of every hour. He refused to talk to her. Not only had she not come back home to Melech, she did not even reach out to him. They needed to get their marriage back on track. Things had to go back to normal, and soon. He missed what they had and did not like seeing his friend suffering.

Melech did have fun at the strip joint, but Levi could not get him drunk every night. Levi knew that he made a terrible mistake in all of this. It was never his intentions to break up their relationship. Feeling Leana's touch just once made him come back for more. She was an addictive, poisonous fruit Levi just had to have.

After their first encounter, Leana became a tease. She flaunted herself at Levi, continually rubbing up against him or caressing him, driving him crazy. The smell of Leana's perfume lingered in his nostrils, intoxicating Levi long after Leana left the room.

Once Leana came home, Levi planned on staying away from them for a while. Leana was going to have to get over whatever she had concocted in her head about them being together. As much as Levi craved her touch, he knew that it was forbidden. Leana was off-limits from this point on. He never should have ventured down this path, and he wanted to take it all back. He did not want to have these feelings for Leana, and most of all, Levi did not want to lose his best friend.

Leana was furious. Not only was Levi ignoring all of her calls, now she had to explain to her father why her belongings showed up to his home. Melech had them shipped to his doorstep. Her father left more than a dozen messages on her phone, even so, she was not ready to talk to him yet. Leana did not know how to explain to her father she left her husband for a man that would return none of her phone calls. How did she fall head over heels for Levi? He had to love her back. Leana felt it in his touch, the way that he looked into her eyes while they slept together. She felt his piercing eyes on her while they were all together. Levi had feelings for her, and Leana knew it. Levi was trying to fight them because of his friendship with Melech. It was not fair for her to lose out on love because she met Melech first. The heart wants what it wants, and Leana's heart wanted Levi. She tried calling him once again.

"Where the hell are you?" Levi finally answered her call.

"Is that how you answer the phone for everyone or just me?" she asked him. "What have I done that was so wrong?"

"I told you to come home. I'm sitting in yo' house as we speak, and I don't see you?" Levi looked around the house as if Leana could see him.

"Then you know that your friend packed up all of my belongings and sent them to my father," Leana stifled her tears.

"He what?" Melech did not tell Levi he was going to do that. He looked around the house and realized that there were no pictures of the two of them anymore. Levi went up to their bedroom and looked in the closet. Everything was gone.

"Levi?" Leana called out his name. He had gone dead silent on her. Leana was not sure if Levi had hung up on her or not.

"Yeah…yeah. I'm here," he answered her. "If you had brought yo' silly ass home, this shit wouldn't have happened!"

"Levi, I want to be with you. Why can't you understand that?"

"No...no...no!" Levi cried out to her. He did not want to keep hearing Leana say those words to him.

"Baby, I know that you feel the same way. I was just brave enough to take action. You can follow my lead. We can leave town if it will make life easier for us." Leana would do anything to get Levi to own what they had.

"Stupid actions, Le!" Levi belittled her.

"No, Levi! I was the brave one in all of this," she tried convincing him.

"You call destroying my friend brave?" Levi went back to the kitchen. He wanted to hear when Melech came back in.

"You didn't seem to mind while you were inside of me," she maliciously snapped to him.

"If yo' hoe ass wasn't constantly pushin' that pussy all up on me, that shit wouldn't of happened," Levi tried humiliating her. "Titties always floppin' out yo' shit. I'd a slapped da shit out yo' ass if you was my wife!"

"Now I'm a hoe, Levi?" The burning tears came streaming down her face, stinging like acid through her flesh. Leana did not want him to know that she was crying. "You slept with this hoe, you know?"

"I fuck a lot of females, don't feel so special." Levi did not know why he was being so malicious to Leana. The self-hate he was feeling, Levi was taking out on her.

"I'm not special to you?" she could not hide the tears in her voice.

"Nah, ma," he said nonchalantly. "You was just somethin' to do."

"You're a fucking liar!" Leana screamed into the phone. "You're a liar," she whispered this time.

"Get yo' husband back, Le! Do whateva it takes. You and I ain't shit. The fuck was nice, but Melech is my boy." Levi hung up the phone on her. He could not leave any room for doubt in Leana's mind. She had to understand that she and Melech were meant to be, not them.

Leana held her phone close to her chest, curled up into a ball, and cried. She could not understand how Levi could say such vicious words to her. They ripped her soul out of her chest. She just knew her sobs could be heard through the paper-thin walls. Leana hoped no one called security. Leana was sure it sounded as if she was being murdered. The pain that she was feeling hurt to her core. Levi's words cut like a knife. Digging deep into her flesh down to the bone.

The run was mind clearing for Melech. It always put him at ease. Walking through the front door, he realized that Leana was not going to be there to greet him. Melech had grown accustomed to their daily routines. He did not consider them to be so dull that his wife would have an affair and leave him because of it. Melech did like order in his life, it just made things simple for him. He thought that Leana felt the same way he did. They discussed their future at lengths before Melech asked her to marry him. These were the surprises he did not want to encounter in life. Leana was not supposed to be the type of woman to do a one eighty on him, especially after they planned out their lives in great detail. When did Leana change her thought process? Melech even agreed not to have children until Leana finished school and got her career off the ground. Melech's parents were not thrilled with the decision in the beginning. He was their only child and they wanted grandchildren, lots of them.

Melech's mother, Halina, finally took Leana's need for success as a sign that she was not a gold digger. Halina had been acting since she was in her early teens. She appeared in almost every great black movie ever made. Not starring roles, but she was recognizable. Strangers always pointed at Halina before she became a soap star saying, *'I know you from...'* then snapping their fingers. Halina started off as an extra while she was doing print work. She moved on to several lines, then the best friend in the movies. She also played on several shows as the token *'black girl.'* She had a perfect look for those roles.

Halina was a young girl of color, but not too ethnic for television. The light bronze tan toned complexion, soft brown eyes, and perfectly curly hair made Halina acceptable for TV land. Her real fame came once she got her role on *General Hospital*. She had a six-episode contract that turned into almost twenty years. Halina was just a nurse when she started. Now she was a full-fledged doctor on the show. The audience adored the romance between her and Halina's co-star during those six-episodes. Over time, he left the show to make movies and returned. The viewers begged for their relationship to blossom once again. This gave Halina's character a whole new life.

Most of her money, Halina saved. Her soon to be husband was on break from college.

Halina just moved into her own little apartment. It was a refurbished backhouse with a tiny small kitchenette, full bath, and the living room doubled as her bedroom. Halina was proud of her new little digs. She was finally out of her parents' home and living on her own in Compton. The little bitty patio gave her a view of the owner's pool, which she was privy too. The only downside was the smell of the horses on the property. Halina almost did not even look at the apartment when she first pulled up to the address. It did not look like much by its appearance. She learned quickly not to judge a book by its cover. Halina was not sure what the front house looked like, she was escorted to the apartment through the backyard, and it was at least an acre of property. In her opinion, this backhouse was safer than any apartment with who knows what hanging out in front of the building. At least here, if someone followed Halina home, the owners had German Shepard's that roamed the yard. Halina had no idea that she would meet her husband that summer when he came home from college. It did not take long for Kaden to make his way to her little apartment on his parent's property. It took even less time for Kaden to spend every night with her in the little backhouse. After college, they stayed together until Kaden found a good job and saved enough money for them to get married and buy a house. Their wedding present from Kaden's parents was all the rent Halina had paid to them. His parents wanted them to start their lives with a nest egg.

"How was your run?" Levi asked.

"Amazing, you should try getting exercise in your life." Melech grabbed water from the fridge.

"These guns right here." Levi showed off his biceps. "Come from that old-fashioned workout."

"LA Fitness is not considered old fashion, bruh."

"I pump iron like I'm on the prison yard, nigga." Levi flexed his chest.

"You dumb as hell." Melech shook his head. "Prison yard…"

"Say, why ain't no pictures up no more wit' you and Le?"

"Don't wanna see her," Melech dryly told him.

"A picture ain't gonna change shit, my man," he advised Melech.

"You got that part right. Sent all Le's stuff to her pop's house. That girl doesn't have a reason to come back here."

"Leek, don't you think you rushing into some harsh decisions?"

"Nope."

"I know you hurtin'."

"Not at all."

"C'mon, man, you not gonna sit here and play games wit' me." Levi was not paying any attention to Melech's answers. He was privy to Melech and Leana's relationship, both the good and bad.

"Leave it alone, Levi." He started towards the stairs.

"You can't just walk away from me and think the convo just ends." Levi followed behind him. "Y'all gonna work this shit out."

"No, we're not."

"The girl tripped for a minute. Go fuck someone and let that girl back in."

"Let it go, man." He was starting to annoy Melech.

"You two are made for each other, bro." he turned around and got face to face with Levi.

"Don't bring her fucking name up to me again! You're either my friend or hers. You better pick a side, right here and right now!" he bellowed. Levi put his hands up in the air, feeling like Melech had drawn down on him.

"Fuck her. I'm always rockin' wit' you."

"Now, if you'll excuse me." He tilted his head to the side. "I'd like to take a shower; an audience is not what I need."

"Are you sure? You took showers with men for years." Levi shrugged. "Naked men in the showers in college, my dude, plus yo' ass been flashing me fo' years. I'm just saying, bro."

"Nigga get the fuck out of my room. You're an idiot." Melech grabbed Levi, pushing him out of his bedroom.

"C'mon, man. Give me a kiss." He tried to hug and kiss Melech.

"Stop playing, fool." He shoved Levi out of his room, closed, and locked it. Melech laughed to himself. Levi was always playing way too much, but Melech enjoyed their friendship. He kept life entertaining.

CHAPTER FIVE

Leana's weary eyes opened to her new surroundings. She may have been in a luxury suite, but it did not feel like home. Leana had become accustomed to the lifestyle Melech provided her. Chester made sure that his daughter had a decent upbringing living in Culver City. Her father doted on her. Nonetheless, they were still two paychecks away from being homeless. When Chester bought life insurance, he was advised that the breadwinner was the only one who needed to have the most coverage. After paying for Leana's mother' funeral, Chester put what was left into a college fund for her. He was still able to give his daughter what she needed and give her the quality time every little girl needs.

Leana rubbed her sleepy eyes, reached her arms to the roof, and stretched her back until it cracked. She looked at her phone, hoping Levi had called. That was not the case. Leana only had three missed calls, and two were from her father. She dreaded having to tell him what happened between her and Melech, but the conversation was inevitable. Leana knew her father was going to be disappointed with her actions. He raised her with values she let blow into the wind long before Leana slept with Levi. Leana made the mistake of not breaking up with her boyfriend before she got involved with Melech. Deep down inside Leana knew a long distant relationship would not last. When he found out, Melech almost left her. Leana had to put on the show of her life to keep Melech by her side. She was not ready to lose him.

At the time, Leana thought Melech was precisely what she wanted in a man. She did not mind him partnering up with Levi to start the lounge. Never in her wildest dreams did she think it was going to be this successful. What Leana was fully aware of was if their business failed Melech had his degree and parents that would pick up the pieces for him. There was no losing with Melech. He was the win, win choice for her. His drive and ambition would take them far in life. Leana covered her face with her well-manicured hands. She had thrown her perfect life away, covered with stability and a future for the bells and whistles of Levi. *'Did I make a mistake?'* she asked herself. The way Levi spoke to her earlier was a blatant sign that he'd used her.

'No…no…no, I saw the way he looked into my eyes.' She tried convincing herself. Leana was so confused. If she had just stayed home Levi would have kept sleeping with her. But she could not continue living a double life any longer. Someone had to take a stand for them to be together, so she took a leap of faith. Leana had no clue Levi would turn on her the way he did.

Leana gathered her emotions, dragged them and herself to the bathroom to take a long hot bath before she returned her father's call. She was going to need some wine before having to listen to the lecture that was surely coming her way.

♥♥♥

"Why are you still here?" Melech asked Levi walking down the stairs. He was not interested in a babysitter. "Don't you have your own place?"

"Just rude, my nig." Levi did not look up from his phone. "You'd think yo' ass would be in a better mood by now."

"I was until I saw you still sitting here."

"You still love me, doe." Levi blew him a kiss.

"Your ass is silly. Don't you have some place to be, some stripper to be in or something?"

"Nah, I like kickin' it with you." Levi finally put his phone down. "What we doing today?"

"We?" Melech was baffled. He had no plans to spend the day with Levi. It was his only day off, and he was not going to sit around with an annoying sidekick.

"Yeah, fool, we. You not 'bout to sit around all day sulkin'. I know you. Yo ass play the blame game real good."

"I don't blame myself for what, Le did. Shit, I never cheated on her ass."

"Yeah, okay." Levi got up from the island and patted his friend on the back. "You been asking yourself a thousand times, *'What didn't I give that girl,'* and you know it." Melech just stared at him, wondering how could he possibly know that? It was his mission to give Leana any and everything to ensure she was happy. So how could she fall in love with someone else? "I'm right, ain't I?" he tapped his shoulder and pointed at Melech.

"Shut up, man. I gave that girl everything!" he protested.

"That ain't what I said."

"Leana's ungrateful. I didn't know she had these tendencies all these years. She blindsided me, bro. I thought she was a sweetheart."

"She is Melech. The girl made a mistake."

"Don't defend her, Levi."

"I'm not trust me. I just don't wanna say shit wrong just in case y'all get back together."

"You definitely don't have to worry about that ever happening." Levi shrugged his shoulders. He went to the refrigerator and grabbed a beer. Levi went to the store while Melech was on his run. If he was going to be spending more time at the house, Levi needed to put some alcohol and good chronic in it. This new brooding Melech was depressing.

"Want one?" he asked Melech.

"Sure." He had no plans for the day. "Didn't plan on spending my day off with a babysitter, might as well get a little buzz if I'm stuck with your ass."

"Pull out the 2K so I can beat yo' ass." Levi gave him a playful shove. They both rushed into the living room like teenage boys.

♥ ♥ ♥

Leana laid wrapped in a towel on the hotel bed with her phone in her hand. She knew it was time to face the fireworks with her father. She took a deep breath and built up the courage to dial his number.

"Daddy."

"Hey, baby. How are you doing? What's going on? I've been so worried about you? Where are you? Neither you nor Melech are taking my calls, and some moving guys brought all your belongings here…" he shot off questions like missiles.

"Daddy," she needed to stop the barrage of questions he was firing her way.

"Melech and I broke up. I'm at a hotel, I just needed a little bit of time to clear my mind."

"Oh, sweetie, are you alright?" he was concerned. "What did he do to you?"

"I...um...I...left him, daddy," she stammered over her words.

"Why would you do that? Was Melech mistreating you?" Chester was not sure what was going on. The two appeared to be happy, and he was impressed with Melech, his accomplishments, and the way he treated his daughter.

"No...no daddy. Leek would never do anything to harm me. He's a good man," Leana defended her husband. "I just needed a change."

"A change?" he was confused. "What does that even mean, child? Buy some new shoes or redecorate your house. You don't change your mind about marriage."

"Daddy..." Her voice trailed off. There was no trying to explain. He was going to hate her.

"Leana, marriage takes hard work. You don't just give up. You buckle down and fight for what's right. Maybe you don't need to be working so much. Spend more time taking care of Melech. Have you two grown apart?"

"Daddy, this has nothing to do with my job. It just got boring."

"You sound like a child, Leana. You're not in school anymore. Grow up, every day is not going to be hallmark cards for you. The honeymoon has worn off. You don't walk away because of that. Do you think that every day was a fantasy island for your mother and me?"

"Can't you just support me, daddy?"

"I love you, Le, and I always will, but you need to go home and make things right with that man. He's your husband."

"Why does everyone keep telling me that?" she was getting frustrated.

"Leana, does Melech hit you?"

"No."

"Does he verbally abuse you?"

"No."

"Does he cheat on you?"

"No."

"Does he take you for granted or ignore you?"

"No."

"So, what's the problem, Leana?" Chester was lost. His daughter found herself a good man, and she wanted to walk away because she was bored. That was not a good enough reason to end a marriage.

"I fell in love with another man," Leana blurted out.

"You what?" Outrage filled his tone. She could feel it burning through the phone.

"I'm sorry, daddy." Leana started crying hysterically.

"Leana, please tell me that you did not step out on your marriage?" She could not respond. The tears flowed down her face, and her heart was in her throat. Leana hung up the phone. She could not speak anymore. Melech, her father, and Levi all hated her. Leana felt alone. Leana left her husband for what she thought was love, now the three men in her life were angry with her tossing her to the side like distasteful gum. Levi and her father thought it was all so simple. They really believed that Melech would just take her back so quickly. She hurt Melech deeply by cheating on him. There was no way he would take her back. *'Would he?'*

Leana sat up. The little voice of common sense was quickly removed from her thoughts. *'I have to try Levi one more time. I know that he loves me. If I can just get him to come see me, look me in the eye and tell me that he doesn't want to be with me- I know he can't do it. Yes, Leana. Get him over here. Levi could never resist your charm.'* She wiped the tears away and started working on her alternative plan.

Melech's cell phone lit up, interrupting Melech and Levi's 2K game. Chester's name glared at him from the screen.

"Better pick that up," Levi paused their game.

"Shit! I've been avoiding him."

"You sent all her shit to his crib, and you didn't expect him to call you?"

"Yeah, I didn't think that one through." Melech stroked his beard.

"Um, no, you haven't been thinkin' much through these days, bruh."

"Fuck you, man."

"Daddies callin' again." Levi pointed at Melech's phone. He shook his head. Melech knew he was going to have to take the call eventually. No time like the present.

"Hey, Chester." Levi motioned for him to put the phone on speaker. He was dying to hear what was going on. Melech did not know why he followed Levi's instructions. He tapped the microphone and sat the phone down on the table.

"What's going on, Melech. I just talked to my daughter. I don't know what to say."

"Not much to say, sir."

"She's a silly little girl. I told her to take her ass home. Boredom is no reason to walk away from a marriage." Melech had to chuckle.

"Is that what she said? Boredom…. Sir, your daughter, cheated on me and fell in love with another man." Levi was feeling uncomfortable. Now he wished he had gone into another room. Trying to be a good best friend, Levi was now feeling like he was sitting in the lion's den.

"I know, son…I know. I'm sorry. Leana's still young in the mind. I told her to go home. Y'all can work through this, my boy."

"No, sir, we can't. Le, made her choice when she left me a letter and walked out of our home. Leana chose him over what we built together."

"She wrote you a letter?" Chester was feeling bad for his son-in-law. He could not believe his daughter could treat a man that cared for her so deeply with such little respect.

"Yes, sir. I went for a run, and when I came home, there was a letter left for me on my pillow."

"I'm sorry, son."

"You did nothing wrong, sir." Melech had a lot of respect for Leana's father. He'd known Chester for a long time, and from the stories Leana had told Melech, Chester was always good to her. He put Leana's needs above him at all costs.

"I raised her, Melech." He was solemn. "You two can work this out, son."

"I don't think so, but thanks for calling."

"I'll talk to you soon." Chester hung up the phone.

"Dude, I can't believe Leana told him the truth." Melech sat back on the couch. "I thought I was gonna have to be the bearer of bad news."

"I'm shocked." Levi was still holding his controller small sweat beads had formed over the top of his eyebrows, dripping into his eye. Levi blinked quickly. "He sounded sincere."

"He's a good man." They both sat in silence.

"Hey, you want another beer?" Levi got up, tossing the controller onto the couch.

"Nah, I'm good." Melech was still in his thoughts over Leana and her father. What made Chester think he would take Leana back after she cheated on him?

"So that's a yes?" Levi totally ignored him. He came back and handed him the opened beer.

"I said I was good." Melech looked up at him.

"Yeah, whatever. Drink the damn beer. Stop being a pussy all the damn time."

"Am I?" Melech grabbed the beer.

"Are you what?"

"A pussy?" Melech really wanted to know. Was that the reason Leana felt the need to sleep with someone else.

"Nah, nigga, I would neva had kicked it wit' yo ass. You just like shit yo' way all the damn time. I'm used to that shit now. It's who you are." Levi drank from his beer.

"It makes life easier."

"Does it, Leek?" He looked at his friend. "I mean, really? Being so damn perfect all the time."

"It's exhausting?" Melech admitted. "This is all I know."

"Yeah, yo' pops is one tight ass muthafucka, I tell you."

"He is who he is." Melech shrugged. "He's a good man." Levi shook his head. He did not care for Melech's father. The demands that he put on his son were too much for a kid to bear. Levi was jealous when they first started hanging out. His dad just got arrested again, and Melech's father was always around. He never missed a game, even showed up to several practices. As time went on, the more he watched the relationship, the more Levi realized Melech was not allowed to fail.

"He gave you, and yo' mom's the world, but y'all couldn't breathe, my man. That's why you turned out to be such a straight arrow. You don't let yo' guards down. Why do you think it was so easy to piss you off this morning when you thought you spent a bunch of money on a damn stripper?"

"Because money should not be wasted."

"See that shit right there is right out of the *'Kaden Book of Laws'*. Levi used air quotes. "He has a list of dos and don'ts that you live by. When does Melech set his own set of rules? Shit, you a grown ass man now. Set your own standards."

"What's wrong with his? He's powerful and successful. My parents have been married for like ever. What has he done wrong not to model myself after him?"

"You're father's a dick."

"Don't!"

"Hey, I'm just telling you to create your own legacy. Don't be a carbon copy of ya' old man."

"If I was, I'd be in a stuffy office building answering to some old white man. I'm not trying to be, my dad." Melech did not know how to have a real conversation with Kaden since he finished college. The two coexisted in each other's life.

"You ain't answering to no old dude, but you stay up in that office. You don't let yo 'self have a good time. You live on repeat day after day. Nigga, this ain't groundhog's day." Melech had to laugh.

"We ain't in no damn movie."

"I'm just telling you to be your own man. Not for Le, fo' yourself. Nigga, I've watched you grow up. Anyone willing to get they ass whoop has some heart, ya' dig. I saw it in you. Leana saw it in you, once upon a time. You just lost that shit somewhere. Find you. The real you. Not some Kaden wannabe." Melech took in Levi's words. He always wanted to be just like his father. He did not want to be a bore.

"I feel you." Melech downed the beer. He had a lot to think about. For now, he just wanted to be free from the pain he was feeling. "Now, get that damn controller so I can keep whooping up on you!"

♥♥♥

Leana struggled to get into her hotel room door with all the packages she just acquired. She decided to do some retail therapy to fill the emptiness she was filling inside. If Leana planned to get Levi back, she needed to look her best. All she took out of the house she shared with Melech was one bag of clothes and her personal hygiene case. Leana did not have time to pack more of her belongings. Melech did the honors of sending her things back to her family home. Leana wanted to be angry with him, but she understood his motives. He was not going to allow her to get close to him again. Melech was not a forgiving man. Leana knew this when she decided to leave. This was the reason she had to make Levi own his feelings for her. The words he spewed at her earlier in the day were painful, yet she knew she had to be persistent. She could not allow Levi to push her away so quickly.

Placing the bags on the bed, Leana kicked off her shoes, threw her purse next to the packages, and flopped on the couch. She was emotionally and physically tired. Leaving Melech was supposed to be liberating-that it had not been. She wanted to stop by her fathers' house; Leana knew he was still angry with her. He would give her another lecture about going home. She did not want to hear the lecture again. Leana could not complain about her life with Melech. Since college, she knew he was something special. Leana was furious with him the moment they met. The charming smile Melech kept on his face while she was yelling at him would not allow her to stay angry with him. Their friendship blossomed so quickly, Leana knew she wanted to be with him forever.

His strength and confidence did not overshadow the tenderness Melech displayed when it came to Leana. She melted into his eyes every time she got upset with him. Melech did not lose his composure with her. Leana could become an emotional wreck, and Melech would pull her into his arms and make life seem simple once again. Even if she was angry with him, Melech did not discount Leana's feelings or tell her she was ridiculous. He listened to her concerns and addressed them with her. Those were all the things that made her fall in love with Melech. Taking him out of his comfort zone was always fun for Leana. She took his clothes one day from the gym's locker room, leaving Melech in only his boxer briefs running through LA Fitness, chasing her all the way back to their car. He was angry with Leana until he caught her, and she was in hysterics. Melech threw her over his shoulder and smacked her bottom until Leana begged him to put her down. Those were the best times. Leana smiled, thinking about the good times they shared.

Leana was not sure when she allowed Levi into her heart. He was one of the few people that brought the laid-back version of Melech out. She liked having him around with his half-witted jokes and playful nature. The three could talk and laugh for hours. Leana would cook dinner while Melech and Levi would play the game until she was finished. They would eat before the two-headed back out to the lounge. They were a little family until that faithful day she and Levi crossed the line. Nothing would ever be the same after that. Leana was not sure if it was the alcohol, the way his cologne suffocated her heart, or how his hand felt on the small of her back when Levi walked past her to get to the cabinet. She needed to feel his mouth on hers, without thinking Leana's pouty lips had overtaken Levi's, gently sliding her wine-drenched tongue into his mouth. Before Leana knew it, she was tugging on Levi's Gucci belt. Throwing all caution to the wind, she could not get him out of his clothes fast enough, knowing Melech could walk through the door at any moment.

All Leana's senses were at their peak. She was not sure if it was the exhilaration of getting caught or if Levi was the best sex she'd ever had. He rushed out of the house before they could talk about what happened. Shaken, Leana went to her room to pull herself together. Melech walked into their room just moments after she did. She was so frazzled, Leana was unable to put words together. Leana got in the bed, pulling the covers over her head. She was sure Melech would be able to see the shame all over her face. Melech being the man that he was, assumed his wife was ill, rubbed her back, and insisted she get some rest. He finished dinner, brought her a plate before heading back to work. Leana promised herself she would never betray her husband again. That was a lie because now she was in a room at the Ritz trying to figure out a way to convince Levi to be with her.

CHAPTER SIX

Levi's adrenaline was pulsating as he pushed his snow bunny threw traffic. He was heading home from Melech's because Leana would not stop calling him. His mental was being disturbed, and Levi was not able to concentrate on the game or trying to keep Melech's spirits up. Leana changed his disposition and anger began to take over. Instead of hitting redial on his phone, Leana was supposed to have some remorse for what had been done to the man she promised to love for life. Through thick, thin, good and bad. Levi was infuriated that she had not once called nor reached out to Melech, her husband. The man whose heart she broke.

Levi knew he had played a part in the demise of his best friend's marriage, but he was right by his side during the hard times. He also kept telling this girl to go home. There was no way Levi was going to sell Leana a pipe dream of them ever running off into the sunset and living happily ever after, while it left his boy devastated. This was not some made for TV movie. Levi was already weighed down by guilt for ever sleeping with Leana. The first time could have been forgiven if he had owned it immediately and told Melech. It would have been a hard pill to swallow, at least Melech would know what he was married to. For Levi, Leana was worse than hustling. You could tell yourself, just one more lick, and you were out of the game, but the hustle would call you back in until you were dead or in jail.

There was a way about Leana that made Levi want to be around her. It was more than the sex with her, which is why he wanted everything to go back to the way it used to be. Leana lightened up the room with her upbeat nature. She could make anyone smile during the worst of times. The beauty she possessed only added to her sex appeal. If that one forbidden day could be taken back, Levi would gladly relive it. If you never taste something you are not supposed to have, you could never desire it. Leana had pulled both men into her web of ecstasy. Melech was cast off due to Leana's betrayal and heartache. Levi wanted out but the damage was done. If he had met Leana first, she may have been the one woman that could settle him down.

His phone went off again, sending rage through Levi's entire body. His eyes grew dark as Levi saw Leana's name flash across the screen. He instinctively wanted to throw his phone out the car window.

"Fuck you want?" Levi answered it instead.

"You," her angelic voice softly sang. "I know that you want me too, baby."

"No, da fuck, I don't!" he protested. "You are starting to make me hate you, Le."

"Don't say that," she pleaded with him. "Come see me."

"Nope. Go home, Le."

"I don't have a home to go to anymore. I ruined all of that for you."

"Hell nah, you ain't gonna blame me for any of this, Le. How many times I tell you we could not do this? I told yo' ass no, so many times, and you kept pushing up on me."

"You kept coming back, Levi." He sat in silence for a moment. Levi had to admit to himself that he slipped up several more times over the past few months. There was no denying she had him hooked.

"You kept pushin' up on me, what's a nigga s'posed to do? Shit Le, you is so fucken foul for all this."

"What does that make you, Levi? You were a willing participant. I did not force you to do anything." Leana did not like the way Levi kept blaming her for everything that took place between the two of them.

"It's all wrong, periot!" Levi did not understand how Leana could not see this.

"How can love be wrong?" Leana did not know when she fell in love with Levi. She could not deny her feelings any longer. All she wanted was for Levi to admit to her he was feeling the same way.

"Because you're married to my best friend, and you're confusing lust for love, baby girl."

"Come see me so we can talk, please."

"Nah, you fucked up my whole mind. I was enjoying my day until you started calling like I owed yo' ass some money or some shit. I'm going home to lay it down."

"With some other female," Leana's tone was shaky.

"And if I do, what's it to you? You gotta husband, go home to him!"

"You just want to hurt me right now. I understand that you're upset, Levi. It wasn't my intention to hurt your friend. I love Leek also."

"You gotta a funny way of showin' that shit. I mean, the first time you pulled up on me, I should have told my nigga, and we wouldn't be here now."

"Well, why didn't you?" Now Leana was mocking him. "Cause you knew you could never hit again, and you know good, and damn well, you've wanted me as long as I wanted you. Stop playing games, Levi. Yes, we hurt Melech, and I hate that we did that to him. I choose you, though, and I can't help what I feel."

"Leana." Levi pulled into his driveway. Why couldn't she see how wrong they were was beyond him. "I don't wanna keep hurting you. How many ways can I tell you, ain't no way I'm goin' against, my man? I made a mistake when I fucked you. I should have told him. Shit, I've been trying to tell him all day. Melech can't deal wit' that shit yet. Go home, make yo' marriage work out. That man loves you in a way I never could."

"Let's tell him, Levi. Then we will be free of this burden."

"Did you hear anything I just said to you? Are you high, cause you ain't listening to shit I said to yo' ass." Leana was actually high and drunk. She was going stir crazy because Levi would not pick up any of her calls or respond to her text messages.

"I heard you say you were going to tell Leek."

"Then what, Le? What else did I say?"

"What do you mean? If you tell him, we are free to be together."

"See, you trippin' right there. I didn't know you were this selfish. I wish that nigga never met yo' ass. This shit ain't all 'bout you. You fucked that nigga's world up, and the only thing that matters to you is being with me? So Melech, can lose you and me at the same time? That's some bullshit. You fucked up as hell."

"I didn't mean it like that. Hurting Melech wasn't what I wanted to do. I just want to be with you."

"Get up off my phone, Leana don't call me again." Levi hung up on her, then blocked Leana's number from his phone. He was so disappointed in the person she had become. The three had become close over the years Levi enjoyed what they had. He realized that a genuine relationship in his life was not needed because he lived through theirs. The lines were not supposed to get crossed. His deeds had destroyed two lives. It was a selfish way of thinking, Levi only cared that he maintained his friendship with Melech.

Getting hung up on was really starting to take a toll on Leana. Levi thought it was his escape from a conversation with her. This was no longer acceptable for Leana. She scrolled through her phone until she found the Uber app, plugged in the information needed to get her to the destination. Her mind was set for this fight as she grabbed the hotel keycard, pulled her jacket over the lingerie she put on. Leana had high hopes she was going to be able to entice Levi over to her room, but he never showed up. She slid on her Air Force One's. No, it was not attractive. But, Leana was on a mission for answers and maybe a brawl if that was what it was going to take. The indigo and wine had settled into her nicely, and she was not thinking clearly. She only had eight minutes before her car arrived. Leana did not want to miss it. She stood in front of the elevator, tapping her fingernails against the keycard. It was the only thing settling down her nerves, Leana's heart was racing faster than an Indie 500 racecar. She did not know what she was in for there was no turning back now. The electric doors slid open, Leana was thrilled the compartment was empty. Small talk was the last thing she wanted right now. Her emotions were all over the place. Leana was not sure if she was angry, scared, nervous, or all of them at the same time. She rushed out of the doors before they were completely open. She saw the black Cadillac pull up to the hotel with an Uber sticker; it had to be her ride. After giving it a second thought, Leana realized she should have ordered a less conspicuous car like a Prius. Melech programmed her Uber account, Leana rarely used it. He wanted Leana to have it for emergencies or if she went out and was unable to drive home. This was the case in her mind. Leana was out and unable to drive. The worst thing that could happen would be if she were to have an accident in her beautiful car driving high and drunk. Leana may have been irrational about the decisions she had been making lately, but common sense took over when it came to destroying that precious car of hers.

"Leana?" The driver asked as she approached his car.

"Yes, that's me." He quickly exited the driver's side to open the door for her.

"I'd rather sit in the back if you don't mind," Leana informed him.

"No problem, ma'am." He helped her into the car.

"I have a lot on my mind tonight. It has nothing to do with you."

"No worries." He gave her a half-smile. The driver could see that Leana was not well put together. Her hair was a wild, curly mess. It appeared that she did not have any clothes on under her jacket, and she was wearing a pair of sneakers. He was not sure if he should make idle chitchat or just turn on some music.

"Are you alright, ma'am? Would you like to listen to anything in particular on the radio?" he asked her.

"I'm fine. Anything you play is fine," Leana told him. "Just not some mushy love songs. I'm not in the mood for that. I think I'm going into a war zone; my mind needs to be ready for that."

"You're a bit small for war," he told her with a half-smirk on his face.

"Love will make you do crazy things."

"It's not my usual playlist for my riders. I have some DMX on deck if you are really ready for something like that."

"I love DMX," she squealed. The driver looked through his rearview mirror. He never would have pegged the young lady for a hard-core rap fan.

"Are you sure, ma'am? You know this is that next level rap. You not going to find this on the radio?"

"Play it…play it. I need my mind right. This man has me in a bad space, and I need my mind right. I have no idea what I'm about to walk into."

"No man is worth you walking into a dangerous situation." He turned on the music, DMX blared over the speakers, *'I got blook on my hands and there's no remorse.'* Leana laid back in the comfortable leather seat listening to the music, revving her up for her next fight at survival. Leana kept making poor decisions in her life, she could not understand why. When she met Melech, it was easy for her to date him without telling her boyfriend at the time, with him attending school out of state made it simple. Here Leana was once again married to Melech, trying to start a new life with his closest and dearest friend. Leana could not understand why she could not be happy with what she had. Her husband was a great person. She could not create a better person if she was the Most High himself. Deep down in her soul, Leana wanted to be with Levi, and she would be damned if he thought she was going to walk away quietly after Leana left Melech for him. If she had to lose it all, so did Levi.

"Miss." The driver called out to Leana. "We're here at your destination."

"That was fast." Leana sat up in the seat. Before she could step out of the car, the driver was at the door assisting her out of the luxury vehicle. "Thank you, sir."

"Not a problem. Are you going to be safe? Do you need me to wait until you get inside?" He looked around the neighborhood. It appeared to be safe, but this was LA. As soon as he pulled back on to the main road, he would be smack dead on Western Avenue which is infested with rival gangs.

"I should be fine," Leana smiled at the driver. "Thank you." She stumbled her way to the door and waved as he drove away. Leana looked around at her surroundings, making sure no one was near her. She pounded on the large oak door, waited thirty seconds before banging on it once more. Only seconds passed when Leana began kicking the door as hard as she could. If Levi did not open the door, Leana planned on breaking windows to find out who Levi had in the house with him. Leana did not take this trip not to be heard by him.

"What the hell are you doing here?" Levi flung the door open. "Are you fuckin' insane? I have neighbors!"

"What took you so long to answer the door?" Leana pushed past him, making her way into Levi's house.

"I was fuckin' sleep. Why are you here?" Levi asked her again.

"I came to see what slut, bitch you had up in here," her words were slurring together.

"That would be you," he shot back at her.

"Don't play games with me, Levi." Leana spun around, pointing her finger in his face. "I know you got some chick in here. That's why you wouldn't come to see me." She struggled to get out of her jacket. Suddenly Leana was feeling extremely warm. Levi sat on the edge of his sleek black suede couch, watching in amusement as Leana drunkenly fought her way out of the coat. "Let me find this bitch, and it's on and poppin'." She continued down the hallway to Levi's bedroom. He did not follow her. Levi was not in the mood for Leana's antics. Choosing to go into the kitchen instead, pulling a bottle of Hennessy out of the cabinet along with a glass, he poured himself a drink. After Leana was done searching his house like a DEA agent, she reappeared in his kitchen.

"You finished, Inspector Gadget?" he asked, looking over the edge of his glass.

"Is that supposed to be funny?" Leana put her hand on her hip. "Your timing is off," she shirked at him.

"You poppin' up at my spot is what's not funny. You losin' it." Levi pointed his glass at Leana. "How da hell you even get here? Yo' ass been drinking."

"You're not happy to see me?" she tried to put on a sexy smile. In her drunken state, it did not come off that way. "I miss you." Leana slivered upon him, gently stroking his cheek with her knuckles. Resisting Leana's touch was not going to be easy for him. Levi could feel his anger towards her drifting away. Standing firm against his desire for his best friend's wife was going to take everything he had. Although Levi would not admit it to anyone, he had fallen hard for Leana. She was that forbidden fruit Levi wished he had never tasted. Regardless of how sweet and juicy it was that after taste left behind, he could not handle.

"Stop!" He removed Leana's hands from his face.

"You know you still want me." She touched his chest, letting her hand travel down his well-structured abdomen into his joggers. This was all it took to make Levi stand up to attention. He had to move away from Leana, or they would end up in the same position that started this whole disastrous situation.

"What did I tell you, Leana?" Levi barked at her, trying to adjust his sweats. Leana took notice at the teepee she created with ease. It was obvious to see that Levi wanted her just as much as Leana wanted him. Levi was trying hard to do what was right because of his loyalties to Melech. She would not make it that easy for him.

"Your body seems to be defying you." Leana gave a cynical laugh.

"That's how I ended up in this mess. My head ain't wit' this shit." Levi finished his drink. "You need to bounce. Get yo' life right, cause you really buggin' right now." Levi poured another glass for himself. "Go make shit right wit' my boy if he'll take yo' dumb ass back. The way you actin' right now," Levi paused, looking her up and down in disgust. "I hope he don't," Levi spat. "You got a fucken screw loose. I don't know how I didn't see that shit before he fell in love wit' you and I fucked up and slept wit' yo ass."

"You played a part in all of this too!" Leana yelled at him. "I was happy with Melech until you took advantage of me!"

"Oh, baby girl, you're delusional. You set me up, and I jumped in that shit headfirst, literally." Levi held on to his manhood. "I know I fucked up…you…you, just keep pushing up on me knowing what it's doin' to yo' husband. A good dude that gives you everything!" To his surprise, Leana broke down and cried. His instincts drew Levi to her, pulling Leana into his arms. He hated what she had done to Melech, watching the tears fall down her rosy cheeks pulled at Levi's heart. The last thing he wanted to do was see her in pain as well. This whole situation had disrupted all their lives. Melech was the levelheaded person in this trio and guided both Levi and Leana into making the right decisions. His absence is why they fell into the ultimate sin. The only pure soul amongst the trio was the one that would be hurt if their secret was revealed.

"Hey, don't cry," Levi gently told her. "It's gonna be all good." He stroked her back.

"No, it won't, Levi," she said through her tears. "You don't want me now, Leek hates me. I just wanted to be with you." Leana's body shook with her cries.

"Why on earth would you walk away from Melech?"

"To be with you. I just wanted to be with you." Levi released her.

"That's the dumbest shit ever," he roared. "Are you that selfish? When did I ever tell you, that's what I wanted? I did some fucked up shit, and after I hit, how many times did I tell you this can't happen?" Levi stared Leana in the eyes. She would not make eye contact with him. "How many, Leana?"

"Every single time," she did not want to confess this to him. Leana knew that they had more than just amazing sex. They could talk about almost anything Levi made Leana laugh. She admired his carefree lifestyle, Levi lived it to the fullest. He did not waste one second worried about what happened yesterday. Levi lived for what was going to happen tomorrow.

"Then why would you throw away a good thing? Walkout on a man that loves you unconditionally?"

"Because I know that you want to be with me. We could have such a good life." Leana cupped Levi's face, trying to kiss him. As her lips touched his, Levi wanted to return the affection and take Leana once again in his kitchen. Instead, he put his forehead to hers.

"We can't do this to Melech. I just love him more than I do you." Leana was not happy with this response. She pushed Levi away from her.

"Does he fuck you the way I do?" she shot out the insult.

"Get the fuck up out my house!" Levi grabbed her by the arm, dragging Leana out the kitchen, through the living room, to his front door. The whole time she was trying to fight Levi off of her. "You dumb as fuck! I'm gonna make sure my nigga neva takes yo' hoe ass back!" he tossed Leana out of his front door, slamming it behind her.

Leana was shocked at how fast Levi turned on her. She cried, banging on the door, begging Levi to forgive her and allow her back into his house. He would not answer her pleas. After over an hour, Leana saw a police car pull up, flashing a bright light on her as she was crutched down on Levi's porch, still knocking and screaming his name. Leana covered her eyes from the piercing bright light's being shined on her. It stunned her that Levi would call the cops on her.

"Ma'am," One of the officers approached her. "Do you live here?" he asked her.

"What?" She looked at the Ken doll look alike.

"He asked you, do you live here." The second cop approached her using his deep raspy voice. Leana focused in on him. He was an attractive man, tall with a Denzel Washington appearance.

"No, sir, I do not. My friend lives here." Leana stood to her feet.

"Have you been drinking, ma'am?" the Ken doll asked her.

"Excuse me?" Venom filled her tone.

"Miss," the Denzel clone got her attention. "We got several calls about you disturbing the neighborhood. "Are you and your husband…mate, having a dispute?" he asked her.

"He threw me out," Leana tried to explain.

"So, you live here?" Ken doll asked.

"No…no, not exactly."

"Miss, have you been drinking?" he asked Leana once again. Her words were garbled, her appearance was disheveled, and the messy ponytail was no longer in place after the thorough search of Levi's house.

"What does that have to do with anything?" Leana snapped at him. "Do you see me driving anywhere?"

"No, I do not, but you are in public, making a whole lot of noise disrupting this neighborhood. You do not have to be driving to be drunk and disorderly." He informed her.

"I am not some gutter rat. Who do you think you are talking to?" Leana got into his face. Levi was watching the entire scene take place through his living room window. It was only a matter of time before one of his neighbors would call the police. He made it a point of buying a house in a neighborhood filled with established elderly people. They had been in their homes for years. Many of them had already paid them off. Levi wanted to lay his head in comfort without leaving his roots.

"We need you to calm down just a little bit, Miss." The Denzel look alike officer was doing his best not to let the situation get out of control. "We've received several calls about your behavior this morning. Do you have someplace to go?"

"I'm just trying to talk to Levi." Leana pointed clumsily at the front door. "He's not listening to me." Leana clasped her fingers together behind her neck, lowering her head, sighing.

"Apparently, he doesn't want to be bothered with you." Ken doll interrupted the conversation. "It's time for you to leave, or we'll take you down to the station. Leave this man alone."

"I don't have a car!" Leana hollered at him.

"Ma'am, there is no way we would allow you to drive," the other officer used a calming voice. "Is there somewhere we can take you?"

"Down to the station. I'm tired of all this now. This chick can dry out and have someone pick her up." Ken doll grabbed her by the elbow, trying to escort Leana to the police car. In her drunken state, Leana was not mindful of who she was dealing with. She snatched her arm away. Instantly, Leana found herself face down in the grass with one of the officer's hands shoving her head deep into the soil, his knee was in the middle of her back. Leana wanted to scream for help; no words were released from her vocal cords.

"That's enough." His partner was pulling on Ken doll's shoulder.

"Eh, man, you doing way too much." Levi finally surfaced from behind his front door. "She a woman, dude!"

"Hey…get back in your house." He quickly rose to his feet, reaching for his firearm. "You hear what I said to you?" Levi put both hands in the air, freezing mid-step. He had several guns pulled on him during his lifetime, never by a police officer.

"Everything is good here. Sir, we need you to go back in your house." The Denzel looking officer had to intervene before this night turned into his worst nightmare.

"I don't want no problems," Levi explained. There was no way he was turning his back on the trigger-happy cop or leaving Leana alone with him, mainly since his pistol was still aimed right at him.

"Then, go back inside and stop talking!"

'This nigga here,' Levi thought to himself. *'Badge and gun got him all beefed up.'* "What's gonna happen to her?" he asked, ignoring Mr. Trigger fingers.

"We're going to get the lady home. Now go back inside." Levi backed his way to his front door, never taking his eyes off of the gun, smiling at Ken doll. "Put that shit away," he scolded his partner, then set his attention on Leana. She was still trying to get the dirt off her face that was now mixed with her tears. "How did you get here, ma'am?"

"Uber," Leana's voice was barely above a whisper.

"She's going in!" Ken doll stormed over to them. The Denzel's carbon copy pulled his partner to the side to be as discreet as possible.

"Maybe, if you hadn't put that tiny woman to the ground and pulled your weapon on that man." He pointed at Levi's house. "How the fuck do we write this up? Hmm, tell me, smart guy?"

"So, she just walks?"

"Do you want her to give a statement?" they locked eyes. "You're a cop, look at her get up, the purse…even her vernacular tells you she is not some run-of-the-mill ghetto girl. She will have her lawyers up your ass so fast!" Ken doll finally inspected Leana. "She got a little tipsy and made a mistake with her dude. Let it go."

"Yeah…yeah, whatever, man. I'm going back to the car. You deal with her then."

"I'm always cleaning up your messes," he yelled out to him.

CHAPTER SEVEN

Waking up alone was still an odd feeling for Melech. The last thing he wanted to do was acknowledge he was missing Levi's presence in the big house he once shared with Leana. Melech's mind would not allow him to give her another thought. Melech had spent way too much time trying to figure out what he had done wrong to make his once delightful wife stray to the arms of another man. He laid awake, reliving their relationship from the time they met up to the dreadful day Melech found the letter.

Leana consistently stood by his side, made him smile during the hard times, and brought out the brighter side to life while she was around. Melech knew his wife had her flaws, yet they did not impede on his happiness. Looking back now, Melech should have seen her need for attention and affection. Overcompensating Leana's needs were only a small part of what Melech did in their everyday life. Losing her mother at such a young age, Melech knew he was in for some abandonment issues with their relationship. He pacified Leana on many arguments to appease her insecurities about him. Melech wanted Leana to see that he was going to be right by her side until one of them died. Never in his wildest dreams did he think she would walk out on him and for another man.

He was given the most prominent warning when she secured a relationship with him before Leana broke up with her high school sweetheart. Melech wondered did she ever spend any time loving herself. The way he was looking at life now, Leana went from one relationship to another. From what he could see, the relationships overlapped the other. Melech realized Leana had never been alone. Her father was a good man and devoted father. Melech knew first-hand that Chester doted on his daughter. She was his first priority. This could have been Leana's downfall. Melech ended up doing the exact same thing. Apparently, whoever Leana left him for did not put her first. Melech dissected her letter. It was burned into his memory now. Leana was looking for adventure and change all of a sudden. Both Melech and her father offered Leana stability and security. The fast lane and excitement is what Leana was seeking. A small part of Melech could understand that need, and Levi had provided that for him.

There would never be a hookah lounge if it were not for his best friend. Melech would be stuck behind a desk in some corporate office, living some mundane life. Leana also gave Melech the spontaneity he needed; she always had something new for them to experience. Why she could not come to him to enhance their lives instead of stepping out on him was beyond Melech's comprehension. He rarely told Leana no, so this newfound freedom she was seeking was mind-blowing to him. Melech enjoyed exploring new things with his wife, stifling her was not what he did. Whoever Leana fell in love with, Melech hoped it was worth it. Not too many men would be willing to deal with her antics the way Melech did.

He understood Leana inside and out. Melech had the chance to walk away from her when she admitted to having a boyfriend while they were in a relationship. Melech forgave Leana because their relationship was long distance, and he was already in love with her. Leana begged him not to give up on her, promising she would prove to Melech she was worthy of giving her a second chance. He was learning now that her word meant nothing. Leana was selfish and only thought about her own needs. This was uncharted waters for Melech. He heard about people like Leana. Melech never thought he would allow someone like her into his life. To him, even Levi knew what loyalty was. You learned that through family or friends. For some reason, Leana did not get the concept.

Melech kept playing the scenario repeatedly in his head; he could work through a one-night stand. Even forgive Leana for the betrayal. The love of his life not only had an affair, but she also fell in love with another man. That was unforgivable. Melech wished Leana kept that secret to herself. Why didn't she just walk out on him without the confession? He knew that people confessed their sins to free themselves of guilt. It was not to make things right. Why did Leana have to drag him down into an emotional turmoil to cleanse her soul? This was information she could have kept to herself, leaving Melech clueless. What you don't know cannot hurt you. Melech would never trust another woman again. When you accept someone with all their flaws, and they stick a dagger in your heart; there is no turning back.

Melech grabbed his keys before heading off to work. As usual, Melech went for a run, then made himself breakfast. After watching a little Sports Central, he showered and touched up his beard. Melech was actually looking forward to getting to the Lounge. It took his mind off of his real-life problems. Levi had brought a real good idea to him about having the locals come out to promote their work at the lounge. Melech planned to jump on that full force. Anything to get his mind off his failed marriage. Leana could not break the goals he set the way she broke his heart. Melech needed to tell himself that several times throughout the day to keep moving forward with his existence.

Levi had many contacts in the community. Melech also wanted to bring in some upscale talent as well. Melech always wanted to uplift his community, bringing in local talent would be an excellent platform. Levi did not have to dig as deep as he would since he had the luxury of reaching out to his inner circle for connections. Melech wanted to go back to his roots and bring in the old school heads. After trolling Instagram, Melech knew there was going to be some talented people who needed to connect with the college kids and millennials. Melech had not discussed it with Levi yet, but he had his mind set on opening another lounge.

Melech did not want Levi out in the streets trying to come up with his share of the funds. They were doing well enough to take out a business loan. Levi was more of the cash upfront type of man. He did not like owing *'The Man'* anything. Now that Melech did not need his enormous home, he was considering selling it. There were no children in his near future, the last thing Melech wanted to do was remain in the house with constant memories of his wife and no children. He would set the house on fire before he lost it to Leana in the divorce. There was no way Melech would allow Leana to move another man into it. He could not deal with Leana starting a new family in the home his parents helped him buy them.

His lawyer informed Melech, Leana moving out of the house was the best thing for him; technically, she now has no claims to it. Melech wasted no time changing the locks and security codes, so there was no way Leana could force her way back in. She was following her heart while Melech was taking directions from his lawyer. Leana did not have one item left in the house. Melech made sure his mother packed up every single item Leana brought into their marriage and anything he bought her while they were married. Leana was now free to be the person she was looking for. She needed to spread her wings…fly butterfly, fly.

The room was spinning around Leana as she held onto the bed for safety. Blinking her eyes wildly, she tried to focus on something. Shaking the woozy, unsteady feeling was difficult for her. Leana was desperately trying to figure out how she got back to the hotel. The night's events were still a blur for her. Attempting to sit up again was unsuccessful. Leana curled up in a fetal position, feeling sorry for herself. All the years of schooling did not prepare her for what was going on in her life. Teaching people not to walk down this path was her job, yet she had made a massive disaster of her own personal experience. All Leana wanted now was her own bed, and to feel a sense of normalcy if only for five minutes.

Leana wanted to be in her kitchen, cooking dinner for her, Melech, and Levi. They would be on the game or arguing over what new flavors they were going to introduce into the Lounge. She would gaze over at them in amusement, loving the way the two went back and forth with the insults. If they had told her they were brothers when Melech introduced her to Levi, she would have believed them. The bond they share is remarkable. None of them had siblings, Leana felt fortunate they both included her into their bond. Levi treated her like family also, right from the beginning. Now, the special relationship they once had was ruined because she was in love with them both. The problem was now neither one of them wanted her. It was a hurt she never thought she'd have to experience.

They still had each other while she was the odd man out. Leana wanted her father to hold her and reassure her that everything was going to work out in the end; she could not call him either. He already told Leana how disappointed in her he was. Chester was only going to give her another lecture; this was not what Leanna wanted to hear while she was feeling this much pain. Somehow Leana found the strength to jump off the once comforting bed and sprint to the bathroom. She felt like she was throwing up her soul for almost fifteen minutes. Laying on the icy floor was the only thing that comforted her. Crawling from the bathroom back into the room, Leana searched for her purse. The one person who had not yelled at her yet was Melech, he was her last option.

♥ ♥ ♥

Levi pulled his Challenger into the Fat Burger parking lot on Crenshaw and Slauson, checking out his surroundings before stepping out. He was not worried about anyone taking his snow bunny of a car; most people knew it was his. Levi made it a habit to take a mental note of who was around him. You never knew when gunplay would happen, even if you were not the intended target. This particular Fat Burger brought in a wide variety of vehicles and patrons. Levi was a regular, it was like a second office for him. Levi closed several deals on this corner, both legal and illegal. He popped his door, standing tall with his six-foot, two sixty frame. He stroked his well-manicured beard, catching the attention of two ladies in a Pepto-Bismol pink Mercedes. Flashing a suggestive smile, Levi winked his green eyes at them. They both giggled in unison.

"How you ladies doing today?" Levi asked them.

"We good. Who you meeting up here?" the chocolate girl with the long ponytail and deep dimples asked him. Levi shook his head, smiling once again.

"I'm waiting on my homeboy. What's yo' name, dimples?" Levi walked closer to her. She intrigued him. Levi had seen this ugly car on several occasions, wondering why anyone would destroy a Mercedes with such a dreadful color. Levi assumed she belonged to some hustler that gave her anything she asked for to keep quiet on the side chicks he kept on his team.

"I'm Candy." She played with the enormous horsetail she was sporting. "This, my girl Mona."

"Does yo' friend look anything like you?" Mona boldly asked.

"That's him right there." Levi pointed at Misfit.

"Why fine nigga's always kick it together?" Mona tried whispering to Candy. Levi heard every word she said.

"Sup, cuh." Misfit took Levi's hand, pulling him in for a hug. "It's been too long."

"Word."

"You snacking before we throw down?" Misfit asked. "You know I'm always up for an appetizer." Misfit sucked in his bottom lip.

"Yo' ass ain't neva gone change." Levi put his head down to hide his amusement. "This is Candy and Mona." He pointed at each girl, respectively. "We just met."

"But we can be friends." Mona was focused on Misfit.

"I got enough friends, ma, but I like to keep some good late-night calls on hand." He rubbed his hand around his fist.

"Ladies, I own a hookah lounge close to UCLA. Why don't you two roll through?" Levi pulled out two business cards. "Ask for me. I'll make sure you get hooked up. My mans and I got some business to get to."

"We will definitely swing by. What's the best day?" Candy took the cards.

"Thursday, Friday, or Saturday, it's poppin'."

"You betta be there." She pointed the cards at Levi before she got into her Pepto-Bismol Mercedes.

"That's her ride?" Misfit asked. Levi shook his head. "That's Payback's girl. Stay away from her. She's trouble."

"I knew when I saw that damn car on the streets, she belonged to someone. Who da fuck does that to they car?"

"He'll go to war behind that broad."

"Don't have time for any more wars in my life. Learning these chicks ain't loyal for shit." Levi's mind went to Leana.

"Got dat shit right."

"How's yo' girl?" Levi asked.

"She good. Tryna get me to get her silly ass pregnant," Misfit huffed.

"You ain't down for being a daddy?"

"Do I look like father material?" He twisted up his face. "I got enough Lil' nieces in nephews to play wit'. Everyone got a bunch of little people runnin' round these days."

"That's why I hit you up. Let's get some food and talk." Levi started walking into the restaurant. "How's Rude doing?" he asked, opening the door.

"Nigga, good. We back out here for a few weeks. He gotta tryout with the Clippers. He's banking on that. I think he's ready to come home."

"Word? I hope he gets that shit. He deserves it."

"That fool don't care if he rides the bench. He just wants to walk on that Staple floor." Misfit told him.

"I heard the shit out of that." They ordered their food and took a seat and talked about old times.

"So whatcha need from me?" Misfit inquired. "We coulda done all this ova the phone."

"You're an ass," Levi chuckled.

"Always have been. Don't mind kickin' it wit' you, but you ain't rolled shit or passed nothin', so I know this is business." Misfit drank from the straw. "Plus, we sittin' at yo' spot. Where you get shit done at." Levi had to laugh.

"You know me so well," Levi conceded. "I actually came to you about Mel, but as we were talking, Rude would be a good fit as well. We wanna start promoting hometown legends in a sense at the Lounge."

"Mel would love it. Everything is about him. Rude…" Misfit frowned. "Not so much. You know how private he can be."

"Still?"

"Cuh, ain't never gonna change."

"You can make him do anything." Levi gave him a look.

"Sometimes. Rude's been mister moody broody for the past few years. Got his heart broke, my man ain't been the same."

"Shit, I feel him on that one."

"Ahh, say it ain't so. A female got to the infamous, Levi?" Misfit burst out laughing.

"Nigga, please. Never. My boy, Melech, is going through the same thing. His wife did a number on him."

"Mister clean-cut is having chick problems. I can't see it. He got everything nigga's like us had to work hard for." Both Misfit and Levi had to struggle in life. They spent more time in the streets than they did at home. They were both blessed with friends who took a liking to them and guided them in the right direction. Misfit had Twin, while Levi had Melech. Without someone fighting for them, the two would have ended up cellmates.

"Trust and believe he gave her everything. All diamonds don't sparkle." Levi shrugged. "He ain't deserve what she did. I blame myself for half the shit he going through."

"You fuck her?" Misfit tilted his head to the side, gazing into Levi's green eyes.

"Why you say some shit like that?"

"You always wanted what that nigga had." Levi sat back in the chair, contemplating the statement. "Yeah…you did." Misfit slapped the table. "Ain't no fun if the homies can't have none." A robust laugh came from Misfit.

"You know you crazy in the head. I ain't neva wanted shit that nigga had. We boys!"

"Yo' secret safe wit' me."

"You always on some bullshit."

"If you say so. You just betta make sure that bitch keeps her mouth shut. Melech seems a little off to me. He wanted in your world just as much as yo' ass wanted in his. He gonna come fo' that ass in a big way."

"It ain't like that and ain't no way in the world I wanna live in his stuffy ass lifestyle. I woulda beat his daddy's ass by now."

"Sure, you would of. Like your pops who fucks you up wit' words from a prison phone."

"We've known each other way too long. I ain't feelin' yo' ass in none of the shit you talkin' bout."

"Ha!" Misfit stood to his feet. "I need to put something in the air." Levi grabbed their trash, tossed it, and followed Misfit out to his car. He did not understand how Misfit was able to read him like a book. Levi spent every day with Melech, how was he the one so clueless about the forbidden relationship going on between him and Leana?

♥ ♥ ♥

"Yeah," Melech answered the unknown number on the office phone. He knew that it was not professional, but he was sidetracked going through the week's supply order.

"Leek?" a soft voice came through the line.

"Hello!" he said again, trying to balance the phone with his shoulder.

"Melech…"

"Yeah…yes, this is he."

"It's Leana…" her voice trailed off.

"What do you want?" Leana could feel the chill through the phone line.

"I'm sorry."

"Don't be."

"You forgive me?" Leana needed some type of comfort from anyone.

"No, Leana, I don't." Melech sat up in his chair. The pain from reading her letter all came rushing back to him.

"I love you so much, Melech. I really do. I don't know what's wrong with me." She threw everything out on the table to him.

"Selfish," came out before Melech thought about it. "After all this time, the only thing you thought about was your wants and needs."

"I still love you, Melech." He held the phone to his chest. Melech did not want to hear anything Leana had to say to him. She ripped his heart out, and that was not forgivable. "Melech…Leek," insecure, she tried to get his attention.

"Goodbye, Leana." He hung up the phone. Melech thought when they finally spoke, he would yell, scream, or curse at her. He just did not have the cruelty to break Leana. She sounded so sad and desperate on the phone. Her wings did not fly her very far. Now she was reaching out to him. Love is a dangerous game. Leana took a leap. From what he heard in her voice, things were not working out in Leana's favor. It was no longer Melech's job to pick up her pieces when they crumbled. When she walked out on him, Melech put a wall up. Not even her tears could bring it down.

"Dayum! Now what?" Levi stood at Melech's office door.

"Leana." Melech did not look at him. He just stared off, trapped in his own thoughts.

"Fuck her, man." Levi sat in front of the desk. "I know I've been pushing for y'all to get back together, but that bitch crazy as fuck." He pulled the blunt from behind his ear. "Stupid ass came to my house last night."

"She what?" This got Melech's attention. "For what?"

"Listen, man, I need to tell you about Leana." It was time to get this out. The guilt was eating Levi up inside. He lit the blunt to give him some relief. "She was acting crazy, drunk, and high, tossing my shit up like 5-0."

"Wait...what?" Melech was not following the story.

"She's lost it, Leek."

"What was she looking for?"

"A woman." Melech held his head in his hands.

"She just called telling me that she loved me."

"You not taking this hoe back, are you?" Levi blurted out.

"Why the hell does she even care if you have a woman at your crib?"

"Because she was tryna fuck, Leek." The entire room went silent. There was so much more that needed to be said, now was the time to put the truth out there. Levi knew their friendship was stronger than any woman. "It's been an ongoing thing for a while." Levi jumped up with a quickness as Melech's desk came barreling at him. Rage had taken over his friend as Levi watched him destroy the unsuspecting room. "Bruh," Levi tried calming Melech down.

"Don't fucken touch me." Melech shoved Levi across the room.

"Melech, there's more."

"Save it!" He stormed out of the office with Levi right on his heels. There was no way he was going to allow Melech out of his sight. There was a temper that laid deep inside of Melech that no one needed to feel but him.

"Melech, where are you going?"

"To kill her!" Levi got an icy chill run up his spine that stopped him in his tracks.

"No...no...no!" he picked up his pace again, catching Melech at his truck.

"Wait…Listen to me, Leek." He wrestled with him, doing his best not to allow Melech in the car. "Not now, not like this. You're angry."

"You fucked her!" Levi froze. There was no way he was going to lie to his best friend. "Don't deny it. Leana gets whatever she wants." Levi stepped back, still not answering the question. "Levi?"

"Man…she…I…she…has a way…fuck!" There were no words to make any of this right.

"Yeah." Melech nodded his head, looking around. He, too, had no words for his best friend. The man he considered a brother. Melech was sure Leana was the one who seduced Levi. In Melech's mind, Levi should have been smarter and more loyal to the friendship. He stroked the back of his head, then socked Levi in the face.

"Fuck!" Levi grabbed his nose as the blood spewed into his mouth and all over his shirt.

"This shit's not over! First, I need to kill this bitch!" Melech tried to get in his truck again; murderous thoughts were on his mind.

"No…Leek." Levi tackled him to the ground. "Beat my ass all you want. I can't let you give up yo' life for that broad." The two rolled around the ground wresting. Melech threw several more blows to Levi's face and abdomen, which he welcomed each painful strike as punishment for his dreadful deeds. Once on his feet, Melech kicked Levi in the rib cage several times before getting in his truck and pulling off. Levi laid there aching all over. This was the first time Melech got the best of him, Levi did not retaliate on this assault, he knew he had no right. All Levi wanted to do was stop Melech from doing something in the heat of the moment. Levi sat up, wrapping his arms around his knees, laughing. Levi could not remember the last time he got his ass whooped. He just let his best friend rip him a new one.

"What the hell did you do?" Rylee walked over to Levi.

"I didn't do shit." Levi spit blood onto the ground.

"So…you let Melech beat yo' ass for no reason at all?" Rylee crossed her arms.

"You saw that, huh?"

"Um, yeah, and you didn't throw one punch."

"He's my best friend." Levi shrugged. Rylee reached her hand out to him, helping Levi to his feet. "Good looking." Rylee shook her head and went back into the lounge. She did not want to get in the middle of what the two of them were fighting about. Rylee knew when best friends came to blows it was about money, drugs, or women.

Levi stumbled over to his car. Getting blood in this beauty made him angrier than the beat down Melech put on him. He would not allow his best friend to do something he was going to regret. Levi grabbed his phone to call Chester. He needed to find out if Melech called looking for Leana's whereabouts before he could get to her.

Confusion, insecurity, and uncertainty all filled Leana's mental space. The composure Melech displayed frightened her. It was not that he did not take on each and every complex situation head-on without the full-on anxious nature the way Leana did. Melech was known for his serene disposition, but this was different. He appeared to be emotionless in his response to everything Leana had to say to him. She did not break down often or cry when she did, Melech moved mountains to ensure Leana was feeling secure in herself, their marriage, or any struggles that came her way. He appeared to be unmoved by any words or emotions that were displayed in the brief conversation. Melech was Leana's last option. She thought deep down inside there was a small glimmer of love left for her.

There was not much keeping Leana focused on the prize. She jumped off the cliff fully thinking Levi would be there to catch her. Never, ever in her mind's eye, did she believe Levi would step to the side and allow her to crack her skull on the concrete. It was becoming clear what she thought was something special between them, was all in her mind. This made him the worst type of man in the world to her. How could he claim to be a brother to Melech and bed his wife? There was absolutely no code of ethics for Levi. If Leana was going to lose everything, she vowed to make sure Levi was left cold and desolate the same way she was feeling at this very moment. Being thrown out as if she were scraps for unwanted slaves did not settle well for Leana. It was time to blow up Levi's world. If she could not have him, neither one of them could have Melech. This was no fairytale in the hood. Leana was determined to make everyone as miserable as she was.

Yes, Melech was a good man and would get caught in the crossfire of her feud with Levi, 'All is fair in love and war,' Leana thought as she glared at herself in the mirror. *'Should have thought twice before loving and leaving me.'* A ruthless grin manifested across her face. She took a long drag from the fresh blunt she rolled. Leana dug through her bag and found the bottle of Xanax she had a coworker prescribe for her before taking a week off from work. Most mental health professionals have a psych of their own just to keep them levelheaded. After confiding in him that she was having a hard time dealing with her marital problems, the medication was way too easy to get. Making sure Levi got what was coming to him was the first thing on Leana's agenda. Figuring out how to let Melech know that she left him for Levi was job number one.

CHAPTER EIGHT

After speaking with Chester, Levi was informed that Melech had not called or come by his home. He sped through the back streets of LA, heading downtown. Leana left him a message to meet her at the Ritz and her room number; his not showing up prompted her tirade on him the night before. Levi was second-guessing his decision to admit his dirty deeds to Melech now. Levi had no clue his friend would lose sight of reality and want to kill his darling wife. Leave her for good was more on the lines of rational.

Levi was also pulled into the web of Leana's seduction but, wrapping his hands around her throat was merely a fantasy. By the look in Melech's eyes, watching Leana take her last breath was something he wanted to make a reality. Not striking back during Melech's assault on him was proof of Levi's regret. If it had become a brawl, Melech would have done his best to do some serious bodily harm to his closest friend and brother. Levi was trying to stop Melech from leaving the lounge filled with rage, disappointment, and pain. The betrayal that was dished out by his best friend and wife sent a murderous instinct flowing through his whole being. If Melech got to Leana first, Levi was not sure what kind of damage he was capable of.

It did not take Levi long to get to the Ritz Carlton. He knew all the back streets from his experience of having one too many drinks and trying to avoid the police. Tossing his keys to the valet, Levi informed them he would not be gone long, not to park his car yet. Taking the ticket, he rushed up to Leana's room, praying Melech had not beat him there. To his surprise, Melech answered the door after Levi's knocks. He did not wait for a formal invite, pushing his way past his friend. Panic-stricken, Levi searched the room.

"What did you do?" he asked Melech.

"I see you rushed right over to save your girl!" he blurted out.

"Nigga, I came here for you. Fuck what she goin' through."

"Did you tip her off?" Melech grabbed Levi by his shirt, lifting him off his feet. This time Levi was not going to take any more of Melech's manhandling of him.

"What da fuck I look like?" he shoved Melech off of him. "I came here to make sure you didn't do nothin' stupid." He adjusted his clothes. "I give two shits' bout your wife."

"You gave some shits while you were digging her out. Apparently enough for her to leave me for you!" Melech tried swinging on Levi again. He maneuvered to the side, grabbing Melech by the waist and tackling him onto the bed.

"The hitting stops now, bruh." Levi held him down on the bed. Melech struggled to get out of Levi's grasp.

"Get the fuck up off me." Melech continued to struggle.

"Nah, man. You gonna calm down first." Levi had managed to get one of Melech's arms behind his back, securing the other over his head. "I know you mad. You got every right to be."

"You fucked my wife!"

"Shit, man, I'm really sorry. I never ever planned it. Leana just...." Melech rolled himself over, taking control of Levi. Guilt diminished his strength, allowing Melech to find himself on top of Levi, ready to start the assault over again.

"Leek, I fucked up." Sincerity overtook all of Levi's emotions. "I really fucked up; I have no other words to say. Leana has a way…" his voice trailed off.

"Yeah, man, I know." Melech let Levi up. They both sat on the bed, side by side. Neither had anything to say to the other. They had allowed a woman to come between their friendship, neither knew if it would ever be the same again. They shared so many things. A woman was not supposed to be one of them. Melech got up and walked out the door. Levi tried calling out to him. It did not make Melech look back or even respond. His heart was heavy. The last thing he wanted to do was talk about what had taken place between his wife and best friend. Knowing that Leana had fallen in love with a stranger, Melech was coping with it. Learning that person was the closest thing he had to a brother struck a core in him, Melech did not know how to handle the whole situation. He wanted to see the life go out in Leana's eyes as he heard her take that last gasp of breath. As for Levi, Melech did not know where they stood. Not having him in his life was going to be difficult. They were family, brothers, and best friends.

Melech felt like he could put a bullet in his head. How the two people he loved and trusted most in the world could deceive him this way he could never understand. His ability to trust was gone.

Laying on the bed gazing up at the ceiling, Levi could not help but wonder how he made such a mess of everything. He was angry with himself for allowing his needs to get in the way of what was right. Melech had shown him nothing but friendship and love. His own mother and father did not support him in the manner Melech had throughout the years. Leana had a way about her that made you want to be a part of everything she was. When Melech introduced them, he did not understand the attraction. Levi warned his best friend that he was moving way too fast. The more time they spent time together, Levi began to understand Leana more.

Leana was like a magnet, pulling you into her soul. Each and every moment, the three spent together was memorable. Levi found himself in love with her. Sharing Leana with Melech was perfectly fine with him until the day he tasted her. That was never supposed to happen. Her touch was so gentle on Levi's face, the whispers in his ear, brushing up against him in that sensual way only Leana could, made the desire to want to be deep inside of her agonizing. Levi fell for it every time he made the vow to never touch Leana again. The smell of her perfume would invade his nostrils, the touch of her lips on the side of his mouth while her hands ventured down to his manhood played on his emotions.

Within minutes, Levi had her bent over and was filling Leana's insides with every inch of him. As good as she felt at the time, regret took over almost immediately. It did not matter how many times Levi told Leana this could never happen again. She gave him a devilish smile and left him in his feelings. They were just words in Leana's mind, something Levi had to say to make him feel better for betraying his friend. The fact that she packed up and left Melech was supposed to be Levi's wake up call.

Never in life would Levi set out to hurt someone he considered to be closer to him than a brother. Her actions actually backfired on Leana. Anger was not the emotion she expected from, Levi. Everlasting love is what she'd hoped for. She thought they would live the happily ever after she read about and saw in movies. The ties that bind the friendship Levi and Melech shared had not been taken into consideration. Levi would never leave Melech's side, especially for a woman. Loyalty came first with him. Having sex with her was of no consequence to him. Leana underestimated genuine friendship over the power of seduction.

Pulling up to the Lounge, Leana witnessed the scuffle-taking place between Melech and Levi. Making sure her car was not seen, Leana stayed glued to the scene in front of her. *'This bastard,'* she thought to herself. *'You got to Melech before I could.'* Leana wanted to get out of her car and kick Levi right beside her husband. Levi was more calculating than she ever thought he could be. Foiling her plans to come to Melech, cry for forgiveness because she was too weak to fight Levi's charms off was now not an option for her. Watching Levi take the brutal lashes from Melech was all the proof she needed to know Levi confessed to his sins, throwing her to the wolves. Leana was sure Levi made sure he came out smelling like cucumbers and watermelon.

Levi would never be honest enough to admit he shared something special with Leana. Throwing her out of his home was devastating for her ego, making Leana want to kick Levi as well. She was also aware his actions did not depict what was in his heart. It was too easy to bring Levi to full erection. The mouth can tell you anything. Levi's touch and the look in his eyes were not deceptive; those were things that came naturally. He could hide what he was feeling for the sake of his friendship with Melech. Playing with Leana's emotions was Levi's biggest mistake, she was a woman scorned. This made Levi and Melech unsafe.

Looking on as Melech finally overtook Levi, Leana decided to follow him. Curious to know where his mindset was, Leana knew that she was not going to able to speak to him until he was calm. She also needed to find a way to flip this whole ordeal back onto Levi. Leana did not imagine Levi would turn against her, it was the furthest thing from her mind. Knowing that Levi was disappointed in her was one thing, putting her out and letting the police mistreat her… *"That damn cop!"* Leana's thoughts flashed to the previous night. All the love she once felt for Levi was turning into rage. Losing everything for a man that was not willing to do the same for her was not a good look… for him.

Leana began to shift her loyalty to herself. She could not be the only loser in this game of chess. She was not sure how she was going to make Levi pay for his sins, but she was going to make sure that he never in his lifetime played with another woman's emotions.

Surprisingly, Melech drove straight to Leana's Hotel, this concerned her. If he knew precisely where she was staying, why hadn't Melech tried to reach out to her by now? He made no efforts at all to fight for Leana after she walked out of their home. She began to question his love for her as well. If Melech tried to walk away from her, any woman Melech thought he was in love with would have a personal visit from her. That affair would end as quickly as it started. Of course, she would make Melech pay dearly for even considering he could have a relationship with anyone but her at any point in his life.

Making Melech miserable would be Leana's number one mission for as long as it took. They would go back to life as usual. Melech was the man you did not let get away. There would be no peace in Melech's life, ever. Leana suddenly laughed loudly in the car alone. *'Yet you walked out of his door,'* she thought to herself. *'What an idiot you are. You had this man all to yourself!'* A single tear escaped Leana's eye. She knew even though she left Melech she would not allow him to be happy with another woman. There was no way her Leek was going to spoil another woman the way he did her.

Watching Melech enter her hotel, Leana planned to follow him until she saw Levi pull up. Confusion took over, getting between these two men was not something she was ready for. Leana wanted Melech all to herself; he needed to know her side to this unforbidden triangle they were all in. Not knowing what Levi had filled Melech's head with was a disadvantage for her. Leana hoped they did not tear up her room. Getting put out of her hotel was the last thing she needed. The room had become her little sanctuary. Going home to her father was not an option she wanted to use. Leana already knew Chester sided with Melech in their separation.

It did not take long for Melech to resurface. Agony consumed his handsome face. Leana wanted to run to him and make things better for Melech, hating that she was the one who caused him the heartache he was feeling. For the first time, Leana understood her role in destroying such a good man. She laid her head back on her seat with a pain in her heart. The ringing of her phone startled her. Looking down, she saw Levi's face appear.

"Now you want to call me?" she yelled at her phone. "Nope! Fuck you now, we aren't friends any longer." Leana hung up on him this time. She sat quietly, waiting for Levi to leave her hotel. Leana needed to figure out her next move. After ten minutes of waiting on Levi, Leana drove to the house she shared with Melech. It was time for them to have a conversation.

Just like clockwork, Melech was home even after an atrocious day. He wanted to have a quick dinner before heading back to the Lounge for the nighttime rush. Not much could ever take Melech out of his daily routine, even a fight with his best friend. Thinking about Leana's letter and Levi's comments, Melech came to the conclusion he was somewhat of a bore. He was not sure if he could shake being organized or like things being done a certain way. Melech made a vow to himself. If he ever found another woman, he found attractive enough to spend any time with, he would not suffocate her with the way he lived his life. In his mind, Melech thought, that is what Leana found attractive. She once expressed to him his drive and dedication to what he wanted in life is what made her fall in love with him. When Leana told Melech that he made her a better person, Melech believed what she was telling him. It was the major reason he paid for Leana to get her master's degree.

If he could help Leana achieve the goals she set out for her future, Melech was going to find a way to manifest them for her. Melech did anything to ensure Leana's happiness. In doing that, she considered Melech to be a bore. Levi on the other hand lost count on how many women he had in his bed, a motel, or in his car. Financially, Levi was hood rich. There was no disputing that. He could never fund Leana's dreams. Levi put away ninety percent of his money for the day he might be brought up on federal charges. He did not want anything he had seized.

Leana put her money on the wrong horse and Melech knew this. Just because Leana was able to get Levi in her bed, didn't mean she could ever get him to part with his money. Many strippers and neighborhood girls had tried. Failure was always the outcome.

Leana did not park in the driveway, she did not want Melech to hear her pulling up and not allow her access to the house. The front door was locked for a change, so Leana pulled her keys out to gain entrance. To her surprise, they did not work. *'This bastard,'* she said to herself. This was not going to stand in Leana's way of getting close to Melech. Knocking on the door would only allow him to slam it in her face. Leana went to the backyard, creeping through the French doors, which Melech always forgot to lock. There was no site of Melech in the kitchen or living room. Peeking into his office, it too was vacant. Tiptoeing up the stairs, Leana heard the shower running in their bedroom. A smile emerged across her face, recalling the fun they once had in there.

Deciding if she should join him or patiently wait in the bed for Melech was a tough choice. Melech fell weak when it came to her body, but he may be upset with her for sharing her gifts with another man, especially when that man was Melech's best friend. She quickly made the decision to wait in the room for Melech; remorse would work on her behalf more than her sex appeal. Considering that Levi had already confessed, Melech was more likely to believe whatever his best friend already told him. Leana was going to have to dig deep to try and find the love Melech once had for her if Leana wanted to win him back.

"What the hell?" Melech was startled when he saw Leana sitting on the bed they once shared. "Get out, Le. I don't want to hear anything you have to say." He wrapped his towel tightly around his waist, heading toward the closet.

"Leek, please give me five minutes," she pleaded with him.

"You lost that five minutes once you gave, Levi one second, we have nothing else to talk about," Melech viscously huffed.

"I have no idea what he has told you, but I'm sure it's not the truth." She allowed a tear to fall. "He used me, promised me things until I got weak, Leek." Leana tried to touch him. Watching Melech cringe when she touched him was heartbreaking. "He's the one who convinced me to walk away from you, baby. I realized he just wanted me out of your life." Leana did her best to lock eyes with Melech. She desperately needed him to believe her.

"So why were you at his house last night?"

"I...what?" the comment threw Leana off. She barely remembered last night.

"You tried to fuck my best friend, and after he tossed you out, your ass tried to run back to me." Fire shot from his eyes.

"No…no…no…" Leana was trying to get last night back into her memory. Being terrorized by the police was still a vague memory.

"And why does it even matter who Levi is sleeping with? You were supposed to be my wife!" If Melech did not have to hold up his towel, his hands would have been around her throat.

"It doesn't matter." Leana could see the hatred in his eyes.

"Get out before I hurt you." Melech walked away to put clothes on. If he had to physically put Leana out, He wanted to be fully dressed if the police showed up.

"Leek," Leana pleaded with him. She was not going to allow Levi to win yet another round. "You know how, Levi is, he takes what he wants." Resurfacing from the closet, filled with rage, Melech walked up on her.

"And I know exactly who you are!"

"We both do." Levi entered the room, interrupting the conversation.

"You can't be serious right now." Melech threw his hands in the air. If his gun were not locked in the safe in his closet, he would have shot both of them.

"Nah, bruh, ain't no way she gone twist some shit up bout me." Levi was ready to go blow for blow with Melech again. "Yes, baby girl, you got me, and I hit that shit. Yeah, I was wrong as fuck. How many times I tell yo' ass to stop comin' round me?" He poked Leana in the head. "How many times you push up on me, and I told you how foul the shit was? Did I once tell you to leave, Leek, that I would give you anything?" Levi bent down to be eye to eye with Leana.

"You damn near took it from me the first time," she protested.

"Did I?" Levi tilted his head to the side, glaring at her. Melech stood in disbelief at the two of them. "I came over for dinner as I…always…do…and you made sure you had booze, charm, and yo' shit all out." Levi pointed at her breast.

"You put me up on the counter and took it!" Leana defended herself.

"After you rubbed all up on me and sticking yo' tongue down my throat. Shit, before I knew what I was doing, my dick was in yo' hand now I'm a fucked-up muthafucka. I hit that shit, not even realizing what the fuck I was doing."

"And you did it again, stroking this kitty with love and affection. You made sure I would fall in love with you, not once thinking about Melech." Levi knew a small part of what Leana was saying was the truth. He did sleep with her again; it killed a piece of him each and every time.

"You're lying -"

"Shut the fuck up!" Melech could not listen to another word either of them had to say. His brain was ready to explode. How either of them could argue over who was at fault was insane to him. They were both wrong on so many levels. "Get the fuck out my house!" He grabbed Leana by the arm, dragging her down the stairs. "How dare you even show your face to me, trying to justify what you did. You're a whore."

"Melech," Leana cried out in pain, feeling each and every step as Melech dragged her down them. "Please listen to me." She finally broke free before they reached the front door.

"Levi will tell you anything, just give me a chance…"

"I did that once before, look where that got me!" Melech pulled Leana to her feet forcefully.

"Let me go," anger filled her voice. "You fucking idiot! That man doesn't give a shit about you. He seduced your wife, and you take his side in all of this?" Leana's true self-surfaced.

"He could never seduce you if you were an actual wife to me. You wanted to be with Levi or else you would have shut his ass down. You opened up those legs willingly. All you wanted was all this right here, you dirty gold digger." Leana slapped Melech for spewing such hateful words to her. Shock took over when he hit her back with such force Leana held onto her face, feeling blood trickle from her nose immediately.

"You bastard!" a flurry of blows came towards Melech. No man had ever hit Leana before. There was no way this would go unpunished. After the initial shock of what Melech had just done and enduring being struck one too many times, Melech pushed Leana. She went flying into the glass table next to the front door, shattering the glass.

"Get out before I slice your throat," the menacing tone scared Leana. She had never seen Melech behave this way with her. Blood was gushing onto Leana's clothes from the glass, cutting her back and hands. Melech showed the once love of his life, no concern for her wellbeing. He snatched Leana up, opened the front door, and tossed her out as if she was yesterday's garbage. All Leana could do was lay on their porch and cry. She could not understand how she made such a mess of her life; happiness seemed to be so far away. Now Leana longed for the mundane life she once shared with Melech.

Levi stood in the shadows watching the entire scene. A small piece of him may have wanted to come to Leana's defense, but there was no way in the world Levi was going to help her. For the life of him, Levi did not understand why Leana destroyed her marriage, and he promised her nothing. No matter how much Levi cared for Leana, the one thing he continually told her was everything they were doing was wrong. Levi loved Melech, hurting him was not something he planned on doing. How Leana did not understand this concept was concerning for him, they had been friends far too long.

"Why are you still here?" Melech snapped at Levi.

"You can hate me, use me as another punching bag, but, nigga, I ain't leavin' you by yo' self."

"You shoulda told me the first time it happened."

"You right." Levi had no arguments.

"My wife?" Melech glared through Levi.

"I fucked up, man. I tried to distance myself from y'all. You wouldn't let me."

"That's bullshit!" Melech hit Levi in the face once again before going back to his room. Levi held his jaw in pain.

"You only get one more of those, my nigga," he shouted up the stairs. The powerful right hook Melech kept delivering was getting old fast, Levi was not used to taking shots and not returning them.

"Fuck you!" Laughing was not the appropriate response. Only Levi could find the humor in the terrible ordeal.

After cleaning up the shattered glass and blood left behind from Melech's outburst with Leana, Levi grabbed a beer from the refrigerator. He was not surprised there was still some left behind; Melech was not much of a drinker. As usual, Levi made himself at home, turning on the TV watching Sports Central. Melech could not hide in his room too long, they both needed to get back to the Lounge. It did not matter what was going on in Melech's personal life, there was no way he would let the business slip by the wayside.

Fury was brewing as Melech paced the floor in his room. Trying to wrap his mind around the fact his wife left him was painful enough; learning Levi was the man Leana fell in love with was devastating. Melech was questioning every decision he had made since allowing both of them into his life. There was nothing Levi could offer Leana that was not already at her feet, both material and emotional. Melech loved both his parents and their relationship. Being perceptive at a young age, Melech knew they had their flaws. His father loved Melech's mother and spoiled her. He was dismissive at times of his mother's feelings, which in Melech's opinion was the reason she was overly dramatic about the smallest things. Vowing to be attentive to his wife appeared to backfire on him.

Levi and Melech were best friends with a lot of similarities. Levi had the air of a gangster about him, while Melech's confidence and athletic build set him apart from most men. They were two men you did not want to have a physical altercation with, especially when they were together. Taking Melech a few blocks away from his comfy suburban block, Levi introduced him to the neighborhood. It did not take long for Melech to become street-smart after spending time with Levi's friends. Both men were meticulous when planning out their lives. While Melech went to college to play football, Levi had been running his own street hustle long before he met Melech. Levi knew how to remain low key, ensuring he did not do any serious prison time.

The only reason Melech could fathom Leana would turn her attention to Levi was that slice of danger about him, the one thing Melech was missing. While he had his gun in his bedroom closet, and another at the lounge, Levi kept his on his person most of the time. Living on the edge fueled Levi; fast cars, loose women, and the best chronic money could buy was part of his daily life. The only thing he took seriously in life was the Lounge. Levi worked hard to save his share of the money to be an equal partner with Melech. They both planned to open a business together once Melech finished school; Levi was the one who brainstormed the Hookah Lounge. Learning how much college students liked to smoke his weed, Levi realized he could flip that habit and make it legal.

Loyalty, brotherhood, honesty, till death do us part-all these things were lost the moment Melech found out about his best friend and his wife. Who was he supposed to have the most hatred for? Hitting Levi only appeased Melech for that split second. As much as he wanted to pull Leana's heart through her throat, out of the mouth that spewed so many lies to him. Melech knew it would not stop his heart from hurting. When it was a stranger, Leana walked out of Melech's life for, moving forward was a struggle, but Melech knew he was able to do it. Learning it was Levi changed everything. The one thing Melech always knew is that Levi would take a bullet for him, even do jail time to spare Melech. This was why Melech did not understand how Levi could not comprehend Leana was off-limits?

His mind shifted to his wife. Leana also knew that Levi was the closest thing he had to a brother. Where in Leana's mind did she think it was a good idea to sleep with him, even worse believing that Levi would throw away their friendship to start a new life with her? Questioning himself, Melech could not figure out how he could be so blind not to see that his own wife was sleeping with them both? There were no changes in Leana's behavior; she did not grow distant toward him or even pull back while they slept together. Sadly, Leana denied none of Melech's advances with excuses. She was always a willing participant, which was the one thing Melech loved about Leana. Pleasing each and every one of Melech's needs sexually was never up for discussion. It was one of the reasons they did not have many arguments.

Leana was a master at calming Melech down when she pushed him too far. Her sensuality and sex appeal could dissipate the emotions that upset him in the first place. Knowing his wife, the way Melech did, he honestly could see how hard it would be for Levi to resist her advances. When Leana wanted something, she went full force in obtaining it. The question Melech still had was why did Leana want his best friend when he gave her everything she could ever want in life, catering to her every need, buying expensive gifts, paying for her tuition, even agreeing not to have children until she was ready. Leana's career came first; Melech understood Leana's rationality, he too wanted to have at least three lucrative business before they had to share their time with a child. Call it selfish, Melech enjoyed the time they spent together. He was an only child to two parents that had demanding lifestyles. Melech wanted to make sure he had free time to spend with a child when they decided to have one.

After wearing a hole in his carpet, Melech finally sat on his bed. Still confused about who his anger was directed at, then he noticed the time. He needed to get back to the Lounge and had not eaten all day. Melech was allowing those two and their dirty little secrets to take him out of his element. Sticking to his daily routine was the only thing that was going to get Melech through the turmoil thrown into his life. Making his way to his closet, Melech thought about the day he introduced Leana to Levi. He should have known then she could not be trusted alone with him. Levi try to warn him about her. He could see that his friend was blind-sided by love.

"What up, my boy?" Levi greeted Melech before he could get out of his bright yellow Mustang with the top down.

"Shit." Melech opened his door to give his friend a hug.

"Wassup, ma?" Levi made eye contact with Leana. She was at a loss, gazing into his eyes. The way the sun hit them, Leana melted in the emerald sea, staring back at her.

"Oh, man, this, my girl I been telling you bout." Melech rushed over to the passenger seat, opening the door for Leana. Shyly, she walked over to him, extending her hand out.

"Heard 'bout you." Levi gave Leana a hug. "You look better than I thought you would. This, nigga keep talkin' bout your smarts, shit I thought you was gonna be some plain Jane." Levi laughed at his own joke.

"I don't date dogs!" Melech huffed.

"When do you date?" Levi looked at him sideways.

"Don't try and play me right now." Melech pointed at him.

"Fool, you had the same bullshit ass girlfriend throughout high school."

"She was fine, though."

"Yeah…yeah, she really was." Levi held his fist to his mouth, chuckling. "Badass body too."

"Do we think I want to hear this?" Leana shot daggers at Melech.

"Don't trip, ma." Levi touched her shoulder. "She left his ass when he wouldn't give her ass a ring after he got dat football scholarship. Baby Girl, thought this nigga was goin' pro."

"Alright," Melech interrupted. He could see Leana did not like this conversation, plus he had never told her about Trina.

"My bad, bro. Ain't tryna start no shit. Shorty, she straight, though." Levi could tell that Melech really liked Leana; he was not going to keep playing with him. "Eh, you comin' in?" Levi stilled lived with his mother on W 62nd St. He was not sure how comfortable Leana would be.

"I thought we'd go get something to eat. Leana hasn't had real soul food. She's from Culver City. They don't come to this part of town." Melech nudged her.

"Really, Leek?" Leana rolled her eyes.

"Y'all don't." Levi co-signed. "But, Melech didn't know his ass had money either until I brought dat ass a mile from his comfy little community."

"You can't be serious!"

"Nah, fo' real, his parents was keepin' it one hundo wit' this one here. Made that ass go to public school."

"Levi, we're not rich!"

"You been rollin' that Mustang since high school, my nig. I'm pushin' an Impala. I'm just sayin'." Levi held both hands out, palms up.

"You pimped that damn Impala up to the nine!" Leana observed the conversation going on, she was under the impression Melech was at UCLA under a football scholarship.

"Whateva, where we eatin'?" Levi asked.

"Dulan's?"

"Word. We rollin' together, or you want me to follow y'all?"

"We can ride together," Melech told him.

"Shotgun." Levi was about to get in the front seat when Leana spoke up.

"I guess that means I'm sitting on your lap," she said with flirtation in her eyes, making Levi uncomfortable.

"Nah, that's all you, ma." Levi glanced over at Melech, who missed the whole thing. He tried putting it out of his mind. Leana had to be joking with him.

After eating, they took Levi back to his house, Leana glared out the window watching the two talking, wishing she knew what they were saying. Being the odd man out was not an emotion Leana enjoyed, it drove her crazy. Melech was going to get Levi's take on her, knowing that Melech held Levi's opinion more important than his own parents worried her. If your boys dislike your girl, the relationship will not last long, Leana knew that firsthand. Her high school boyfriend struggled with his friends all the time because they did not care for her. It was his parents that kept them together. Leana was the perfect wife for their son, Luca was destined to be an NBA first-round draft pick. Luca's father was an assistant coach for the Clippers, and his mother was on the school board in Culver City. They did not want some gold digger getting a hold to their son. This made Leana the perfect wife, his high school sweetheart, who was not looking for a rich man. Leana went to junior high school with Luca. They started dating when they were in the in the tenth grade. Leana's father already had the means to take care of her. Little did they know Leana just met a bigger whale once Melech entered her life.

Melech finally came back to the car, Leana played on her phone, pretending his absence did not bother her. On their drive back to campus, Melech said little to Leana. The pregnant silence was driving Leana insane. Whatever Levi told him was weighing on Melech's mind.

"You know, Levi had a gun on him?" Leana inquired.

"He always does." Melech looked over at her, curious. "How you know?"

"Either he was thrilled to meet me, or that was a piece he was holding," she explained.

"Levi lives a different lifestyle."

"He doesn't seem like someone you would be friends with."

"Don't judge Levi, you don't even know him."

"No judgment on him. I don't think he likes me," Leana sadly told him.

"You're silly," Melech was dismissive only because Levi just told him to slow the relationship down.

"I think he's just jealous you found happiness with me and don't have time for a person like him anymore." Leana sat back in the car seat. Breaking up this friendship was now on her agenda.

"Yeah, no. That's so far off base. Get to know him better, you'll learn the only thing Levi wants is for me to be straight. It's what we do."

"I didn't know your mom was an actress?" Leana learned this piece of information while Levi was telling stories about their childhood.

"Didn't think it was important. It's a stupid Soap Opera."

"Hmm..." Leana wanted to choose her next words wisely. "Your best friend is a drug dealer, and your mother is an actress. Is there anything else I need to know about you?"

"You have a lot of assumptions about my friend, and no one needs to know what my mother does. All it does it draw out a bunch of unwanted fans in my life."

"Did you see how your friend was looking at me?" Leana batted her eyes. Melech gave out a deep laugh coming from deep down from his gut.

"Now, that's funny." He wiped the tears from his eyes. "You are so out of his league."

"What is that supposed to mean?" Leana found the comment to be an insult.

"Baby, you're the type of woman men marry. Levi messes with strippers, video vixens, and the baldest hoes Compton has to offer because he's not calling you tomorrow."

"Oh." Leana felt better with Melech's explanation.

Melech could see now, Leana had a fascination for Levi the first day they met. He and Levi were only pawns in her game.

The drive back downtown was horrific for Leana, attempts to call her father went unanswered. She tried to leave her father a message, but only painful sobs escaped from an unknown place. Feelings of loneliness was aching deep inside the essence of Leana's soul. Quickly rushing to her room, Leana needed to escape her bloody, glass filled clothes and soak in a hot bath. Glancing in the mirror, Leana did not recognize the person staring back at her. She was a mere shell of herself.

Dark rings hung under her eyes. Her once well-kept wavy hair wildly flowed about her face, making her cheekbones protrude. Leaning carefully into the image in the mirror, Leana's once milk chocolate skin tone had a gray hue with speckles of blood from the shattered glass. Tears rolled fiercely, burning her skin as they fell. Emotionless Leana ran water in the tub, then slowly removed her clothing, dropping them to the bathroom floor. Suddenly feeling the aches of her body, Leana absentmindedly reached for the glass on the bathroom sink, then filled it with water, then she opened the bottle of Motrin and removed three pills. Noticing the Xanax, she realized just how much her heart was aching as well. Leana popped the top dropping two in her hand. Placing all five pills into her mouth, Leana drank the water until the glass was empty. Sliding into the soothing bathtub, a disturbing pink overtook the water from the blood Leana had not realized was all over her body.

The day's events were still replaying in her mind. Leana could understand Melech assault on Levi. But how he treated her was shocking. Even though Leana had never struck Melech, him slapping her back took her by surprise. Shoving Leana and physically putting her out of the home they once shared proved to her Melech hated her. The whole time they had been together, Leana had never seen such ruthlessness aimed at her. Leana was fully aware of Melech's temper.

On several occasions, she had to calm him down once others had pushed him to that hostile point. Usually, Melech was a levelheaded man, nurturing when it came to her. It did not matter what Leana did or how upset she became, Melech was able to take a step back, assess the situation, and bring a loving disposition to resolve any issues that came their way. Even when Melech became aware, Leana was still dating her high school boyfriend. He calmly told Leana their relationship was over without an outburst, questions, or any type of anger displayed by him.

Leana took this for granted when she wrote the letter, leaving it behind without an actual explanation. Melech taking Leana back in the past gave her a false sense of security. Looking in his eyes, Leana realized Melech had shut off the emotions he once held for her. The one thing Leana thought would never happen. Being able to manipulate Melech with her words was Leana's power over him. After learning Melech had more to offer Leana, holding on to her relationship with Luca was a moot point.

Even if Melech did not make it onto a professional football field, he was still going to be well off, because of his parents. Why Melech did not tell her that his mother was an actress and his father an investment banker, was a little bit concerning to Leana. The fact Levi enjoyed giving Melech a hard time became beneficial to her. Leana was not going to allow Melech to break up with her without a fight. That was never going to happen in Leana's lifetime. He checked all of her boxes. Most men could not do this, even Luca fell short. Leana would have still married Luca, nonetheless. The problem was she met Melech.

Leana watched her father work too hard to make sure she always had what she needed. Living an average life was not in the plans for her future. Melech had the characteristics every woman wanted in a man. He was goal-oriented, put his woman's needs first, handsome, intelligent, came from a respectable family, faithful, and knew what he was doing in the bedroom. Falling in love with Melech just made life easier for Leana. Levi was the icing on the cake for her. The succulent, creamy, sweet goodness that makes your jaws tingle once you've taken a bite. You know you should only eat one, but your taste buds are begging for just one more taste. All that goodness comes with a price. Leana did not have the funds to pay for the debt she just incurred.

CHAPTER NINE

Over the next few days, Melech did his best not to be in Levi's presence, but his efforts were futile. Every morning he awoke to Levi on his couch as he left for his morning run. This was not at all helpful to Melech; it was becoming more aggravating than anything else. Words were only exchanged if it was work-related. The sight and sound of Levi only brought visuals of him with Leana, which brought on the need for Melech to strike Levi again. He had taken heed to Levi's warning. The next time the two came to blows, Melech knew it was going to be an all-out war. How Levi thought his actions were forgivable baffled Melech.

The fact Levi did not feed into Leana's delusion of the two running off living happily ever after did not redeem the fact he crossed every boundary imaginable. Not to mention, he did not say one word while Melech was racking his brain trying to figure out who the other man could possibly be. Levi's first mistake was not telling him the first time Leana made an advancement toward him. Melech had an aching feeling it was not the days they slept together, the three spent too much time together. Frequently, Melech came home, and Levi had beat him there. They went on outings alone, and Levi spent the night on many occasions. In his mind, Levi looked at Leana as if she was a sister.

He was never short on women; Leana should have been off-limits without even speaking those words. The two often found the same women attractive, *'That's all you,'* Melech usually conceded, only because casual sex was not his thing. The women Melech knew he could spend more than a few random nights with, he often pushed Levi out of the way. It was a game they played while they were young and having a good time in life. Melech grew up, found Leana, and settled down right out of college. Spending most of his free time with Melech and Leana, Levi was supposed to follow suit, not share Melech's wife. This is what made Melech so angry.

Levi refused to give him the space Melech was looking for in fear he would not be allowed back into his best friend's life. No woman in this world would tear down the brotherhood he had formed with Melech, not even the woman he thought was righteous and faithful to him. Leana was replaceable in Levi's eyes, not Melech. He told Leana several times to go home and repair her marriage; she did not listen to him. Levi had no choice but to tell Melech about them. Leana had gone too far when she showed up to his house, causing the police to show up. Where Levi laid his head was sacred to him, nothing, not even the police were supposed to come to his sanctuary. Levi owned an apartment building where he did a lot of his dirty dealings for a reason.

"Leek," Levi stood in the office doorway. He tried giving Melech his space. Now it was time for them to have this uncomfortable conversation. Their staff was noticing the tension between them. It was time for them to set Leana to the side. Neither one of them had heard from her since the night Melech physically put her out. "We need to clear the air."

"I'm busy, Levi." He stepped into Melech's office, closing the door behind him.

"Nah, my nigga. That shit ain't gonna fly no mo'."

"So, you want me to just forget you slept with my wife?"

"Never that. I'm fucked up for that one. Shit…." Levi chucked. "I took that ass-whoopin' for that one. I can't make no excuses. She got me, I fell for it, but it don't change shit between me and you."

"You can't be serious?" Melech was now vested in the conversation. "You fucked my wife, she left me for you, and I'm supposed to just move on with life? Act like it never happened?" Levi put his hands on the top of his head.

"Shit, man, nah. Le, she crazy for that shit she pulled. It wasn't like that, Leek."

"So how was it, Levi, tell me? I need to know how my best friend fucked my wife so well she kicked my ass to the curb!" hostility filled his words.

"C'mon man, I fucked up, but that girl loves you, not me. She ain't thinkin' right." Levi tried to explain.

"Hmmm, let me see..." Melech stroked his beard, squinting his eyes. "If I'm not mistaken, Leana clearly said she was in love with another man. "You read the letter, right? Then sat in disbelief as if you didn't know she was talking about your ass."

"Wait, hold up, Melech. I swear I didn't know this dumb ass bitch was talkin' 'bout me." Melech was filled with confusion.

"What does that mean?"

"Damn, bruh. I told yo' ass to slow down when y'all first started out. You didn't listen. When you found out 'bout dude in New York, I told you don't forgive so fast, but yo' ass didn't listen. All you can see is perfection in Leana. She gotta sad story, beautiful eyes, and some bomb ass pussy. You ain't neva been able to see straight when it comes to her." Before Levi could get through to his friend, he was staring down Melech's .45. He forgot just how quick his friend was after all these years. "If you pull that muthafucca, you betta use that bitch!"

"You seem to forget I'm a man that don't have shit to lose right now." Levi pulled his nine from the small of his back; how Melech would think Levi would ever leave home without it was his mistake. He pressed the nozzle to Melech's temple.

"Nah, cuh, I'm the one who ain't got shit to lose. Don't eva forget that shit. You got muthafucca's that care 'bout you. I love yo' ass like you gave me a kidney, but I'll dead dat ass in a minute, befoe' I let you put a hot one in me!" The two were at a stalemate, neither refusing to lower their weapons, standing toe to toe eye-to-eye.

"Melech." Chester burst into his office. "What the hell is going on in here?" This was an odd situation he just walked into. Both guns were now aimed at Chester. Holding his hands up, fear whisked over Chester. "Can you two take those off of me?" Neither knew why Chester was even there, or if they felt the need to lower their weapons, Leana could be right behind him. "I don't know what I walked into, Melech, I'm just looking for my daughter," he tried explaining. "Don't shoot me."

"I would never shoot you, pops. Come on in." Melech walked back over to his desk, placing the gun in front of him before he sat down. As long as Levi was in possession of his, Melech was not taking any chances.

"What you mean, you looking for yo' daughter?" Levi returned his gun to the small of his back. "We ain't heard from Leana in days."

"Neither have I. She left a message on my phone, crying in hysterics. I could not understand one word she was saying. Now her phone is going straight to voicemail."

"I don't know how to help you. Leana showed up at the house, I put her out once I found out she left me for my best friend here." Melech pointed at Levi.

"Oh, no! Don't put that shit on me. We ain't one hundred percent sure on that one yet. I made the mistake of fuc…sleeping wit' your daughter. She neva eva once told me she was leaving, my man, for me."

"Okay, wait." Chester was confused with the information being thrown at him. "My little girl. Slept with, Levi?" He was getting overwhelmed.

"Yes, sir. In my own home," Melech curtly told him.

"This is some type of mistake. Leana wouldn't do something like that."

"She did," Levi, added his two cents. "Yo' little princess had a plan to seduce me, then thought I'd run off with her. She been tryin' since the day I met her ass." Shock came over Melech. This was the first time he heard Leana had feelings for Levi for so long. Melech did not know why she even married him.

"She what!" Melech's attention went straight to Levi.

"Yeah, man. Little inappropriate jokes, way too long hugs, accidentally brushing her lips on mine instead of my cheek. I ain't think nothin' of it. You know pretty girls always need that extra indulgence. Leana married you. Y'all was happy. She ain't neva cross too far over the lines, till that day she had that dark liquor on deck and you was runnin' late. Shit, yo' ass drove right past me after I drove away. It was like she wanted you to see me diggin' her ass out. A little too crazy fo' my ass. I wasn't tryin' see a body bag."

"What the fuck!" Melech flew over his desk, tackling Levi to the ground. If Chester was not there to intervene, the two would have fought to the death. Levi had made the mistake of falling for Leana and her seductively devious ways. Now he was paying the price for it.

"Stop comin' for me, loc. That girl is the problem!" Levi roared frustrated.

"You shoulda told me!" Melech was trying to break free from the hold Chester had on him.

"Would you have believed me?" Levi yelled at him. "The first day I met her, I told yo' ass she was doing way too much, but you brushed me aside. If I told you that girl let me hit that shit, yo' bitch ass woulda blamed me fo' that shit. All yo' ass can see is what da fuck she want yo' ass to see. Wake da fuck up. When reality sets in, my nigga, call me. We boys, fuck dat bitch. She worked my ass too. I was just smart enough to see through her before yo' dumb ass. Hope you signed a prenup, cause she gonna eat dat ass up."

Levi stormed out the office, slamming the door behind him. Those were words Levi never intended on speaking to his best friend. It was time Melech heard the truth. He believed somewhere down the road, Leana fell in love with Melech, but it never started that way. Learning Leana left Melech had been driving Levi crazy. He did not have close to what Melech had to offer Leana, so why now? Did she actually love him, or was Leana up to something? There was no way Levi was going to track Leana down and ask her. She had a way about her that could melt the heart of an Eskimo's igloo.

"She's not that bad?" Melech asked his father-in-law.

"I hope not, son." His mind drifted off to his daughter and where he went wrong raising Leana. Deep down inside, Chester knew every word Levi spoke was accurate. He had given Leana everything after her mother's death. That may have been a grave mistake. His daughter kept looking for the next best thing. Chester was disappointed when Leana broke things off with Luca, but he really adored Melech. He did not approve of the way Leana went about the relationship with Melech. He truly believed she was in love. With Luca away in New York, it opened the door for Leana to explore her options while in college. Chester realized that most high school romances do not transpire into marriage. Luca was an excellent fit for his daughter, the family he came from, and his morals were in line with his. After meeting Melech's family, he found them to be very pleasant. Leana could not have chosen a better partner.

Chester did not want to admit it, his daughter had actually moved up by marrying Melech. Now he was wondering if it was a strategic move on her part. What was concerning to Chester is that his daughter cheated on Melech with Levi, he was a small-time hustler in partnership with Melech in a successful business. Levi could not afford to give his daughter the lifestyle Melech had. She obtained a master's degree with no debt. A man such as Levi was on a tightrope with the law. Fast money usually brought on long prison sentences or death. Chester had taught Leana better than that.

He did not understand her decision-making skills when it came to Levi. As close as Melech and Levi were? Chester just walked in on both of them, guns drawn on one another. He was not sure if Melech had what it took to pull the trigger on his long-time friend. Levi, on the other hand, would not hesitate to put Melech six feet under and have a restful sleep. That was not the type of man Chester ever wanted his daughter with. Levi had no soul encased in the body that walked the earth, killing was in his nature. At a blink of an eye, Levi would take great pleasure in ending your life for no reason at all. Fear for his daughter became alarming. Finding her whereabouts became essential. Something told him Levi would have no problems eliminating Leana because she just became a problem in his world.

"I need to find Leana. Do you have any idea where she's staying?" urgency filled Chester's tone.

"I tracked her phone to the Ritz, downtown. I paid her a visit, but she wasn't there. Then she popped up at the house. I hate to admit it, pops, I physically put her out. Listening to her and Levi argue over whose fault it was they slept together sent me over the edge." Melech remorsefully told his father-in-law.

"Yet, you keep this man close to you."

"He's my brother, I love him." It embarrassed Melech to utter those words.

"Leana, was your wife," Chester tried to enlighten him.

"My wife seduced the one person who would die for me. Leana didn't care she was going to hurt me when she walked out. She tried to take my best friend with her, knowing full well he's like my brother. My own father will not step in front of a bullet for me."

"Are you sure?" Chester was puzzled.

"Chester. Levi's a lot of things. I could literally kill him myself right now…" Melech looked down at his gun, resting on his desk. "I love my dad and all, but no one else will come to my defense the way Levi does. It's in his blood, embedded in his soul. You cannot be taught that. One must be born with it, that's Levi. Oh, trust and believe he will make mistakes. But, when it comes to me, there's no wavering. If any other person had pulled out a piece on him the way I did today, they would not live to speak on it. He's my brother until the day I die. One day I'll forgive him for what he's done to me. Leana, I just cannot do it. Le, is one of the few people who had firsthand knowledge of how close we are, yet she tried to come between me and Levi. Not cool, pop."

"I understand friendship. I don't know what's going on with my daughter, but she doesn't bear all of the blame. It takes two, son."

"I get that."

"I hope you can forgive her one day." Melech shrugged. "I'm going to check out her hotel room." Melech fished around his desk, finding Leana's hotel room key.

"Here," He tossed it on the desk. "Don't ask how I got it." Chester shook his head with great sadness, exiting the office. In his mind, Melech and Leana belonged together. He was going to do his best to put their marriage back together. Chester was sure his daughter was in hiding due to her embarrassment.

Melech was over the whole situation. Chester and his blind faith in his daughter, Leana, for her pure existence, and Levi for just being Levi. Where would they have ended their standoff if Chester had not shown up? As much as Melech wanted to put a bullet in Levi's heart, there was no way he would have pulled the trigger first. Chester could speculate about Levi being able to take his life and sleep with ease, Melech knew better. Every night, his own demons would haunt Levi until they drove him insane. The one life he felt bonded to was Melech's. Leana felt their connection; a small part of her was envious of it. The two were more than best friends, they were brothers, this ordeal they would someday recover from.

Melech leaned forward, placing his head in his hands. He was not sure how much more he could endure. Levi storming out meant he was going to do something reckless. Under usual circumstances, Melech would have gone to the block to locate his friend, ensure Levi was not a sitting duck for stray bullets or some youngster trying to find a come up. He grabbed his keys and headed out the door. His truck led Melech home instead of a search and rescue mission. Selfishness was his new outlook on life. Both Leana and Melech would have to fend for themselves from this point on.

The day had not turned out the way Levi had planned. In his mind, after a heart to heart conversation with Melech, he would have his friend back. It was challenging to find out your wife was not the woman you once thought she was, Levi understood that he too had to fall out of love with Leana. There was no way Levi could own his genuine feelings for her. Leana had been toying with his emotions for years, long before they ever slept together. She made it a point to keep Levi close to her and Melech, including him in their day-to-day lives. Leana also pried her way into Levi's personal life without Melech. She helped him furnish and design his house, took him out to eat with her, and made sure she knew all of his favorite things. Melech did not notice they were both dating his wife, he was the only one benefiting sexually until that faithful day.

Misfit's words were ringing in Levi's head. Did he really want his best friend's life, or did he genuinely love Leana? The only thing Levi was sure of was that Leana had destroyed something he never had with another person. Levi's father once told him, *'When you find someone you trust, hold on to them like a squirrel with a nut. They come far and few.'* Levi found that with Melech. He wanted nothing but the best for Levi. Melech did not put him on the block, never asked for anything. He even got upset when Levi spared him from the neighborhood beat down in high school. Melech was the type of man who asked for nothing and gave you his all. Levi hated himself for betraying Melech's loyalties by sleeping with his wife. As much as he loved Leana, Levi wanted to take her life just to ease the pain she was causing Melech.

Pulling up to the Ritz Carlton, Levi handed the valet a hundred dollars not to move his car. This was becoming a habit. Levi never had intentions of being there long. Someone needed to shake some sense into Leana, Levi planned to fill that position, even if he shook her head right off her perfect little body.

To Levi's surprise, Chester walked up behind him as he was knocking on Leana's door.

"What are you doing here?" Chester asked him.

"Someone needs to tell yo' daughter what's she's doin' to my boy is shity as fuck."

"I don't think that's your place, young man."

"Look, old head, I ain't tryna disrespect yo' ass, but yo' daughter got some screws loose. All you gonna do is pacify her ass and make her think she ain't done shit wrong." Levi stood his ground knowing a father could not see who their child really was.

"Considering you soiled, my little girl, you're the last person I need to take advice from." Levi bellowed with laughter.

"You don't know that girl at all. The first day she met me Leana was tryna get at this right here, buddy. I ain't the one who soiled dat ass. Check her resume', old man." The blow was a hard one to take for Chester. The more Levi spoke, made Chester realized there was a lot he did not know about his own child. Pushing Levi to the side, Chester unlocked the door with the key Melech gave him. Opening the door, the two walked into Leana's room in search of her.

The room appeared to be lived in, but there was no sign of Leana. Her purse and phone were still on the bed. Levi picked it up, noticing that it was dead. Looking over his shoulder, Levi noticed Chester was not in sight. Finding Chester in a frozen state in the bathroom is when panic took over Levi. There was blood on the bathroom sink, glass, and cloudy pink water in the tub. The bloody clothes she wore the night Melech threw Leana out of his house were lying on the bathroom floor. Levi's mind started working overtime.

"What happened here?" Chester's words were meek.

"How did you get that key?" Levi asked him.

"Melech." Panic took over Levi. *'What the hell did this nigga do?'* Levi thought to himself.

"Okay, where would she go? Do y'all got a safe house? I know she pissed and all."

"What?" Chester was confused.

"Vacation house?" Levi forgot who he was talking to.

"No...no, we can't afford anything like that." Chester was still looking at the bloody scene in the bathroom.

"Family?"

"What?"

"Damn, man! Do y'all got family, Leana would run to cause she's upset?"

"No, none she's close to." Chester blindly walked out of the bathroom, making his way to the bed. He needed to sit down. Noticing his daughter's phone, panic struck him. Reaching for his phone on the table next to the bed, Chester tried to call 9-1-1. Levi slapped the phone out of his hand.

"What da fuck is you doin'?"

"Calling the police!" He grabbed his phone off of the floor. "My daughter is missing."

"Or she's up to some bullshit, tryin' to get everybody in a tailspin ova some dumb shit."

"Leana wouldn't do that," Chester came to his daughter's defense.

"Do you see a muthafuckin' struggle in this bitch?" Chester looked around the room. There was not one, but he was not going to take any chances. This was his daughter.

"Leana's begging for attention, man. Melech's mad at her, you disappointed in her actions, and I won't fuck wit' her ass. Yo' lil' girl is sick in the fuckin' head!"

"We'll let the police determine that," Chester made his call to 9-1-1.

"I'm sure this fancy hotel gonna appreciate all the fucken attention. I'm out homie." Levi rushed out of the room. He wanted no parts of what Chester was stirring up.

For the first time, Melech felt relaxed. He stopped by the market, picked up some salmon, wild rice, asparagus, and a six-pack of Corona's. Melech planned to treat himself and watch some basketball, taking the night off. He left instructions with Rylee, the assistant manager, just in case Levi did not come back in for the night. Malech had handpicked Rylee in the hiring process and knew that she could run the Lounge without either of them. Trevor was on duty also; he was the bar back and bouncer. Melech knew they would be in excellent hands without him. Peace and quiet was all that Melech wanted for just one night.

His life had changed so much over the last month, Melech wanted to settle into the single man's lifestyle. In all actuality, he was looking forward to his new life. Melech enjoyed being married and having his beautiful wife to come home to every night. Levi's carefree way of life was intriguing to him. Not having to consider someone else's happiness first was becoming freeing to Melech. Just as he sat down in front of his Sony, fifty-five-inch 4k TV with his meal for some me-time, Levi came bursting through his door.

"Leek!" he shouted out. "Nigga, you not gonna believe this shit." Melech sat his food down and took a long drink from his beer, understanding why so many people drank. "Where you at, fool." He finally reached Melech in the family room. "Damn, man, it smells good as hell in here." Taking an asparagus off of the plate as he sat down. Levi went on talking as if they had not drawn down on one another earlier in the day. "That father-in-law of yours is buggin' out." Melech slapped his hand as Levi tried to reach for his plate again.

"What are you talkin' about, Levi?"

"This dude, showed up to Leana's hotel."

"Why were you at her hotel?" Melech was surprised to hear that was the first place Levi went after their altercation.

"I wanted to break her face! Shut up and listen," Levi was not going to make him lose focus on the bigger picture. "Guess she ain't been there since the day you put her ass up out of here," Levi continued. "This girl done staged her room to look like she missin'. Phone and purse on her bed, bloody bathwater, and blood on the bathroom sink and a glass up in there." He used a finger to point each statement out for Melech.

"Wait, what?" Melech was not following the story.

"The old man done called five-o, my nigga. Yo' wife is up to some crafty shit." Levi took another asparagus.

"Have you been smoking, cause I'm confused as hell?"

"Okay, peep game. Leana is gone like da wind. She left bloody clothes in her bathroom, blood all up on the sink, and a water glass. Like she been watchin' the ID channel way too much."

"Why you just didn't call her?" Melech asked, still trying to understand why Levi went back to his wife's hotel room.

"Oh, that broad left her cellie and Gucci sittin' upon her bed. What chick do some shit like dat?" Levi's green eyes opened wide, trying to send a telepathic message to Levi.

"You sure, Leana is up to something? What if she's really in trouble?"

"It's the same clothes you put her ass up out of here in?" This got Melech's attention.

"Really?"

"Yup, she settin' dat ass up. Don't you watch all them crazy women shows on Lifetime?"

"Yeah…no," Melech told him. "Who has time for all of that?"

"Yo' bitch ass wife, that's who and her sappy, pappy over there eatin' that shit up. Called the cops and everything."

"I didn't do shit, so I don't really care." Melech brushed the whole thing off.

"Nigga, the husband is always the first one to go down. OJ, Chris Brown, Ocho Cinco, Bobby Brown, Ray Rice, Bow Wow…"

"Dude, them nigga's were all guilty," Melech cut him off.

"Okay, terrible examples." He held his right hand up. "William Montgomery." Levi pointed at him.

"Who?" Melech squinted his already slanted eyes at Levi.

"The rookie Lakers player turned sports agent. Nigga, you remember when his wife came up missing, them cops was so focused on him they didn't even look fo' no other suspects, and he didn't even do da shit. Some damn stalker grabbed her up."

"I vaguely remember that story. Dude was supposed to be the next Shaq, got hurt his first year playing."

"Yup, that be him. She had to save her damn self. Fuckin' po po was tryna put that nigga under the jail cell. Cops ain't looking at who really did the shit. Leana set dat ass up fo' real, fo' real. That bitch out fo' blood."

"Don't call her that." Melech may not have wanted to be back with his wife, he could not sit back and allow anyone to call her out of her name, not even Levi.

"Yeah, whateva, she a cold piece, and yo' ass bout to take the fuckin' fall on some bullshit."

"Levi, I didn't touch that girl. You were here all night after I put, Le out."

"Shit yeah, I'm yo' alibi. Who da fuck gonna believe me? I'm yo' best friend, they could say we did this shit together." Levi enlightened him.

"But, we didn't."

"Get a fucken lawyer, they comin' for you," Levi warned him. "I need to go back ova y'all's foyer, I cleaned it up wit' that organic bullshit y'all got. The whole thing needs a bleach overhaul. Leana's blood is everywhere from when she fell into that glass table."

"Why?" Melech was confused as to why Levi was so concerned about his wellbeing.

"Do you really have to ask?" Levi knew how wrong he was sleeping with Leana. Melech is his day one. He still did not understand why Melech would pull a gun on him, but bygones would be just that, bygones. "I'll be back in a few, don't let no one in this muthafucca till I get back. You got me?"

"Yeah," Melech answered Levi even though his mind was a thousand miles away.

"I need to make a phone call to someone who can get you cleaner than Windex. 'You got cash on deck? If not, I can hold you down."

"Yeah, yeah, bout five hundred grand in the safe." Not all profits from the lounge were logged into the books. Melech knew that he needed to report a loss on the business for at least three years. Levi also cleaned his dirty money through the club, he did not own up to it. Melech was a wise man and picked up on it three months into opening the Lounge. He was a mastermind when it came to numbers and keeping his books, not even Leana knew what was going on behind the scene.

"Okay, cool. I'll get my boy, Q on this shit right away."

"Right…right."

"Oh." Levi tossed Leana's phone at Melech. "I snatched this up when the old man wasn't lookin'." Melech caught the rose-colored iPhone with one hand. "I figured yo' ass could get in there and figure out what, Le was up to after it charges."

"Yeah, it's how I tracked her to that hotel," Melech admitted.

"To think, I just thought you followed the credit card receipt. You know she wanted to be found."

"Ha!" Melech let out. "I'm learning more and more about my wife every day." He never thought to go through the credit card statements.

"Hope that phone don't break yo' heart, bro." Levi's eyes softened. He was not sure if it was a mistake to hand over Leana's lifeline to Melech before looking at it first. He honestly did not want to be hurt either. Something was missing in this twisted tale of Leana's. Being the bearer of bad news for his friend brought not only agony to Melech, but it was also tearing him up inside as well.

"Can it get any worse?"

"Yeah." Levi left him with those haunting words. Melech put Leana's phone on the charger, warmed up his food, then sat down to eat his food and watch the game. His mind kept venturing to the cell phone. What wonders would be found inside of his darling wife's phone? Unable to focus on the food or the game, Melech ventured back into the kitchen to check if there was enough battery life for Leana's phone to light back up. Keying in her password, Melech went to the recent calls first. Before she slipped away with a whisper early in the morning, who had Leana spoken to? The number was all too familiar to Melech. Confusion took over as to why it was the last call Leana would make from her cell phone? Something deep inside of him made Melech tap the number.

"Why are you calling me right now? I said I'll see you in an hour or so."

"Dad?"

"Melech? Son..."

CHAPTER TEN

Making his way to his son's house was all Kaden had on his mind. The phone went dead after Melech realized it was him on the other end. Kaden had no clue what was going through his son's mind, considering Melech hung up on him so hastily. Kaden was aware Melech and Leana were separated. Still, Melech had yet to reach out to his father for advice or even a conversation about what was going on between him and Leana. He spoke to his mother, only because Melech needed her help in getting Leana's belongings out of their home. Kaden was accustomed to Melech keeping his life personal to himself unless he needed something. Melech had been the same way since he was a young boy.

This was not an issue for Kaden; he raised Melech to be a strong man with the capacities to overcome all the struggles that came his way. After getting hurt in college, Melech continued on with his education, and his Plan B. Not playing professional football did not hinder Melech's goals in life. The fact his son did not come home and have a breakdown proved to Kaden that Melech could handle anything that came his way. This situation deserved of a face-to-face meeting because Melech would not answer any of Kaden's calls.

Entering Melech's house without knocking, Kaden called out his son's name.

"He ain't here? Who are you?" Q asked suspiciously.

"Where is Melech, and why are you in his home?" Authority filled the air.

"Hey, Mr. B." Levi walked up behind Kaden. "Did you hear from Leek?"

"What do you mean?" Kaden was skeptical of answering the question. He knew that Levi was Melech's best friend; however, Kaden was not sure just how much of his private life Melech shared with him.

"The cops took him down to the station for questioning. I pulled up as they were putting him into their car. They wouldn't tell me nothin'."

"What kind of trouble have you gotten my son into?" Kaden was outraged.

"Me?" Levi pointed at himself. "That wife of his is the one who has your son in pig shit."

"Excuse me?" Kaden twisted his head to the side. He did not know what Levi was referring to. His wife, Halina informed him that the two were having marital problems. Melech told her Leana was unfaithful to him.

"Yeah, that girl came up missing. That father of hers called the police, they came up in here and took him down to the station."

"Why would Chester send anyone over here for, Melech?"

"Cause yo' son talk too damn much and gave Le's hotel key to him. That girl done set that room up to look like someone hurt her."

"Leana?" Kaden was trying to piece together what Levi was telling him.

"Look, you need to talk to Leek. I'm not tryna tell you some shit he don't want you to know." Levi left the foyer walking into the kitchen.

Kaden pulled his phone out of his pocket to call his lawyer. "Do you mind?" he snapped at Q."

"Asshole!" Q shook his head then followed behind Melech.

"What do you mean you're not trying to tell me my son's business?" Kaden entered the kitchen after sending his lawyer to find Melech and get him home. Levi chuckled.

"Where you been, Mr. B?" Levi gave him a dirty look. "I been right here every day even when your son won't say one word to me. Where you been? You ain't even called this, lil' nigga."

"He's a grown man, not a child."

"Yeah." Levi rubbed his hands together. "He's your child, asshole."

"My son calls when he needs something, and I give it to him if that makes me an asshole." Kaden threw his hands in the air. "So be it."

"You a cold piece, my nigga." Q stood right next to Kaden. "Yo' own seed gets his heart broke, betrayed by his best friend, his wife turn up missin', the cops come fo' his ass and his pop's say, he's a big boy." Q patted Kaden's shoulder. "Make me want to body yo' ass myself."

'Betrayed by his best friend,' is what ran through Kaden's mind, not all the other things Q said to him. Kaden felt Q was an insignificant person in his world. "How did you betray my son?" He turned his attention to Levi.

Shamefully, Levi responded, "I slept with Leana." Kaden put his hand to his forehead as the words sunk in.

"You piece of shit…" Kaden attempted to grab Levi. Lightning struck the back of his head through his eyes. Falling to the Spanish tile floor, echoes of voices rang in his head.

"Damn, man!"

"What was I supposed to do?"

"Not pistol whip the old dude."

♥ ♥ ♥

After receiving a call from the family lawyer, Halina rushed downtown on sixth street to meet with him. There was not too much information he could give her over the phone at the time. In all actuality, Jim was trying to locate her husband. Surprisingly, Chester was standing in front when Halina found a parking spot trying to rush in. Almost missing him altogether, Chester called Halina's name and got her attention. Looking up from her phone, Halina walked over to Chester with a warm smile, giving him a gentle hug.

"You heard?" she asked.

"They still don't know where she could be?" sadness filled his voice.

"Who could be?"

"Leana…missing," Chester told her, now confused as to what she was referring to.

"Oh, that's terrible," she gasped. "Is that why Melech is here? Is he trying to help them find her?"

"I haven't seen him at all," Chester informed her.

"This is crazy, my husband told our lawyer to come down here and get my son."

"Oh, no...." Chester looked to the sky.

"What...what is it, Chester?"

"They may be asking him some questions. I don't know why they brought him down here, though."

"Chester!"

"After talking to, Melech." Guilt was suddenly weighing on Chester. "They had a tremendous fight. He may have been the last person Leana talked to."

"You told that to the cops!" Halina's tone was almost a scream.

"I didn't think they would..."

"Do you really think my son would hurt, Leana?" anger spit from her mouth.

"No…well…not intentionally…he's hurting, Halina."

"Hurting and hurting someone are two totally different things." She pointed at him. "Your daughter hurt my son!" Halina stormed off. It took all the strength she could muster not to slap Chester across the face for putting her child in the hands of any police officer. She questioned her son's naiveté for telling anyone that he had an argument with his wife. Halina prayed Melech was smart enough to remain silent during his questioning. She knew Jim would have her child out of there in no time.

♥ ♥ ♥

Finding himself lying on the couch, Kaden rubbed the back of his head. As he attempted to get up, dizziness took over. Levi was standing over him and handed Kaden a bag of ice. Reluctantly Kaden took it.

"Eh, my boy was outta pocket for crackin' you like that. He wasn't gonna let shit happen to me. I'm sure you can understand that." Kaden nodded his head. Still, angry learning Levi slept with Leana; he was trying to form questions that were running rampant in his mind.

"It just happened," Levi told him. "Leana's got away 'bout her. She pulled me in, and I feel like shit. It ain't gonna change nothin' for me. Melech's gonna have me by his side no matter what."

"You…" Kaden managed to say. "You're the reason they broke up?"

"That's what she says, but I never promised that girl anything. I still don't know why she would blow up her world the way she did. Melech loved, Le. He gave her everything."

"I see." Kaden put the ice on his head.

"Yo, man." Q interrupted their conversation. "Melech just pulled up with some man and woman."

Levi rushed to the front door. Recognizing Halina, he gave her a hug. The other man with Melech he was unfamiliar with. Halina embraced Levi, giving Q a once over. Noticing her husband in the background, Halina made her way to his side.

"You straight?" Levi addressed Melech.

"Yeah…" He shook his head. There was no way in the world Melech was okay with everything taking place in his life.

"Why they take you downtown?" Levi asked.

"To ask me if I knew where Leana was. If I've seen or talked to her since I put her out of the house."

"They couldn't ask you that shit right here?" Levi was hostile.

"It was a scare tactic," Jim intervened.

"A what?"

"If they treat Melech like a suspect, he might slip up and say something incriminating," Jim explained.

"He ain't do shit," Levi huffed. "Did you tell them we was here all night?"

"Yeah."

"You didn't tell em' nothin' else, did you?" Levi whispered.

"Her father pretty much told them everything." Melech was exasperated with the entire ordeal.

"What I tell you." Levi pointed at Melech. "It's crystal clean up in this bitch, don't trip." He whispered nodding towards Q, winking. "Not even luminol is finding shit in this bitch." Melech did not like that Levi brought yet another person into his private life.

"Son." Melech shot daggers at his father. There were several unanswered questions he had before Leana's phone went dead again. There was no way Melech was going to let the police know that his own father was in contact with his wife, but his father had a lot of explaining to do. "I tried calling you back," Kaden did his best not to alter the tone of his voice. No one knew that he took a call from Leana not knowing it was actually his son.

"I was too busy being hauled down for questioning on a woman that seems to be playing even more games with my life." All eyes went back and forth between the two men.

"Yes, I've learned some interesting details over the past few hours."

"He's all caught up on the Levi thing," Q stepped in, adding to the conversation.

"I see. So, my life is just an open book suddenly," Melech smirked.

"No, son. Not at all. We are all just concerned."

"Are we, though?" He looked around at them all.

"Melech, baby, you need to eat and get some rest," his mother lovingly told him. "Let me make you something to eat."

"How about everyone gets out of my house? That sounds really good to me."

"Son."

"Dad!" Melech fired back.

"That's enough, young man. Get in your office, now! You are out of line, and you will not speak to your mother in that tone." Kaden sternly spoke to Melech.

"I'm not fifteen anymore!" Melech was defiant. Kaden marched to his son, grabbed him under the arm, and escorted him to the office.

"I don't give two flying fucks how old you are, boy! You seem to forget I'm your father. This house you're trying to get bold in, all me! I brought your disrespectful ass life and I will fuck you up in front of all your friends if you speak like that again to your mother or me like you have lost your mind." Kaden shoved Melech. "Do you understand me?" Melech could feel his father's fiery breath on his face. Grabbing him by the throat, Kaden asked again. "Do I make myself clear?"

Pulling his hands off of him, Melech finally answered. "Yes."

"You are letting that girl mess with your head."

"Why are you talking to her? Why are you even meeting up with her?" Melech felt sixteen years old again. Kaden knew he was about to step on land minds if he did not take his time answering his son's questions.

"She asked me for help."

"Why you?" Melech was suspicious.

"Why not? You haven't told me anything. I only know that you two are separated because of your mother."

"That should be enough for you to stay the fuck away from her." Melech got in his father's face.

"Watch your mouth." Kaden put one hand on his waist, pointing at Melech with the other. "She called crying because you wouldn't talk to her. Leana told me, Levi had turned you against her. Chester was upset with her because things weren't working out with you two. All I knew is Leana wanted some time to think where no one knew where she was."

"And look where that got me, father?" Kaden clasped his hands together.

"Melech, I had no idea." Hands still folded; Kaden pointed his two fingers at his son. "I just found out about, Levi."

"Yeah, that's a whole different problem. Levi was right about one thing. She damn sure wanted it to look like I did something to her." Melech rubbed his beard. "Damn cops, came right to my door."

"Well, you don't have to worry about it. Jim will handle everything." Kaden reassured his son.

"You know where she is!" Melech raised his voice. Jim did not need to handle anything. His father needed to stop playing games with his life.

"That too," Kaden paced the floor. "I still cannot believe she slept with, Levi."

"Oh please, Dad, keep saying it." Melech fussed at him. "It's really making me feel good about myself right now."

"Yeah…yeah…I see how troublesome that can be." Kaden was wrapped up in his own thoughts.

"You think?"

"Yet he's right here, in your house, running shit. How stupid is that, Melech?" His father looked at him. "You forgive him? How weak does that make you?"

"No! Hell, no I haven't forgiven him. Don't call me weak! He's the one who has been right here even after I beat his ass and still won't say shit to him." Melech looked directly into his father's eyes. "What he did is unforgivable."

"Then why, son?" Kaden needed to understand. "You two fought over this girl and Levi is still right by your side."

"I don't know, dad. He just is. I can't explain it to you. You wouldn't understand, anyway. You've always hated Levi."

"Not true."

"Okay." Melech had listened to his father complain about his friendship all these years. Nothing he could say now was going to change that.

"I saw that Levi was your missing piece. He provided something you were looking for in life." Kaden shrugged. "I also knew the boy would keep you safe."

"Wait, what?" Melech could comprehend nothing his father was saying to him.

"Oh, Melech. Levi is everything you want to be…"

"That's so not true." Melech did not know where that was coming from; he was the one who kept Levi on the straight road. "You seem to forget I am the one who went to college on a football scholarship and came home with a degree, plus the business was my plan."

"Yes, son. You have done very well for yourself. Levi allows you to play in the gutter from time to time. Gave you the street cred you were looking for. You will seek his advice before mine, yet I am educated and successful."

"Do you see why I don't?" Melech was getting angry at his father's assessment of him. "You know everything. You even knew what was best for my wife. Right, dad? Hey, does mom know you have my wife held up somewhere?" Melech facetiously asked. "Let's go ask her how she feels about it, shall we?" he headed toward the office door.

"You're acting like a child, Melech."

"Am I, dad?" Melech knew he was acting petty; it was the only way to strike back at his father. Being Levi was never something Melech ever wanted to be. Those words hit hard especially after Leana left him for a man like Levi.

"Son," Kaden knew this was going to be a touchy conversation. "I'm not trying to upset you. What do you want me to do regarding your wife?"

"Father knows best. Do whatever you want. Just don't send her back to me. I don't ever want to see that woman again."

"Melech." This was the first time he could see the pain his only son was in.

"Don't give her any more money, either!" Melech stormed out of the office, slamming the door behind him. Not wanting to deal with anyone taking up vigil in his home, Melech went up to his room, locking the door behind him.

Making his way down Century Blvd. to the H Hotel, Kaden's mind was consumed with the day's events and everything he had learned. Fully aware he was hurting his son, Kaden had not taken everything into account until he looked into Melech's eyes earlier. He and Halina did their best to ensure their son would never have to deal with law enforcement. By no means did they spoil Melech by giving him the same privilege his neighbor's friends received. Halina was very insistent that Melech remained in public schools, even when they had the finances to enroll their son in the best institutions private schools had to offer.

Kaden was not born with everything handed to him. The one thing Levi did not realize is Kaden knew exactly who his father was. They ran the same streets, attended the same schools, and had equal opportunities. Kaden's father worked for General Motors's until the plant closed down. It was a tough time for their father until he got another job driving trucks while his mother was a schoolteacher. Kaden wanted to be in the streets with all his friends doing small jobs making quick money as well. That was not the plan Kaden's father had for him. If it killed Kaden's father, he was going to make sure his son went to college and made something of himself. If Kaden could live up to his father's expectations, there was no way Melech was not going to do the same. Meeting and falling in love with Halina just made life so much better for him. Doing what they always expected of Kaden is what made him somewhat vulnerable over the past few years.

Approaching the room at the H, Kaden was still unsure how he was going to handle the Leana situation. Tapping softly, the door flung open with a woman who had crept into his heart without permission, encouraging him to make one wrong decision after another. One part of his heart wanted to sweep her up in his arms and make sweet love to her, the other wanted to drown her in a tub of freezing cold water.

"You don't seem happy to see me." Leana stood in only a bright red thong, and black, red bottom heels. Her voluptuous breast stood at attention, anticipating Kaden's full attention. Taken aback by the lust he had for Leana, the day replayed in his head. Grabbing Leana by the throat, Kaden drug her to the bed.

"Oh, yes, baby. I've been waiting all day for this," Leana cooed.

Fire in his eyes, Kaden asked her, "How dare you sleep with that little thug!" She was beginning to hate Levi more and more.

"What are you talking about?" Leana was trying to pry Kaden's hand from around her neck. It was no longer sensual Kaden struck fear in her.

"Both Melech and that…that boy confirmed it today. You actually left my boy for Levi's ass."

"No…no…no!" she pleaded. "That's not true!" Finally, breaking free. "That's some way-out story, Levi told Melech. I just told him I fell in love with someone else. That's you, baby. I fell in love with you." He sat thinking about Leana's words.

"But you slept with, Levi?"

"Yes," she humbly admitted. There was no point in lying since Melech and Levi already told Kaden.

"Pack your shit and get out of here. I'm done with you," Kaden said with disgust.

"You don't understand, Levi threatened me. You know that he has, Melech's ear. He was turning him against me. I only did it so I could keep my husband. Then you came along, and I didn't care about my marriage anymore. I just wanted to be with you." The waterworks fell like clockwork. Leana was learning to cry on command.

"None of this is helpful to my son. You and I are worse than what Levi did to, my son. Melech would never forgive me if he ever found out."

"Baby, I won't tell if you don't. You see, I let him think it was Levi. They've already had a fight about it. Levi made it clear as day he would not be with me, he would always choose, Leek."

"See, now that's starting to sound as if I was not your first choice."

"You are my only choice." Leana crawled across the bed to get closer to Kaden. Sliding her hand down his chest, she whispered in his ear, "It's you that I love, Kaden." Nibbling on his ear, "You make me feel like a real woman." Leana sucked on his earlobe. Easing on to Kaden's lap, she tried to take his lips into her mouth. Turning his head, Kaden did not want to confuse the way he was felling with her sexual advances. Kissing and sucking on his strong jawline, Leana kept whispering, "It's you, baby." Noticing how hard he was trying to fight off her advances, she caressed her own breast, circling the ripe nipples with a pink tongue. "You can leave me, baby. Melech is what's important in all of this." She softly pecked his lips. "Can you just touch me one more time? I need to feel you one last time. You are the one I fell in love with. Can you do that for me?" Leana guided his hand into her thong. Immediately he could feel the wet, hot goodness leaking from between her thighs.

"I can't," he murmured, even though it was exactly what his body yearned for.

"Oh, but you can." Leana slowly moved her hips in a circular motion, forcing his fingers to play with her. "Um, can you feel what you do to me," Leana hummed.

"Why is it so damn hot?" Kaden wiggled his fingers around, allowing two to slide into Leana.

"Only you can get her to purr like this." She quickened her pace. Cupping her own breast Leana leaned backed, giving Haden access to put them in his mouth.

"No…no…no…" Kaden took Leana off his lap. His son had to be what was more important than sexual gratification.

"Okay, I understand." Leana sat next to him. "Do you want to at least watch for old time's sake?"

"No, you need to pack up and go to your father's place." Leana did not abide by Kaden's demands. She removed the red thong which was blocking the view of her glistening goodness.

"I like it when you touch me right here." Leana began pleasing herself for Kaden to watch. Sliding her fingers in and out and stroking her lips and clit only produced a wave of radiant juices. As much as Kaden wanted to turn and walk away, he was in a trance. Her hips moved faster and faster as a thick white cream made her fingers sticky every time they exited their precious hole. "Do you wanna taste it, baby?" she said erotically. "You won't be doing anything wrong, just tasting this goodness.

Leana had won. Kaden lost all his common sense. His mouth went right to Leana wet, creamy wonderland. Kaden was out of his clothes before he had a handle on his emotions, pounding every ounce of his manhood into her stomach.

Satisfaction instantly turned to regret for Kaden. Once again, he had violated the constitution of his marriage, and his sons as well. Leana was the first woman he had been with since he met Halina, she was the love of his life. It was not that Kaden did not have the opportunity to step out on his wife; he made a conscious choice not to. Somehow, Leana worked her charm on him as well. After Melech brought her home to meet his parents, they both gave their approval of Leana. She was charming, educated, and doted on Melech. It was apparent that she adored their son and that made them like her even more. Halina treated Leana like a daughter; they spent time together planning the wedding since Leana did not have her own mother to share the special day with her. Leana also confided in Halina when it came to her career goals and marital issues. Kaden felt this would give his son's marriage longevity until Leana began warming up to him.

Leana was always a space invader in Kaden's opinion. He chalked it up to being raised by her father and losing her mother at such a young age. He felt Leana was in need of affection. The hugs seemed to last a little too long, or Leana's hand would linger on his leg while they talked. She did not try to hide these actions from Melech or Halina, making Kaden brush his uneasiness about it to the back of his mind. A year ago, Leana began calling Kaden for personal advice, inviting him to lunch and showing up to his office. Needing a male perspective was her reasoning for reaching out to him. Kaden looked at Leana as a daughter. If he genuinely wanted to know what was going on in his son's life, Leana was going to tell him.

They were both concerned with Melech's relationship with Levi, Leana, more so than Kaden. It affected him hearing that Leana had slept with Levi after she had informed him of his drug use, illegal activities, and womanizing. She was fearful her husband was being influenced by Levi's lifestyle. Being pulled down a road Leana would not be able to save Melech from. Kaden knew that Melech had stars in his eyes when it came to Levi, but Kaden felt his son had his own mind. During their friendship, Melech still went to college, started his own business and married a lovely girl.

Reassuring Leana became difficult for Kaden. She came to his office distraught one day informing him, Melech was distant, spending more time with Levi than her. Leana felt Melech was changing. She suspected her husband entertained women at the Lounge, the same way Levi was. While comforting Leana, Kaden found himself embraced in a passionate kiss. Becoming embarrassed, Kaden fought her off at that time. Leana rushed out of the office. Feeling guilty, Kaden attempted to call her for days. How he allowed it to happen was weighing on him heavily. Up until that moment, Kaden had not felt any attraction for his sons' wife. But the way she made his body come alive with her kiss, Kaden could not stop thinking about her. Leana appeared to be a simple girl. She was sweet and innocently looking for love that his son was not providing her with. Kaden's heart went out to the young girl, losing her mother so young, expecting Melech to fill the void she desperately wanted to fill.

"You're upset with me?" Leana looked up at Kaden. She laid her head back on his chest. Looking into her big brown eyes only hurt more knowing the words he needed to tell her.

"I'm mad at myself," he said, stroking her long curly hair.

"You didn't do anything." Leana snuggled closer to him. "You take good care of me." She kissed his chest.

"No, sweetie, I haven't." He sighed. "I have made your life more complicated. This has to end. I love my wife and son. This never should have happened. That's my family and with them is where I need to be."

"I don't understand." Leana sat up so Kaden could see the tears in her eyes. "What did I do wrong?"

"I saw the sadness in my son's eyes." Haden wiped the tears from Leana's face. "This is wrong."

"What about me? What about how Melech hurt me? You saw the bruises." Leana tried hard to contain her anger only showing sorrow to Kaden.

"Wait." The reality of it all was coming back to Kaden. "That was after, Melech found out about you seeping with Levi." His body became rigidly erect. "I was under the assumption he lost control because you fell in love with someone else."

"It is," Leana tried to explain. "I told him that when I left. Levi ran and told him we slept together and…and…now, Leek thinks I walked out because of him." For Kaden, something in Leana's story was missing.

"I still don't understand this, Levi thing?"

"He made me." Leana started crying.

"Made you, how? Raped you?" Kaden did not like the words Leana was using.

"No…not…by force."

"What does that even mean?" He demanded.

"He threatened me," she yelled at him. Kaden was asking Leana questions she was not prepared to answer.

"With what a gun?"

"Huh," she was getting frustrated with all of Kaden's questions.

"Did Levi hold a gun to your head, Leana? How did he threaten you?" he commanded an answer from her.

"No…no…he…um…said that," she stuttered. "He said that…he would turn, Melech against me. Levi…he said he'd make, Melech…he'd make him leave me." Leana was trying to put her lie in order. "Yeah…divorce me and leave me with nothing," she paused. "I got to the point I didn't care anymore. That's why I walked out, baby."

"Don't you know how ridiculous that sounds?" Kaden got up from the bed, Leana was lying to him, Kaden needed to know why.

"He knew about us…." Leana blurted out. "He was going to tell…tell, Leek, if I didn't give him what he wanted." Putting his clothes back on Kaden froze momentarily.

"So, you fucked that, little thug, after you were with me?" he calmly probed Leana.

"Baby, I had no choice," she pleaded with Kaden.

"There's always a choice!" he roared. "I would have squashed that little boy like the little punk he is, you know that!" Leana was quickly learning where Melech got his anger from. "What kind of game are you playing?" Kaden was now in her face.

"None…baby…I swear." Leana tried to touch his face. "You have to believe me."

"I would have believed everything that came out of your mouth until you whored yourself out," he spat with disgust.

"I what?" The words stung worse than when Melech slapped her back.

"Get your shit together. I'm taking you back to your father, he's worried, and you have the cops thinking my son did something to you." Kaden sat down to put his shoes on.

"Kaden, baby, please…" she tried one last time to get him back on her side. "I love you…I gave up everything for you."

"No, little girl, you used me for far too long, and I fell for it. Now I need to beg my wife for forgiveness and hope my son will put this behind him someday."

"No one has to know about us."

"I know!" Kaden yelled at her." How he fell for Leana's innocent act was beyond him. Kaden saw what he wanted to see in her. Levi did not have to threaten a woman to have sex with him. The one thing Levi would love to do is prove to Melech what a terrible father he was. He would have been sure to announce the affair to both Melech and Halina while they were all together today. Leana made the biggest mistake when she told that lie. Levi would confront Kaden, not blackmail Leana. She slept with Levi because she wanted to. Kaden was not sure why or who Leana left his son for. At this point, it did not matter to him; she was not worth losing his wife over.

"Okay…" Leana sadly went over to her Gucci suitcase and took a deep breath. She did not know how all of this went sideways. All Leana knew is that she was tired of losing at this game called love.

CHAPTER ELEVEN

Levi woke up to banging on the front door. Melech had not been seen since the fight with his father. Rubbing his eyes, he staggered to the door.

"Hold on," Levi yelled. Opening the door to two poorly dressed detectives, Levi got uncomfortable. "How can I help you?" he asked them.

"Mr. Buckley?" One of them asked.

"No."

"Is he here," The older disheveled one asked.

"He's sleep," Levi informed them.

"We need to have a word with him."

"His lawyer ain't here. Shouldn't y'all wait on him?" Levi asked.

"I don't think that will be necessary," the detective told him.

"Oh, it's always necessary."

"Sir, can you retrieve Mr. Buckley, please," the clean-cut detective asked. Levi closed the door on them both and went upstairs to wake up Melech. To his surprise, he was not in his room or bathroom. Levi rushed back downstairs to get his phone. Trying to call Melech to find out where he was when his phone rang in the house. Levi turned around, seeing Melech's phone on the kitchen counter charging.

"Damnit!" Levi did not know what he was going to tell the detectives. He honestly did not hear Melech leave. Hesitantly he went back to the door. Opening it, Levi saw Melech's truck pulling up in the driveway. Relief took over.

"What's going on?" Melech asked, walking up to the trio.

"Mr. Buckley?" The older detective asked.

"Yes." He looked back and forth at the two men.

"They just got here. I thought you were sleeping."

"I went for a run," Melech told Levi.

"Can we come in and have a word with you?" the younger detective asked.

"No!" Levi inserted himself.

"What's going on?" Melech wanted to know.

"It's about your father."

"What about him?" Melech asked.

"Sir, may we come in and talk to you?" The younger man asked once again.

"Tell me what's going on?" Melech wiped the sweat from his head and face with his small towel.

"Sir, he's in the hospital with a gunshot wound."

"What?" Melech did not know how to take this information.

"How…When…Where is he?" The question flew out. Melech was not sure which one was more important.

"I'm going to need you to calm down, sir," the older detective told him. "We have a few questions for you."

"Fuck dat!" Levi snapped at them. "Where is Mr. B? We need to go see him!"

"We understand your concern, guys, but we need to find who did this to him."

"He's a banker?" Melech was baffled at who would want to hurt his father.

"He wasn't at work, Mr. Buckley. He was at a Hotel."

"A what?" both Levi and Melech said in unison.

"Did your father have an outside relationship?" The shabby detective asked. A cold chill came over Melech.

"No…no." He put both hands on his head, holding back his tears. "My wife…"

"Excuse me?" The younger detective was not sure he heard Melech right.

"What?" Surprise took Levi.

"My father was not having an affair," Melech tried to explain. "Leana, my wife and I are estranged. My dad was trying to talk some sense into her. The police thought she was missing, but Le's not. She was hiding out, playing games."

"I'm confused," the younger detective told Melech.

"My wife, Leana, went missing, so her father thought...."

"Yeah, he's done talking," Levi cut Melech off. "Where is his dad at?"

"What's the problem, son? If his wife did this, we need to find her."

"Yeah, I get that," Levi told them. "Does his mother know about this yet?"

"We have officers en route to her," the scruffy detective informed them.

"Give us your info I'll make sure he calls you after we see his dad."

"Please do." Both men handed over their cards. "Time is of the essence," the unkempt detective replied.

"Where's my father," Melech asked again.

"Centinela," both men responded. Levi pulled Melech into the house, closing the door behind him.

"What the fuck?" he pushed Melech.

"I need to get to the hospital." Melech tried to go up the stairs.

"Oh, hell, no!" Levi grabbed him by the shirt. "What the fuck does your pops know that got him shot?"

"You don't think Leana had something to do with this?" Melech was shocked by the question.

"C'mon, man. How dumb are you?" Levi could not believe Melech did not see the writing on the wall.

"Look, my dad was helping Le because she told him a bunch of lies. He was going to make sure Leana brought her ass back to stop the nonsense with Chester."

"My dude, she's fucking yo' old man. He turned on this crazy girl, now he's in the hospital. What you missin'?"

"What? No…my, dad?" Melech shook his head.

"Leek, Leana is running on desperation now." Levi tried laying the facts out for him.

"My dad?" Melech was finding the tidbit of information hard to accept as real.

"Me!" Levi pointed at himself. "She got me…"

"I need to shower. I have to go see my dad and check on my mother." Melech had his suspicions but did not want to think his father could do this to his mother. "Don't you dare say this shit in front of my mother!" he ordered.

"She gonna figure the shit out, trust and believe. That lady ain't as blind as yo' dumb ass." Levi walked away from the stairs to get dressed. There was no way Melech was leaving him behind on his trip to the hospital.

♥♥♥

"That was interesting," Detective Kelly, the eldest of the two Detectives said.

"Tell me about it," Detective Anderson confirmed the assessment.

"What do you think they're hiding?" Kelly asked.

"The son seems oblivious to what's going on. Sad to say, he's in for a rude awakening."

"Do you think they know the father was sleeping with the girl?" Kelly took a puff from his cigarette.

"The friend picked up on it, that's why he stopped Buckley from talking to us."

"I think the son knew, I wouldn't be surprised if he walked in on them and shot his father," Kelly told his partner.

"I don't think so. The Buckley boy was willing to tell us all he knew until his friend stopped him."

"His wife is missing, his father knows where she is, and he doesn't find that odd?"

"What son would think their father is having an affair with their wife?" Anderson questioned Kelly's logic.

"True, it's a real-life soap opera."

"Something his mother would be acting out on her show," Kelly gave a small chuckle.

"This case is going to be interesting. I hope Mr. Buckley survives, he's the only one who can tell us who shot him."

"He better hope he doesn't. His wife and son are going to want to kill him." Kelly was snide.

"You are so wrong for that."

"This is a man that is cheating on his wife with his son's wife. Would you want to live to tell that tale," Kelly threw the question out there.

"I'm still focused on the son. He was certain that his father was trying to help bring his wife home, he had no idea."

"Well, we have the murder weapon." Anderson pointed out.

"We already know it belongs to the boy."

"It doesn't mean he pulled the trigger. His wife had full access to it as well." Kelly flicked the cigarette.

"So, you think that tiny woman is capable of shooting a man?"

"We don't give women enough credit for murder," Anderson informed his partner. "This family is hiding something."

"The one thing we do know is that the girl and young Buckley were separated. What we need to find out is why?"

"I put my pension up that it was infidelity. That man does not look like the forgiving type," Anderson added his opinion.

"His friend is the brains between the two."

"That he is, did you get his name?" Anderson realized he did not ask.

"No, let's do a search on all of young Buckley assets and acquaintances. I can see that young man being a problem."

"I'll get on it when we get back to the station." Anderson knew if Melech's friend was not there, they would have gotten more information from him. This was going to be a compelling case.

♥ ♥ ♥

Melech made it to the hospital to see about his father, with Levi in tow. No matter how much Melech tried to distance himself from his long-time friend, Levi would not allow it to happen. Levi knew he made a grave mistake by sleeping with Melech's wife, but he refused to let it get in the way of his friendship with Melech. Levi owned his mistake; there was no way he was going to lose his brother over a woman who had an ulterior motive. Yes, he had fallen in love with a scorpion and learned a valuable lesson. Losing his best friend and brother would not happen on his watch, no matter how much Melech tried to fight it.

Melech noticed that his mother had beaten him there. Halina did not look like her usual beautiful self; an aura of sadness surrounded her. Melech wanted to make everything better for her. He just didn't know how. He too, was feeling a sense of melancholy while his father was fighting for his life.

"Mother." Melech took her into his arms while she was still sitting in the uncomfortable waiting room chair.

"Hey, baby." Halina cupped his face with her hand.

"How's dad doing?" he asked with concern.

"I don't really know. He's in surgery. All we can do is pray and wait." Melech did not like seeing his mother so vulnerable.

"Hey, moms." Levi gave her a hug as well. Halina held on to Levi's hand, giving him a warm smile.

"I tried calling you," she addressed Melech.

"I didn't have my phone."

"The cops came to his door," Levi softly let her know.

"They're not as gentle as a mother." She lovingly looked at her son.

"I'm okay, mom." Melech tried to comfort her.

"How long has Mr. B been in there?" Levi was curious.

"I'm not really sure," Halina told them. "When I got here, they had already been working on him." The calm she had was concerning for Melech.

"He's going to be fine." Melech gave a warm smile to his mother.

"I'm not so sure, son. Just prepare yourself for the worst. If he pulls through, we can be grateful." Halina stared down at her hands. The last thing she wanted to do was give her child false hope. The nurse on duty told her it was touch and go for her husband. What Halina could not understand is why her husband was in a hotel room. She had never known Kaden to be a cheating man. With his life hanging on the edge, there was nothing she could do. Halina tried not to think about anything else.

"He was trying to get Leana to come back home." Melech could feel that his mother was questioning her husband's whereabouts. "He was the only one that knew she was fine."

"Excuse me?" she glared up at her son. "Your father is in there because of your wife?" Levi did his best not to give his views on the matter.

"She filled his head with lies about me, dad was just trying to help." Melech wanted to put his mother's mind at ease.

"I see." Halina digested the information her son had just fed her. Not trying to sound the alarm to him, she sat in silence. Now she understood why her poor husband was fighting for his life. Leana was at the end of her timeline, and her husband paid the ultimate price. Unaware of what she fed Kaden to assist Leana in her deadly plot, Halina knew her husband had tasted the wild springs of the young girl. She was not aware of the conversation that took place between her husband and son. Whatever it was struck a core in Leana. Halina knew she was the one who tried to take Kaden's life. Whatever Leana had between her legs, Halina knew it was not enough to tear Kaden away from his own flesh and blood. It may have disrupted their marriage momentarily. Excitement could always lead a man to stray for a short time. A bond with your own child changes things.

Kaden was not the most affectionate father the lord could have blessed Melech with. The one thing Kaden did was support his son with any goal he had in life. Barely missing a game since childhood, sponsoring his lounge, paying for Melech's wedding, even helping to secure the home Melech and Leana moved into after they got married. Melech may have come to his mother for personal advice-but he modeled himself after Kaden. That was the man Melech wanted to be. Halina noticed that Leana had taken an interest in her husband. However, she turned a blind eye to it. In her mind, Leana was a child seeking acceptance. If at any point, Halina thought Kaden would succumb to Leana's charm, she would have stopped the entanglement immediately. Considering Halina had treated Leana like a daughter, she felt the young girl had some type of morality about her.

"Mom, are you okay?" Melech asked her.

"Yes, baby," she lied, wondering if her son had connected the dots. The two officers that informed her Kaden was in the hospital from a gunshot wound tried questioning her. Halina did not have time for them. All she wanted to do was be by his side. What stayed in her mind was that Kayden was shot in a hotel room. This was out of character for her husband. Pulling up their credit card information, Halina realized there were two different hotels Kaden was paying for. He did not take any precautions to hide any of it from her. This saddened Halina. Kaden was aware of the trust she had in him, which made him careless.

"He's gonna pull through," Levi added. He could see Halina's mind working overtime, she was putting the pieces together the same way he had done. Levi took his phone out of his pocket and sent a text. If Melech was not willing to find out what was going on with his wife, he was going to get to the bottom of what she was up to.

"We'll be fine." Melech was not sure if his father was going to pull through all of this, he wanted his mother to know he was there for his mother no matter what.

Noticing the same two detectives approaching them, Levi quickly sprung to his feet. He would not allow them to upset Melech or Halina while they were waiting to find out if Kaden was going to live or die.

"This is not the time." Levi was hostile.

"Son, we just have a few questions," Kelly kept his cool.

"You can wait on that. They don't know if Mr. B is gonna live or die."

"What's your name and how do you fit into this family?" Anderson asked in his always-professional matter.

"My name is *'fuck off,'* and I'm associated through *'fuck off.'* Does that help you out?" Levi shrugged his shoulders.

"Not one bit." Kelley's whole face contorted. "You're making this harder than it needs to be."

"Am I?" Levi tilted his head to the side. "This family is on pins and needles waiting to find out if Mr. B is gonna be good or not."

"We just want to find out who pulled that trigger. Can you understand that?" Anderson genially asked Levi.

"Nah, you tryna pin this shit on one of them. How dumb you think I am?" Levi crossed his sculptured arms over his chest.

"I think you're as dumb as a Teddy Ruxpin," Kelly told him.

"A what?" Levi did not understand the reference.

"A pet rock." Anderson changed the analogy.

"Oh…" Levi chucked. "You think I'm some dumb ass nigga?" He pointed at them both. "No, sir. I ain't no dumb ass coon y'all can take on down to a tree and hang up on a noose and confess to some shit I ain't do fo' a coke a cola. I's a smart boy ova yonda. I know I got sum kinda rights, foe you shoot me in my back, sir. Me and my, folks, we gonna wait right here, Massa and see if dis here man live or die, foe' we answer em der question y'all got foe' us. Oh, and Massa, I'm gone make sure, dim der folks gotta lawyer foe' de talk to y'all pigs, sir. No disrespect, Massa."

"You're a funny guy." Kelly found no humor in Levi. This was not racial at all.

"We understand how difficult this is for the family…" Anderson was searching for Levi's name; he was not willing to give it to them. "We just want to know who shot Mr. Buckley. You do understand that, right?"

"I understand that you guys are self-serving, and you are not gonna make them feel worse than they are feeling right now."

"Very well." Anderson was not going to get into a sparring match with Levi. "Please make sure they get in touch with us as soon as possible.

"Yeah...whateva." Levi waved them off. Standing his ground, Levi stood in the hallway until both detectives were out of sight. He needed someone to find Leana before she hurt somebody else. Now Levi wished the officer had locked her up the day she made a spectacle of herself at his front door.

Chester rushed into the Central police station, looking for some assistance. He had been on the phone for several hours before he was able to get in touch with anyone who would listen to him. The police officers who made the initial report regarding his daughter's disappearance had passed the case on. Patiently waiting was not one of Chester's strong suits. Being told to have a seat and wait yet again was not the kind of help Chester was seeking when he made a personal appearance to the station.

Glancing down at his watch once again, Chester heard his name being called. A tall, clean-cut gentleman was standing next to the worn-down wooden door.

"That's me." Chester waved, walking in Anderson's direction. Adjusting his tie, the detective took stock of Chester's appearance. He couldn't help but notice he needed sleep, a shower, and a shave. A fedora covered his uncombed graying hair while smudges consumed the lenses of his glasses that barely stayed on the bridge of his nose. Usually, an attractive man, Chester, had been overwhelmed with anxiety over his daughter, Leana.

"I'm detective Anderson." He reached his hand out to him. "What can I do for you?"

"Yes…yes, sir." Chester shook his hand. "It's my daughter, she left me another disturbing message."

"Who's your daughter?" Anderson was unclear about which case Chester was referring to.

"Leana, Leana Buckley." Chester retrieved his phone, looking for a picture of his daughter to show the detective.

"The Buckley case, yes…I know it." Anderson put his hands in his pockets. "Where exactly is your daughter? It's imperative that we speak with her."

"That's just it." Chester scratched his arm nervously. "She's missing. I've been down here several times. They asked her husband questions, but they…"

"Melech, right?" Anderson cut him off.

"Yes…uh huh. The other officer didn't tell me anything about what he knew. They haven't been getting along since she left him…"

"So, she left the marriage?" The detective reached for his notepad.

"Yes…but, she called me again…"

"Why did she leave, Mr. Buckley? What type of problems were they having?"

"She was being silly. You know how young people are. I'm really worried because she was crying and told me she…"

"Can you elaborate, sir?" he cut him off once again. "Silly, how? Was it money or…" Anderson left it open, waiting for Chester to fill in the blank.

"Why does that matter right now?" Chester was getting annoyed with the questions. He wanted to find his daughter.

"The minor details are always important," Anderson explained.

"My daughter thought she was in love with someone else." Chester hated to admit.

"I see."

"On the message, Leana was crying. She said someone hurt her…"

"Hurt her, how?" Anderson looked from his pad.

"Raped her." Chester removed his glasses, wiped his eyes with the back of his hand before the tears escaped.

"Did she tell you where she is?"

"No, that's why I'm here. My baby girl is out there somewhere. I need to find her." Chester wiped his eyes again, putting his glasses back on.

"I understand, sir. We have been looking for her as well."

"Yes, I know, the other officer told me they handed the missing case off to detectives." Anderson got a blank look in his eyes.

"That's not me," he told Chester.

"Huh?" This concerned him. "Why are you looking for, Leana?"

"Mr. Buckley is in the hospital. We believe she was the last one to see him before he was shot." Chester was drained of all his emotions. He did not know exactly what questions to ask next.

"I know they had some problems, but my girl would never hurt, Melech." He tried his best to defend his daughter.

"No, sir, the father." Anderson anticipated Chester's reaction. There was a sense of sadness and disappointment that took over his face as his eyes blinked slowly. "What can you tell me about Mr. Buckley and your daughter's relationship?"

"Um," Chester shrugged. "Not much. She spent a lot of time with his wife. Halina treated her like a daughter. Leana lost her mother when she was very young."

"I see." Anderson kept taking notes. "Oh." He pointed his pen at Chester. "Melech…his friend. What's his name?"

"Levi?" Chester was unsure of the question.

"Hmm…Is that a street name?"

"No, that's his given name. Why?"

"Do you happen to know his last name?" Anderson did not look up from the tiny notebook.

"I don't talk to the boy much, he's trouble."

"I see. Okay, thanks." Anderson pulled one of his cards out of his pad. "Give us a call if your daughter calls you again."

"I thought you guys were looking for her?" Chester desperately asked.

"Yes, yes. I will locate the detective on the case." Anderson started walking away.

"Don't you need my number?"

"Sure." He had given him some valuable information. Anderson was not sure if Chester would call him if Leana turned up. "For your daughter's safety, make sure you contact me if she shows up." He was firm. "If she was raped, we really need to get her some medical attention."

"Right…yes." Chester took note of the *'If'* in his comment. "Sir," he got Anderson's attention before he disappeared behind the door again. "Where is Kaden at?"

"Centinela Medical Center."

"Thanks."

CHAPTER TWELVE

Everyone was sitting around quietly when Chester made an appearance at the hospital. He did not want to hear bad news about Kaden over the phone. Levi was the first person to notice Chester slowly approaching them; he wasn't sure how this was going to play out.

"Hey, Halina, how's Kaden doing?" removing his hat Chester leaned in to give her a hug.

"We aren't sure yet."

"He's been in surgery for over three hours," Melech added.

"I'm so sorry to hear about all of this."

"How did you find out?" Levi was interested to know who called him.

"The detective."

"They came to your house also?" Halina was still upset with Chester for sending the police to question her son over Leana. He should have known that Melech would never do anything to harm her. Because of his child, Kaden was the one in danger unbeknownst to them.

"No, I was at the station when they told me what happened." Levi blew out a long sigh. He stroked the back of his head with his hand.

"Say what?" Halina leaned forward in her chair.

"Do they have, Leana?" Melech wanted to know.

"They don't. It doesn't seem like anyone even cares if they find, my girl." Chester felt guilty talking about his problems while Kaden was having surgery. "The detective was more interested in asking me useless questions that didn't pertain to where she could possibly be."

"Like what?" Halina glared up at him.

"Her and Melech's marriage. Her relationship with you and Kaden." Chester pointed at Halina. "Um…oh, his name." He tilted his head back where Levi was sitting.

"You gave them answers?" Levi jumped out of his seat, poking his finger deep into Chester's temple.

"What's the big deal?" Chester tried to slap Levi's hand away.

"You stupid, old man. Mr. B is in there cuz yo' daughter." He poked him in the forehead. "Yo' ass just tied the knot to help hang her ass, stupid." Levi pushed past him to make a phone call.

"When did you get so trusting?" Halina asked him.

"What are you talking about? My daughter…" Chester had to compose himself.

"Your daughter started this mess." Melech stood to his feet. "I gave that girl everything. She threw it all away for my best friend. Now my dad is in there." He pointed toward the double doors nurses and doctors were coming in and out of. "Fighting for his life. Why? Because he was trying to help her. Leana didn't disappear the way you think. She ran to my dad; she was hiding out."

"They said she was the last person, Kaden talked to." Chester did not want to believe the obvious.

"Because she shot him, Chester."

"No…no…no…" Learning Leana was making grave decisions did not change the fact she was still Chester's little girl. "She called me hysterical, telling me she was raped yesterday." Halina leaned back in her chair. The words Chester just uttered hit like a grenade exploding in her chest.

"Chester, I know you are not accusing my father of such a heinous act!" Melech waved his hands in front of him.

"I'm…I'm not…no…I would not…Halina," Chester needed her help.

"I don't know what happened to your daughter, Chester. I do know that Kaden would never do something like that." She did her best not to pass judgment on Leana, especially not knowing what was going on in the girl's life. "We were unaware, Leana was with him last. Melech knew that his father was helping her hideout."

"Why did she go to him and not me?" Chester was still upset with his daughter for her actions.

"That's something you're going to have to take up with her." Halina crossed her legs in the uncomfortable chair. There was so much more she wanted to say on the subject. There was no concrete proof on her suspicions. Melech had been vocal on his perspective of his father's relationship with his wife.

"I don't know where her head is right now, Halina." Chester sat next to her.

"She lost her way somehow." Halina touched his hand, trying to give him some type of comfort. Chester was not the same person he was a few weeks ago. The wholesome, handsome man had aged years in such a short time. His once naturally graying well-kept beard was overgrown as well as his hair. It used to define him as a handsome, humble man, unlike Kaden, whose soft chocolate hue tranquilly nestled behind his rugged beard. The wrinkles on his forehead overshadowed his deep-set eyes that screeched confidence when Kaden glanced in your direction. He and Melech looked more like brothers than father and son; both specimens were a work of art.

"Yes, she has." Chester was ashamed of Leana's behavior. He did not raise his daughter to be the type of woman who would cheat on her husband, especially with his closest friend. Chester tried calling Leana several times before he arrived at the hospital. Her phone was still going to her voicemail. Chester prayed Leana was somewhere safe.

Levi needed air from the madness that was taking place in the hospital. Why everyone was sidestepping who Leana truly was, aggravated him. Kaden was not his favorite person of all time. The way he treated Melech as an afterthought had been a source of Levi's contention for years, no one seemed to notice it but him. An outsider would think Kaden was the greatest father of all times; any man can buy their child whatever they wanted. Real fathers give some type of affection to their own flesh and blood. Kaden spoke at Melech. Not with him. This was the reason Melech did not confide in his father the way a son should.

It did not surprise Levi that Kaden slept with Leana at all. Melech was the toy Kaden put up on the shelf once he stopped being fun. Once football was over, Kaden had no more use for Melech. Levi knew he didn't have room to criticize anyone because he did the same exact thing with Leana. The difference was Kaden was supposed to be wiser than both him and Melech. Still, Levi did not want to see Kaden die, Melech could not take too many more losses at this point in his life. Once Melech came to terms about his father and Leana, Levi knew it was going to hurt Melech more than what he had done. He was going to need time to forgive him; Kaden could not die before Melech had a chance to do that.

"I knew you would be out here smoking?" Melech startled Levi as he walked up behind him in the parking lot.

"You know I needed to clear my head. Ya' boy is dumb as hell. I wanted to knock his ass out. He's too old. Might have a stroke on my ass."

"He doesn't mean any harm. Chester just loves his daughter."

"Who seems to love everybody." Levi hit his blunt.

"Really?" Melech leaned up against his truck.

"My bad, bro. I wasn't thinking," Levi apologized.

"You weren't lying." Melech shrugged it off. "Why didn't I see it?"

"Man, Leek." Levi did not like the question. "You love Le. I hate to admit it, cause she turned out to be pure evil; she loved you too. Something just snapped in that head of hers, man."

"Yeah…" Melech looked up at the stars. Trying to wrap his mind around his father getting shot was affecting him. Somehow, he felt it was his fault. "I said some terrible things to him."

"To your pops?"

"Yeah." Melech hated that Levi was the one person he turned to when his heart was heavy. He was still upset over what was done to him. Yet, it was always Levi that was by his side through good and bad.

"Hey, yo' ass is only human. You got a lotta shit going on. Pop's laid some real shit on you. You went off. Don't blame yo 'self fo' that shit. You ain't pull no trigger. Getting shit off yo' chest ain't a bad thing, Leek. Pop's understood, trust me."

"Her phone…"

"What about it?" Levi put his blunt out.

"I saw his number on it and called him. He thought I was Leana."

"Word?" Levi was wondering why Kaden suddenly made an appearance at Melech's house. Melech did not tell him about the argument the two had in his office. It had slipped Levi's mind that he gave Melech Leana's phone.

"That's how I found out she wasn't missing."

"Why?" Levi did not know what else to ask.

"I don't know, man. My dad said something about her telling him she needed space. I hurt her and she was scared…some stupid shit, so he helped her out. I don't know, he was waiting on me to call him or he was about to call me when the cops hauled me in for questioning. I forget what he said, I was so pissed."

"Rightfully so," Levi confirmed Melech's feelings. "You know, Le can spin a tale."

"I'm learning that more and more each day."

"Shit, I got hoe's in all these area codes." Levi twirled his finger in the air. "Even six-six-one, my nigga and she pulled one over on my ass. Don't blame yo 'self." He patted Melech on the shoulder.

"Yeah, but you didn't marry her and pay her way through school."

"That I didn't do," Levi couldn't help but chuckle.

"You paid a few strippers way through college here and there, it has to count for something." Melech could not help taking the personal dig.

"So, know you got jokes?" He shoved Melech. "You Kevin Hart to my Eddie Murphy, homie."

"I'm Martin Lawrence to your Eddie, fool." Melech finally got a small smile on his face.

"Nah, nigga, you Arsenio Hall."

"That's hella wrong. Why I gotta be a sidekick?" Melech asked.

"Been my side bitch since high school."

"You really have life twisted, Levi. You sat at all my games and hung out at my college. That makes you a tag along." Melech laughed.

"I was yo' bodyguard, nigga. Yo' scary-ass woulda been jumped every day if it weren't fo' me."

"Ahh, you can't be serious. Can't none of your homies see me, and you know this, man."

"My homies don't fight head up, nigga. I ain't taught yo' ass nothin' in all these years?"

"I don't take lessons from the runner-up." Melech jabbed him in the shoulder.

"Imma let you have this one, only cause yo' pop's, cuh." Reality set back in for both of them.

"Damn, man. Pop's gotta make it through this." Melech leaned back up against the truck.

"He will." Levi touched his shoulder. "Bastard too stubborn not too."

"You right about that." Melech shook his head. They both quietly went back into the hospital. Neither one saw Leana watching them from her car. Seeing that their relationship had fallen right back to normal burned her soul. She walked out on her beloved Melech to end up with nothing. Levi wanted nothing to do with her, and Kaden might be dead. Leana could not feel anymore useless than she was feeling all alone in her car.

Melech walked back into the waiting room just in time to notice Halina and Chester embracing one another. It caught him off guard and instantly made him anxious. He thought maybe they were comforting each other because his father had taken a turn for the worse while he was outside trying to regroup with Levi.

"Is everything alright?" Melech asked, walking up to the pair.

"Oh, baby." Halina hugged her son. "Your father is stable." Tears fell from her eyes. "The doctor said he lost a lot of blood; however, the bullet didn't hit any major organs." She held her fist to her mouth, trying not to cry. "It came very close to his spine. They are pretty sure he should be able to move his lower extremities. They will know more once he comes to."

"Can we see him?" Melech asked.

"No, not yet. He's still in recovery. Soon though."

"Damn, man." Levi gave him a hug. "I told you he was too mean to leave this earth."

"You know that man isn't done torturing people," Chester added.

"I'm just glad he's going to be fine." Melech kissed the top of his mother's head, holding her close to him. "Go home, mom. Get some rest. I'll let you know when we can see him."

"No…no." she waved him off. "I want to be here the minute he wakes up." Halina was still upset with Kaden. She was not sure if he was cheating on her with Leana, but he was still her husband, and she needed to be by his side right now.

"Let's at least get you something to eat," Chester told her.

"Coffee. I need some caffeine in my life right about now."

"Okay, I'll take you down to the cafeteria." Chester took Halina by the hand, leading her away from the two men.

"You think that nigga knows where Leana is?" Levi said as soon as they were out of earshot.

"If he does, that man wouldn't tell us. He may think Leana was wrong to walk out on me, but blood is thicker than water."

"Not always," Levi stroked his beard. Melech was not any blood relation to him, yet he would side with him over his own father any day.

"True." Melech had in the back of his mind the true nature of his father's relationship with his wife.

"I'd kill a muthafucca for you."

"Sadly, I know that to be true." Although Melech was disappointed in Levi for sleeping with Leana, he also knew Levi would kill her if Leana ever tried to do anything to him. His father making it through was a good thing. Melech had taken notice of Levi texting and making phone calls since they found out Kaden had been shot. He was pretty sure Levi was up to no good and Leana was no longer safe. Chester better hope the police found her before one of Levi's friends did. Q was a quiet storm that cleaned up dirty work for high paying clients. He stayed out of the limelight, making sure he did not have a record. Levi was either paying serious money or Q was a master at staying under the radar; this was a question Melech did not want the answers to.

After making sure Halina was fed and fueled with coffee, Chester headed home. When he went inside something in his house did not feel right to him. He turned on the lights as he walked through his house. Chester noticed that the boxes in Leana's room had been moved about and tampered with. He started to say her name, but Chester was not sure if Leana was the one who came into his home. Getting the bat out of the hall closet, Chester searched his house for an intruder. No one appeared to be there except for him, insuring the home was locked up tight Chester went to his bedroom closet to check the safe. Using the combination, he opened it up, noticing someone had tampered with it also. The only two people that knew the combination were him and Leana. Going through the contents immediately, Chester knew she had taken one of his credit cards and half of the cash. Her passport was also missing.

"Girl, what are you up to?" Chester said out loud. Locking the safe back up, he started to call the detective. Levi's words danced in his head. He needed to stop giving the cops information to hang his only child. Leana would reach out to him when she was ready. He could not help the police put her away if she was the one who shot Kaden. Chester tried calling her one more time before taking a shower and getting some well-deserved sleep.

Anderson was pleased with the information he got from Chester, it filled in some blanks for him. Kelly was sitting at his desk, feet kicked up, drinking coffee.

"I just spoke to the Buckley girl's father." Anderson sat at his desk. "Interesting man."

"Did he give you anything?" Kelly sat his cup on the desk.

"More than he realized." Anderson flipped through his notepad. "The Mrs. is the one who left the young Buckley."

"Tell me more."

"Apparently, she was in love with another man."

"Hmm…the old man?" Kelly inquired.

"He didn't say, but we know she was staying at the hotel from what the cleaning ladies have told us."

"The guy at the front desk also confirms she was in the room. He accepted a food delivery for her."

"And the room was paid for with Mr. Buckley's card, so it's a given they were in the room together." Anderson was trying to put the pieces together.

"Well..." Kelly sat up. "That's speculative at best. "We need someone to verify they were having an affair. It's too easy to dismiss the old man as just helping the girl."

"Who's going to believe that?" Anderson wasn't convinced.

"It only takes one person to think the old man is a good guy, then he'll walk. We need real evidence he was sleeping with the wife, or we can't prove the son shot him."

"I'm still not on board with that theory."

"It's his gun," Kelly protested.

"Exactly, who's that sloppy?"

"A scared kid who caught his daddy poking his wife." Kelly tried getting his point across.

"That's just it, Melech did not appear to be shaken or nervous at all when we met him. He wouldn't leave a gun behind."

"You have a point there. He does seem calculating. The friend, on the other hand." Kelly rubbed his hands together.

"Oh!" Anderson almost forgot. "His name is Levi."

"As in the jeans?"

"I think it's biblical." Anderson shook his head. He learned a lot working with his partner even though his mind was narrow.

"Oh," Kelly chuckled. "You know I haven't opened a bible since Catholic school."

"That's why you can't keep a wife!"

"Who's trying to make them stay?" Kelly reached for his coffee. "You'll learn, kid."

"Yeah, anyway. Mr. Stone told me his daughter called him crying."

"He talked to her?"

"No, she left a voicemail saying she was raped," Anderson, informed him.

"Now, that's a reason to shoot someone."

"Why would you have your husband's gun on hand?" Anderson questioned Kelly. "Premeditation, maybe?"

"Or protection." Kelly pointed out.

♥♥♥

It felt good for Levi to be at home finally. He had been away far too long. He did not plan on staying long. Levi was driving Melech's truck. He tried to get Melech to leave the hospital since they were both in desperate need of showers and clean clothes. He wouldn't budge. Levi wanted to check his mail, and make sure his house was secure. He also had a few people to see before he went back to the hospital.

Setting his keys on the kitchen counter Levi got an eerie feeling. Slowly he reached for his gun resting snugly in the small of his back. Levi walked back into the living room, pistol at his side. There was no sight of anyone still not feeling safe Levi went down the long hallway to the bedrooms. This was the reason he did not want anyone knowing where he laid his head. Levi wanted to feel safe any time he was home. Checking his home office and guest room, a small sense of relief started to come over him until Levi opened his bedroom door. It had been ransacked. Someone had gone through his drawers, spewing clothing all over his room. His bed was unmade with the pillows sliced up, leaving cotton and feathers strewn about the place. Levi held his head, confused as to what provoked the assault on his belongings. Entering his bathroom, Levi saw the shattered glass from his shower and mirror covering the length of the floor along with his cologne, body wash, and personal hygiene items. Suddenly horror overtook Levi's whole being. Rushing to his closet dropping the gun beside him, Levi moved several shoe boxes, lifted the carpet, then the wood floorboard to make sure his money was still safe in its hiding place. A sigh of relief came over him only for a slight moment. Putting everything back the way it was, Levi went to his kitchen.

Opening up his pantry, Levi removed all the can goods, exposing his safe. Entering the security code, the door popped open only to reveal the money he had in there was gone.

"Ain't that a bitch?" Levi stared at the safe only housing jewelry and his important papers. "I'm gonna kill this bitch." There were only three people knew about the safe. Him, Melech, and Leana. The password was her birthday, common sense should have taught Levi better. Frustrated, Levi closed the safe, put everything back in its rightful place, and left his house. The cleanup would have to wait. Levi needed to make a personal visit to a friend.

'Not as smart as you think you are,' Leana thought to herself as she watched Levi drive off in Melech's truck. *'You're supposed to have some type of street smarts, and I've been right next to you this whole time.'* It was not difficult getting into his house. Levi always forgot to close his bedroom window. Leana knew this about him from spending as much time as she did with him. Opening his safe was even easier. When Leana had it installed, she told Levi to use a code he would never forget. After only two attempts, she was in. Why Levi thought he was so different from Melech was mystifying to her. Leana entered her husband's birthday first then her own, bingo she was in. They were both very predictable on almost everything. Leana won both of them over with her good girl charm. Levi only surprised Leana when he chose Melech over her. Underestimating their connection was her flaw in the situation. Kaden's love for his son was understandable to Leana. It was only a matter of time before his conscious took over. Leana did not know why she ventured down that road.

Taking Kaden from Halina was not a challenge; the guilt Kaden had over Melech was a problematic tie to break. Kaden shared with her his love for his son. Not being able to bond with Melech once he got to high school always bothered Kaden. More so because he did not give his all to connect with Melech. Once his son started pulling away, Kaden allowed it to happen. He felt that he laid down a good foundation for his son. When Melech was ready to come back to him, Kaden would be there and willing to be a father. Unfortunately, that day never came. Kaden did not know how to fix the relationship, especially after Levi befriended Melech. At that point, Kaden just gave Melech anything he asked for. To Kaden, it was the only way to show his love to his son.

Taking forty thousand dollars from Levi is what he deserved, in Leana's opinion. He had caused her too much pain. Leana felt she had lost way too much while Levi was still in Melech's good graces; she was not the only person involved in the affair. If Leana had anything to say about it, no one was getting a happily ever after.

CHAPTER THIRTEEN

Melech had not felt so drained since he was doing two-a-days in college. How his mother was still holding on was surprising to him. The hospital moved his father to a private room in ICU. They were both by Kaden's side, but he had not woken up yet. Melech tried to get his mother to go home and get some rest, Halina would not hear of it. She wanted to be there when Kaden finally opened his eyes. The doctors tried to explain to her they did not know when that was going to happen.

"Mom," Melech rubbed her leg. "Do you want me to get you something to eat?"

"No, honey, I'm fine." She smiled at him.

"You really need to eat and get some rest. I'm worried about you."

"Sweetie, I'm fine," she tried to sound upbeat for her son. "Why don't you take a quick break? This must be difficult for you."

"Mother, I'm a lot stronger than you are," Melech teased her.

"I'll still bend you over, boy." She gave him a warm smile. They both turned their heads when a knock was heard on the door. Detective Kelly entered the room first, followed by Detective Anderson.

"Hello, how are you guys holding up?" Anderson asked them both.

"My father can't answer any question right now."

"The nurse explained that to us," Kelly told them. "May we speak to you, Mr. Buckley?"

"Why?" Halina did not allow her son to answer. "He has nothing to tell you, Melech was not even there."

"We know that ma'am," Anderson politely addressed her. "This is about his wife, Leana. We are trying to locate her."

"My son doesn't know where she is."

"Yes, um, we understand that. It's just that your wife's cell phone is pinging at their residence. Do you know if she is back home?" Halina looked at her son.

"I haven't been home since you told me about my father." Melech forgot he had Leana's phone.

"We sent a patrol car by," Kelly informed them. "Your place appears to be empty. Do you mind if we take a ride over there?"

"Are you serious right now?" Halina ranted at him. "Do you see my husband lying in this bed? My son is not going anywhere until his father opens his eyes!"

"We're just trying to locate Mr. Buckley's wife, ma'am. We're here to help," Anderson tried to defend their actions.

"Don't you want to find your wife, son?" Kelly challenged both of them.

"No, not really," Melech replied nonchalantly. His response surprised both detectives.

"What if she did this to your father?" Anderson inquired.

"Then she needs to rot in hell," Melech revealed his genuine feelings. Once he learned the true nature of Leana's relationship with Levi, all the love he once felt for her dissipated.

"If you hear from your wife…"

"Get out!" Halina demanded cutting off detective Kelly. Both men quietly walked out of the hospital room.

"She kind of scared me," Anderson admitted.

"We may need to add her to our suspect list," Kelly looked back at the ICU room door. "She could kill anyone and get away with it."

"She is an actress," Anderson confirmed the suspicion.

"Do you think she suspected the affair with her daughter-in-law?"

"I," Anderson drug out the word. "I'm not sure. Would she be sitting at his bedside?"

"If you want to look like the dutiful wife, you would," Kelly advised his partner.

"Yeah, okay, but I can't see her leaving her son's gun behind. Whoever did this wanted us to focus our attention on the son."

"Or the kid pulled the trigger," Kelly offered up his theory once again.

"I keep telling you, he is too calm about all of this."

"Then why is his wife's phone at his house?" Kelly reminded his partner.

"You have a point on that one."

Levi cruised down Slauson Ave blaring the music in Melech's truck, feeling at ease behind the tinted windows. His car would have stood out in this neighborhood. Moving in the shadows is what he aimed to do, even though his mission led him to Fatburger as usual. Turning on Crenshaw Boulevard, Levi noticed the car he was looking for before he entered the parking lot. Tapping on the horn to get Q's attention, Levi parked next to him.

"Rollin' incognito, my boy?" Q climbed into the truck.

"Switching things up, ya know me."

"Dippin', I feel you." Q pulled a Black & Mild from behind his ear. Levi handed him a lighter. "How's your boy's pop's doing?" he lit the Black.

"He straight."

"Cold piece of work that nigga there. Didn't need to catch a hot one, though."

"He's an ass, but Leek and his moms don't need to be going through all this right now." That was the worst part of it for Levi, watching everything his friend was going through. "You know my shit got hit?"

"Word?" Q was surprised. "I ain't heard nothin', I was just round there earlier."

"Nah, man, my crib," Levi explained.

"Damn!"

"Who the fuck…"

"That damn bitch…girl." Levi cut him off. "Tore my shit up and robbed my damn safe."

"C'mon on, my nigga, how the hell you get caught slippin' like that? Her shit that good?" he joked with Levi.

"Don't play." He snatched the Black from Q. "Money is money, no pussy ever trumps that shit." Levi inhaled the soothing tobacco. "She put the shit in," he added, releasing the smoky cloud.

"She got all y'all niggas by the nut sack."

"For a minute, she on borrowed time now."

"That's what your mouth say. All Leana has to do is bat those sexy brown eyes, shake dat ass, and wiggle that tight ass at you and yo' ass gonna be a sucka once again." Q had never known Levi to let anyone get close enough to steal his money, not even Melech. He was still running weed out of his apartment building on East Arlington. Q thought for sure Melech was unaware of it.

"I'll shoot that bitch while she sucks my dick." Leana had pushed Levi too far. "Fuckin', then lighting the old man up. Hey, I can give you a nice ass-whoopin' on that shit. Taking over forty racks from me? Nah, man." Levi shook his head. "That deserves a toe tag."

"Fuck, man. She got you like that?"

"I separate my shit, so that was just play money. Dumb ass didn't know the jewelry she left behind was worth more." Q grabbed his chest, letting out a hearty laugh.

"Where do you find the humor in this shit?" Levi wanted to smack Q but that was not an option for him. Q would kill him faster than any man Levi knew. He was aware just how dangerous Q was.

"The girl was tryna get under yo' skin, nigga not come up," Q advised him. "She's out for blood. Ever hear of a woman scorned?"

"What?" Levi turned in his seat to make eye contact with his friend. "You do realize Leana started this mess? Melech is the one who has the right to come for me, not her crazy ass!"

"You right 'bout that. Takes a hell of a man to fuck his boy's wife." Q winked at Levi.

"Shut up!" Q was starting to irritate Levi.

"Now, you wanna be mad?" He reached for his Black, noticing Levi smoked the whole thing. "I still got yo' back."

"Whateva', nigga. What you find out for me?"

"Big ass baby," Q teased him. "My boy caught up with your girl. It wasn't hard at all. She's still driving her car."

"Leana, ain't street smart, got a bunch of letters behind her name, but don't know to change cars when you on the run." Levi shook his head.

"He's been tailing her."

"Where she at right now?" Levi was eager to wrap his hands around her neck.

"Are you sure? I don't want yo' ass locked up. Let me handle it."

"Nah…" Levi shook his head. "This one is all me, cuh. All mine."

"Alright, man." Q handed Levi a burner phone. "Hit em' up, and he'll give you details."

"Cool, I'll get that money to you." Levi took the phone.

"We straight, you just took a big loss." Q tapped him on the shoulder, exiting the car.

"You got jokes," Levi called the only number stored in the phone.

"What up?" the caller answered.

"You got eyes?" Levi asked.

"Yup. Check yo' messages." Shock took over when the address came through. Levi needed to get to Leana before she did something else irrational.

"Hey." There was a tap on the window.

"Oh, what's up wit' you?" Levi rolled it down.

"You remember me?"

"Of course, I do, sexy." Levi saw the disaster of a pink car next to him.

"I see you be dippin' in different rides. Who you hidin' from?" Candy flipped her ponytail.

"Never that."

"Don't look at me like that, those eyes get me going," Candy flirted with him.

"Ma don't get me shot out here. I know who yo' man is."

"So, you was checkin' on me?" she smiled at him.

"Haaa," Levi saw that Candy had flattered herself. "I know this ain't your part of town. Why you always up over here? Ya, man, still gone find out what you doin'."

"My girl, she lives down the street, and he ain't my man no more." Candy put her hand on her hip.

"Yeah, sweetie, when you stop rollin' in his ride, pull up to the lounge." Levi touched her chin. "I need to get up outta here. My boy's pops is in the hospital."

"Oh, wow! Okay, I will see you soon, cutie pie." She waved at Levi doing her best to walk away as sexy as she could.

"Women." Levi pulled off without haste; he was on a mission.

♥♥♥

Gazing at his mother, Melech was getting worried about her. She was aging before his eyes. The stress of his father being in a coma was taking a toll on her. Halina was a stubborn woman, doing as she pleased whenever she wanted. The only person who could tell her what to do was Kaden, and right now he was in a deep sleep. Melech was not sure if it was because his father did not want to face what was sure to come to him when he came to.

"Mother," he softly got her attention.

"Yes, dear."

"I need you to go home."

"That's not going to happen, son."

"You haven't eaten, slept or showered in days. I need you healthy if I'm going to get through all of this." Melech tried to reach her as a mother. "If I lose you both, I…"

"Melech!" Halina stopped her son before he could finish his sentence. "I'm not going to leave you in this world alone."

"Yes, mother, you will if you don't start taking care of yourself. I know how much you want to be there for dad. I love you so much for that. I really do." Melech hung his head low. "I wish my wife was more like you. We both have doubt, yet we sit here." They did not have to talk about the reason Kaden was fighting for his life. It was a given neither of them wanted to admit there was more to him and Leana's story. "I love you more than anything in this world."

"I know, son." Halina did not want her son to speak the words she was already thinking.

"Please go home, get some rest and a good meal, for me," Melech pleaded with her.

"I want to be here..."

"I will stay by his side, promise." Tears filled Melech's eyes.

"For you." Halina got up from the chair. "I will take a break." Kissing his forehead, she headed towards the door.

"Mom," Melech stopped her before Halina walked out of the door. "I love you."

"I know you do, son. You are my life." She put her fingers to her lips, blowing Melech a kiss. As much as he wanted his mother by his side, Melech was happy to see her go.

"It's just you and me now, dad." He scooted the chair next to the bed reaching for his father's hand. "It's safe to wake up and talk to me." Melech looked on as his father lie in the bed. He didn't look like the man who was able to overpower him just days ago.

Levi parked Melech's truck down the street so it would not be noticed by anyone. The element of surprise was always the best way to catch someone off guard. Spotting Leana's Mercedes parked a few houses away; Levi crept up on it, finding it empty. This was disappointing to him. He really did not want to have an altercation with her inside of the house. Carefully making his way into the backyard, Levi saw Leana through the window sitting at the breakfast island drinking a glass of wine. *'Making yourself at home,'* Levi thought to himself. *'Typical of you.'* Knowing the Buckley's as well as Levi did, he went in search of the rock they kept their house key hid under. To his dismay, it was already gone. *'Fuck, she knew about it also.'* Plan B had to be set in motion. Levi went to every window, hoping one was left unlocked. *'Bingo!'* The master bedroom bathroom window was wide open. Halina must have left in a rush, forgetting to secure the home. It was challenging, but Levi maneuvered his way in. Before he made it out of the bathroom, there stood Leana in the master bedroom's doorway.

"What a surprise to see you, my love." She sipped the glass of wine. "You were not what I expected, but you're a sight for sore eyes."

"Always a pleasure," Levi mocked her.

"What brings you to the Buckley house?" Leana inquired. "And through a window no less."

"I don't know, taking on a new profession." Levi glared at her.

"You always were a funny guy," sarcasm filled her words.

"And you a lying, cheating bitch."

"Tsk, tsk, tsk…Such harsh words," Leana played with the wineglass. "You used to love my cheating ass until you found out Kaden was just a little better at it than you are." She taunted Levi.

"Was he now?"

"Oh, yes, baby. I never knew how well trained an older man could be." She put her hand on her thigh. "They know exactly where to touch you. Ummm." Leana closed her eyes, biting on her lower lip. "Did you know they take their time with your body?" She pointed the wine glass at him. "Always making sure I was pleased several times before he ever let loose."

"Cute." Levi refused to allow Leana the satisfaction of letting her know how her words were affecting him.

"You know, his son was almost as good in the bed. Melech was never selfish with this." She ran her hands over her breast.

"Yeah, whatever, Leana. I get it; you're a hoe." He did not want to hear any more from her. "What the hell are you doing here?"

"See." She walked closer to him. "Levi, I loved you, but you did not appreciate that, now did you?" Leana tilted her head to the side. "I was willing to give up all this great dick and money just to be with you."

"Miss me wit' that bullshit. What da fuck are you doin' up in here," Levi demanded.

"Wouldn't it be nice to play in their bed?" Leana tilted her head to the Buckley's California king-size bed. "That shit is making me wet just thinking about it." Leana got close enough to put her lips to Levi's. "You know you want me." Leana let her hand slide down Levi's chest to his torso. As she tried to stroke him, Leana felt Levi's hands around her throat.

"Don't fuckin' touch me." His bright green eyes burned into hers. A smile came across her face.

"I didn't know you were into the kinky stuff, Levi. You so enjoyed looking deep into my eyes as you were pleasing me."

"I will snap your fucken neck. Ain't shit, you got I want. How many times I have to tell yo' ass ain't nothin' special 'bout you?"

"Are you sure," a wicked laugh came out of her.

"What the hell is wrong with you?" Levi let her go. "What happened to you?"

"You happened to me!" Her words were cold and filled with venom.

"Are you serious?" Levi was unsure of where this was coming from.

"So, you're mad at me, now you're sitting up in Mrs. B's house to do what? How's that gonna hurt me?"

"Oh, I just wanted to let my mother-in-law know who her husband really is." Leana gleefully announced. Levi could not understand what he was listening to.

"Are we going to make use of this bed?" she pointed in its direction.

"You're fuckin' crazy."

"So that's a no?" Leana looked at him for a moment, turned, and walked away. Levi was not sure if he should shoot her in the head or put Leana in a mental institute. Following behind her to see how far this game was going to play out, Levi found Leana back in the kitchen, refilling her wine glass.

"So…." She spun around, smiling at him once again. "How long do you think it will take for Halina to get here?" Leana sat back down.

"Why are you doing this to her? You already shot her husband!"

"Me?" Leana pointed at herself. "Why I would never…"

"Cut the shit, Leana. What happened? Kaden found out I had already tapped that shit and didn't want no parts of dat stank ass no more?" Leana's demeanor changed instantly.

"You shut up, Levi. You ruined everything!"

"Is that why you broke into my shit?"

"Someone broke into your house and got you? Guess you need to stop breaking hearts," she was snide.

"Hmmm, how you know it was my house?"

"You said…"

"No, …fuck no. I said my shit!"

"Oh…maybe, I should call mommy in-law. That should get her here sooner." Leana reached for her purse.

"You ain't doin' shit!" Levi grabbed her by the arm.

"Why are you so concerned? You and my husband are closer than ever." Tears stung her eyes. "He'll always choose you." Leana pulled away from him.

"That's why you want to destroy, Mrs. B? What did she do to you?" Levi fussed at her. "You slept with her husband and shot him!"

"You don't know…" Leana wiped her eyes, trying to calm herself down. Drinking her wine, she finally told him, "You have no idea what happened."

"You just told me, 'What he did to your body'." Levi said facetiously, using air quotes.

"I was just trying to hurt you." Leana put her glass down. "He wasn't so nice to me, Levi."

"C'mon, man." He was not falling for her antics.

"Actually, I came here to get Halina's help. Really, I did." Leana turned childlike. It was the same innocence that pulled Levi into her web for the first time. "Kaden isn't the man you think he is." Leana put herself into Levi's arms. "He hurt me."

"What are you saying?" Levi was trying to understand where Leana was going with her story.

"He made me do things," the sobs grew deeper. Levi contemplated what she was saying to him.

"Like rape?" Leana would not say the word; she only cried harder. This was disturbing to Levi. The affection he had for Kaden was slim. In Levi's eyes, Kaden was not the sort of man he would give any father of the year awards to. The problem he was having with what Leana was saying to him was that Levi had a first-hand view of the way Kaden treated his wife, Halina. He was always kind, gentle, and loving. Halina on most occasions was the superior one in their marriage. Levi did not care for Kaden because of how he treated Melech, yet he had the utmost respect for the way he catered to his wife. It was the reason Melech bent over backward to give Leana the world. He gave her everything her heart desired, almost always compromising his own need to ensure Leana's happiness. Melech would have been content in a two-bedroom apartment somewhere downtown but Leana wanted a house close to her husband's family, so Kaden made it happen. She was ungrateful for everything they had done for her in Levi's opinion.

"I can't see that happening." Levi pulled her from his arms. "That man doesn't have it in him."

"You're gonna take his side?" Leana was astonished.

"What are you talking about? There ain't no sides in this."

"Levi, baby," Leana pleaded with him. "He knew about us; Kaden was so angry…"

"If this was so, why didn't he cap me? He had plenty of chances."

"I…don't know, Levi." Leana hung her head. "He took it out on me, maybe because I'm weaker than you." The sad girl act almost worked on Levi. Deep down inside, he still loved Leana.

"I call bullshit."

"Huh." This caught her off guard.

"I don't think that's what happened at all, baby."

"What are you saying to me?" Leana was still full of tears. "Levi, when are you going to get it?" She covered her eyes with her hands. "You." Leana ran her hands through her wild curly hair. "You're the only person who means anything to me. Once Kaden found out I wanted you and not his son, it all went sideways." Levi did not know if anything Leana had to say was truthful. Even if it was, she did not understand there was no future between the two of them.

"See, every word that comes out of your mouth comes with a double-edge sword."

"No...no...no, not when it comes to you, baby." Leana stroked his cheek with her knuckles. "Levi, I love you so much it hurts." Her words and the look in Leana's eyes proved everything Q said to him. As much as Levi wanted to put a bullet in Leana's brain, he still loved her.

"I can't..." Levi turned his back to her.

"I know you love me too," her words were like a symphony playing for a full house. Levi wanted to take Leana into his arms, let her know everything was going to be alright. Then make sweet love to her regardless of everything she had done.

"Leana?" Levi turned back around, ready to throw everything away for her. Unexpectedly, he was met with a custom-made Louis Vuitton Glock that he gave Leana for her birthday. Melech was angry with Levi for giving her a gift that could only cause bodily harm to others.

"Man, you need to chill," Levi brushed Melech off after Leana opened her gift.

"How does a gun sound like a great gift idea?" Melech scolded Levi.

"I gave you your first gun," Levi reminded him.

"Is that shit legal?" Melech grabbed him by the shirt, pulling Levi close to him. "Cause the one you gave me wasn't."

"Yeah, fool." Levi pushed Melech's hand away. "I gotta guy. It's in her name and all, chill. You know she spends way too much time away from us. What if some nut-job is following her when she gets out of class? What if someone tries to snatch her lil' ass up?"

"Okay, pepper spray or a taser would have been a better gift," Melech opposed the gun idea.

"I love it," Leana beamed over her new toy.

"You know I had to doll it up for you," Levi bragged.

"This girl loves her some Louie." Leana pulled her new Glock 42 out admiring the signature Louis Vuitton emblem on it.

"Babe be careful with that thing," Melech warned her.

"It's not loaded yet," Levi let him know. "I'll teach her how to use it before she can take it out, promise." Melech did not agree with the gun, but Leana was so thrilled with it, he did not have the heart to take it away from her. He kept the gun locked in the safe next to his. Melech believed in protecting himself, which is why he possessed two of them, one was registered, and the other was not.

"What, you gonna do shoot me?" Levi laughed at her. "Pull the trigger!" he barked. "Do it!" Levi walked up on her. Suddenly, Leana wasn't as sure of herself any longer. The small hesitation allowed Levi to lunge at Leana, knocking her to the ground. "You stupid bitch. If you gonna whip yo' shit out on a muthafucca,, you betta damn sure let loose!" He snatched her once prized possession out of her hand, raising it over his head to strike her with it.

"Not here!" Q interrupted Levi mid-swing.

"What the fuck?"

"I didn't think you had it in you. I almost had to shoot this girl when you got soft. Told yo ass, ya think with yo' dick and not your brains." Q took the gun from Levi. "Get her up, my boy's waiting out front."

"Levi?" he heard Halina's voice. "What is going on in here?" All three turned to look at her.

"Mom's," Levi did not expect her anytime soon. "I found Leana here with a gun." Snatching away from Levi, Leana fixed her clothes.

"I just wanted to talk to you, Halina."

"In my house?" Halina was too tired to deal with Leana's antics. "Kaden's in the hospital."

"He is?" Leana covered her mouth, tears filling her eyes.

"If you don't knock it off." Levi wanted to backhand her. "You doin' too much."

"I can't right now. Levi why is this boy in here with you?" she asked.

"Mom, you remember Q? He came in as this girl pulled her gun on me," Levi felt like a child being reprimanded. He did not answer to his own mother since he moved out of her house.

"This is my home, Levi. How did all of you even get in here?" That was the most disturbing part of it all.

"We followed her here, moms. She was trying to get to you." As Levi was trying to explain his way out of being in Halina's house, Leana took the opportunity to grab her purse and ease out the back door.

It only took Q a second to notice her absence. Bolting after her got Levi's attention. "Damn it!" he yelled. "Lock the doors." Levi went out of the front door trying to cut Leana off; he was not going to let her get away again. She did not get far. Q's guy was waiting out front. He swooped Leana up before she made it to her car.

"Help me!" Leana started screaming. "Help!" Two elderly ladies were walking their little dogs. They both stopped to watch what was going on.

"Shut up," Q told her as Levi ran up to them.

"Rape! Rape!" Leana shouted again.

"What are you boys doing to her," one of the ladies asked.

"It's okay, ma'am," Levi replied. "She broke into my mom's house."

"He's lying, please help me," Leana begged.

"Shut yo' ass up," Levi warned her. "I swear I'll put a bullet in yo' head." People started coming out of their houses due to her screams.

"Call the police," one of the neighbors expressed concern for Leana. That was not the outcome she wanted.

"If you don't let me go, Levi, I will make sure the cops put all three of you away for trying to kidnap me," She hissed at him.

"Let her go," Levi felt defeated. There were too many strangers out here watching what was going on.

"Fuck that!" Q told him. "Let the cops show up. That lady in there." He pointed at Halina's house. "Knows this girl was up in her crib. They looking for her ass, anyway."

"But, I wanna put this hoe in a body bag." Levi's emerald eyes were icy cold.

"You're hurting me!" Leana yelled out again. "You don't love me anymore, baby? It felt so good having you on top of me again." A fiery inferno overcame Levi. Thoughts of sending Leana to the pits of hell suddenly consumed him. Leana's feet were dangling; her hand instinctively went to her throat where Levi's hands were wrapped tightly. Each breath was labored as Leana tried clawing away at his hands while gasping for air. She had finally pushed Levi into a murderous rage; the darkness took over; he would not be satisfied until he felt Leana take her last breath. It did not matter one bit that all of Halina's snobby Baldwin Hills neighbors were watching him. The echoing screams to let her go rang in his head, but they did not penetrate Levi until a fierce full blow hit his rib cage. Leana's limp body crumpled to the ground. Q slammed Levi to the ground bringing him out of the deadly trance that had consumed him.

"You lost your fuckin' mind?" Q scolded his long-time friend. "I told yo' ass this girl got you all twisted up." The only reason Q did not plan to end Levi's life was because they were friends since grade school. Q also knew Levi's father would be sure to put him six feet under instead of behind bars. Levi was untouchable only because of who his father was.

Leana laid on the ground, coughing as her lungs slowing filled with oxygen. Actual tears emerged from her eyes as the blurry vision of police cars appeared. This did not go the way she had planned. Leana just wanted to get away from Levi and his goon patrol.

"Why did you stop me," Levi asked. "Killing her would have been worth it."

"You gotta get yo' shit together and don't say shit to these damn cops."

"I'm already knowin'," Levi assured Q as he got to his feet, watching the officer rush to Leana's assistance. Levi knew she was going to play the victim role to the fullest, especially with all the whiteness her bellowing drew from their quiet sanctuaries.

"Hello," an officer approached Q and Levi.

"Sir," Q responded.

"Can you tell me what happened here?"

"The young lady broke into my friend's mother's house. We were trying to hold her until you guys showed up." Was all Q was willing to tell them, knowing that he had Leana's gun he took away from Levi in his possession.

"The young lady says you chocked her," he addressed Levi.

"Hmmm," he replied.

"Is this true?"

"Sir," Q interrupted. "There seems to be a misunderstanding here. Can we talk?" Q led the officer to a quieter location. Levi watched as the two men engaged in a conversation. The officer walked over to Halina's house while Q came back to where Levi was standing. An ambulance was giving Leana assistance while she was being questioned. Bystanders were quickly dispersing as the police arrived. They may have spent a lot more for their homes, but most of them were still black and did not want to speak to law enforcement. None of them knew who the three men were that were holding Leana hostage and did not want any unwelcome problems.

"What was that all about?" Levi asked Q.

"He's gonna deal with it. Don't worry and don't talk."

"Yeah." Levi was going to follow instructions, but he still wanted to know what Q said to the officer. Q took this time to dispose of Leana's gun.

♥♥♥

Looking down at his watch, Melech was getting worried about his mother. Typically, she would have called him half a dozen times by now. He was hoping she had finally gotten some sleep. Melech knew how worried she was with his father still not awake. The doctors kept telling them it was normal, Melech felt there was something they were leaving out. Every twenty or thirty minutes, a nurse came in to take Kaden's vitals, yet they told them nothing except everything looked good. This was not reassuring to Melech. A nurse came in again to check on his father, smiled at him, and began to walk out. This time Melech stopped her.

"Miss."

"Mona," she told him her name.

"Mona." Melech stood up, reaching his hand out to her. "Melech." She found it amusing most men did not do things like that anymore. "Is there anything you can tell me about my father besides it looks good?"

"Is that the only thing they've told you, Melech?"

"Yes, and it's getting frustrating now."

"I completely understand." Mona took a good look at him. Underneath the fatigue, wrinkled clothing, and overgrown beard, she could see a good-looking man in Melech. "Protocol and all." She pulled his fathers' chart reading through it. "Honestly, I don't see any complications from the surgery. He honestly should have awakened by now." Mona kept reading. "I'm just an RN, so you didn't hear this from me."

"No, I get it." Melech wanted Mona to know he could be trusted. "We never had this conversation."

"Your father may have had a stroke they missed or something. I'd request an MRI of his head."

"Oh, wow." Concern took over.

"Now it may be nothing at all, so don't panic. You just want to be safe, you feel me?"

"Thank you, Mona. No one else has taken the time to tell us anything."

"I'm not like these people here." Mona gave a bashful smile. "I'm just a girl from around the way, trying to save enough money to do better for me and my little girl."

"You are what you make of yourself, Mona." Melech encouraged her. "Probably better than most of them because you're fighting for something important. You took the time to think of someone besides yourself."

"It's just what I do." She gave a fake curtsey. Melech was able to have a joyous moment finally. "I'll come back soon and check on you guys."

"Thank you again, Mona."

"No problem." Melech watched her leave the room. "Nice girl." He sat back down next to his father, looked back at the door, and smiled to himself. He planned on contacting the doctor after Mona's shift was over.

The ambulance took Leana away and all three men were taken down to the station. They were sitting on a bench when Ken doll and Denzel look-alike approached them. Levi sat up straight, remembering their last encounter.

"So, we meet again," Ken doll hissed. Levi just stared at him "What they got you for, criminal misconduct?"

"You know this clown?" Q asked.

"He came to my house."

"House, house?" Q whispered.

"Yeah."

"Let's move on," Denzel suggested to his partner.

"I want to see what they have on this looser," he pushed back. Levi shook his head, disgusted. He was the type of cop everyone disliked. The kind that couldn't see a man beyond his race. Levi was just another black man that must be involved in something criminal. Denzel did not follow his partner; he lingered with the three men.

"You straight," he inquired.

"I'm good, man," Levi informed him, watching as Ken doll talked to the other officers down the corridor.

"Get this," Ken doll said to his partner. "You remember the crazy chick we picked up from his place." He pointed at Levi. "They got into an altercation. She claims he choked her."

"What?" Denzel, look-a-like, replied. "Did you tell him we know the case?"

"Of course, I did. That bat shit crazy chick had to have started the whole thing." This was the first time Levi appreciated the arrogant officer.

Denzel pulled Ken doll to the side. Levi saw the two engaged in a heated discussion. He predicted the two did not complete any paperwork after the overzealous officer acted inappropriate with Leana the other night. Mr. Denzel left his partner to speak with the officer. The two went behind closed doors. After twenty or thirty minutes, they told Levi, Q, and his partner, Omar, they were free to go. They questioned not one of them about what happened at the Buckley residence.

"Can somebody explain what just happened in there?" Omar asked.

"I knew we wouldn't be charged. I at least thought they would go through the motions." Q talked to the officer at the scene, breaking down what happened inside of the Buckley house. He also dropped a well-known name; the officer verified his connect and he deposited an acceptable amount of cash in the officer's car. "What you know?"

"The two officers that walked up to us did some real shady shit at my crib. I'm guessing they didn't report it." Levi shrugged. "Dumb ass rollin' up braggin' must have set some alarms off."

"What they do?" Omar asked.

"Ruffed up Leana pulled heat out on me. A few neighbors were lookin' on."

"That, dude, put hands on a girl?" Q fumed.

"Like she was a grown-ass man."

"He needs a bullet in his skull," Omar ranted about the ordeal. "She off her rocker, but damn."

"I tried to stop it, but it's not time for no *Black Lives Matter* ticker tape on my ass yet," Levi defended his decision. "Besides, his partner checked ol' boy."

"His ass still an Uncle Tom to me," Omar objected to Levi's assessment.

"Nah, man. That white boy needs a leash on his ass. Imagine if he had a partner with the same mindset?" Q had to add his viewpoint on it all.

"Guess you, right?" Omar had not thought of it like that. "What we up to next, boss?"

"Quick temper?" He glanced over at Levi.

"I need to get my boy's ride back to him and check on Mrs. B before I head back up to the hospital."

"Gotchu. I got someone headed this way. We'll get you back to Baldwin Hills. We both need to grab our shit too."

"What you think they gonna do with Leana?" Levi still did not know her status or what she may concoct next.

"I got someone at the hospital; she's a nurse. She's playing lookout so if she ends up there, we'll know."

"Word." Levi knew Q would be on top of everything.

♥ ♥ ♥

Getting back to the hospital, Halina and Levi found Melech alone in Kaden's room. They were both uneasy; fearing Kaden had passed away in their absence.

"Where's your father?" Halina was hysterical.

"Mom, calm down," Melech tried soothing her. "He's fine. They took him down for a cat scan of his head."

"Why? What happened while I was gone?"

"Nothing at all, mom. It's just some random testing." Melech did not want to upset his mother with what Mona had told him. It could all be for nothing.

"Okay, okay." Halina calmed down.

"You straight?" Levi nodded his head at Melech.

"I'm good."

"Let's talk." Levi opened the door for Melech to follow him out.

"What's going on?" Melech wanted to know what the secrecy was all about.

"Leana," Levi started.

"The cops get her?"

"Not in a good way. She was up in mom's crib, waiting on her to get home. I got to her first."

"Say what now?" Melech was stunned.

"Yeah, I got the drop on where she was and took my ass up over there. You was right about that gun. She pulled it on my ass." Melech held both arms over his head, clutching the back of his neck with his hands.

"I told you when you gave it to Leana, it was a bad idea!" Melech hated to say I told you so. "Why was she there?"

"Get this," Levi did not want to pass bad news on to Melech, but he was going to find out eventually, it might as well be him to jab another dagger into his heart. "She claimed your pops raped her."

Turning in a disgusted circle, "Are you serious?" Melech tried dismissing the comment.

"As a triple bypass, my dude!"

"Why…why would he ever do that?" Melech could not understand why Leana would make such a disgusting accusation.

"Same thing I said. Leana planned on telling moms that nonsense."

"My mother does not need that crap right now."

"Who you telling? Moms walked in as all hell was breaking loose, and Leana tried to run. Q went after her."

"Q? What was he doing at my parent's house?" The story was getting more and more outlandish for Melech. He could not fathom how his world turned into a bad Tyler Perry made for TV drama.

"Stopping me from cracking her skull," he explained. "She almost made it to her car. Stupid ass started screaming and some nosy neighbor called five-o. We ended up down at the station, Le left in an ambo."

"This just gets crazier and crazier." Melech wanted it to all stop. Leana may have thought life with him was mundane, but Melech would take his boring life over this any day.

"Yeah, I kinda tried to kill her with a bunch of ya mom's neighbors watching me."

"And they let you out?" Melech was surprised.

"Ya boy, like a cat, I got sixty lives."

"Nine," Melech corrected.

"I don't know none of them mafia's," Levi rebuked the word entirely.

"You're silly for that." Melech did not want to laugh. Nothing about what was going on was funny.

"I'm a hood nigga," Levi joked, trying to bring some humor to what they were going through. "You know she's coming like a semi-automatic, right?"

"For what, though?" Melech did nothing to Leana.

"For some reason, this girl feels like she's been wronged."

"Are you kidding me?"

"I'm afraid not. Leana blamed me for losing your father." Levi knew this was going to be a hard one for Melech to take in. "She bragged how he satisfied her better than I ever did."

"In bed?" Melech quizzically inquired.

"Oh, don't trip. You almost as good as your old man."

"Mr. Buckley?" Dr. Oliver walked up to the pair." He could not have come at a better time. Melech's brain was about to explode from the words coming out of Levi's mouth.

"Yes." Melech was still digesting what Levi just told him.

"We had to send your father up to surgery."

"Excuse me?" The news could have knocked Melech over with a pebble.

"You were smart asking for the head scan because your father came in with a GSW, no one ever checked his head."

"What does that mean?" Levi interjected.

"He sustained a blow to the head. It's been slowly bleeding," Dr. Oliver explained. "Your quick thinking may have saved your father's life." Levi grew nervous; his heart went into overdrive. Who would've thought Q pistol-whipping Kaden would cause this much damage days later?

"Dr. Oliver, is my dad going to be alright?"

"I'll do my best to make sure of it." He touched Melech's shoulder before walking away.

"That's crazy." Melech fell into his own thoughts about Mona.

"What?"

"The nurse from earlier is the one who told me to ask for it. She thought they may have missed a stroke. If I hadn't talked to her today, my dad…he would have died."

"That was a blessing." Levi was not going to give a full confession right now; he needed Kane to pull through first.

♥♥♥

"Interesting. The young Mrs. Buckley shows up now," Andrews said, standing outside of the Emergency Room waiting to question her.

"What's more fascinating is that she was at the old man's house when they picked her up. Why do you think she was there?"

"You think she was looking for the wife. That's why she's having them do a rape kit on her now." Anderson added to the scenario.

"Blackmail."

"Huh?" Anderson was confused.

"Think about it. From the wife's statement, the girl was at the house with a gun when she got home. This Levi character, was there trying to get her out of the Buckley house?" Anderson was trying to make some kind of sense of what happened before the street unit showed up on the scene. "How does, young Mrs. Buckley, get from the house to the streets? And where is the gun?"

"Mrs. Buckley said the girl snuck out the back while she was talking to, Levi." Kelly could only rely on what the officer told him. "They never located her gun."

"I'm trying to figure out why she didn't just stay and talk to her mother-in-law." Anderson pointed out.

"Fear for her own life, maybe? You have two intimidating men threatening her." Anderson was not fully understanding the story. There were too many holes in what they were getting from the officers who responded to the incident.

"Let's just say, the young lady was able to speak with the elder, Mrs. Buckley. She knows that the son caught her with the father. Buckley loses control then shoots his own father. What mother would not move heaven and earth to protect her son, especially if that's their only child?" Don't you think the mother would give anything to keep that secret under wraps?"

"I'm not buying it, sorry. I'm still not putting the gun in the hands of the son."

"If it walks like a duck, and quacks like a duck my friend, it's a duck," Kelly pointed out.

"Yes, but we also know when everything is set up so perfectly for us, we need to take a closer look. There are no perfect crimes. This one keeps laying out too many clues, pointing us in the son's direction. My gut says it doesn't feel right. Who hands us a case this cut and dry?"

"Let's see what the young lady has to say before we decide on a suspect."

"That's the smartest thing you've said all day." Several times it had crossed Anderson's mind to request a different partner. Kelly was still set in his old ways of thinking. Anderson could not deny Kelly had taught him a lot about being a detective. The problem was when he focused on a suspect, Kelly did not look at the evidence that pointed in any other direction. Anderson learned this the hard way with the Montgomery case. Kelly was so sure the husband was involved with the kidnapping. They wasted precious hours that could have been used to find the man's wife faster.

Nurse Mona let them know Leana was available to see them.

"After you," Anderson reached his hand out to let Kelly walk into the private room first. Nodding at the woman's advocate standing next to Leana, he gave her a warm smile.

"Ladies," Kelly greeted them both. "I'm detective, Kelly; this is my partner, detective Anderson," he made the introductions. "Mind if we ask you a few questions?" Leana nodded her head.

"She's been through a tragic situation," Tracy softly informed them. After assisting her best friend cope with being kidnapped and raped, Tracy began volunteering her professional psychiatric counseling to the hospital for women in crisis. "Not only did she have to endure a rape kit, which is difficult in itself, but the days' events have also taken a toll on her."

"We understand completely," Anderson expressed concern for Leana's mental state.

"This won't take long, miss…"

"It's just Tracy." She brushed her blonde curls out of her face, showing gratitude with a slight head nod.

"Mrs. Buckley, we've been trying to locate you for a few days," Kelly started off gracefully. Leana only nodded at him. "What can you tell us about what took place today?"

"I went to see my mother-in-law," she paused.

"Go on."

"She wasn't home, so I let myself in just so I could wait for her to get back."

"Were you aware she was at the hospital?" Anderson asked.

"I...I wasn't really sure where she was." Leana did not make eye contact with him.

"Did you know, Mr. Buckley was in the hospital with a gunshot wound?" Leana's shoulders began to shake uncontrollably while tears dripped from her eyes.

"It's alright, sweetie." Tracy rubbed her back.

"Melech," she forced out between the sobs. "Is...he... Kaden, okay?"

"He's stable for the moment," Anderson informed her.

"What were you saying about, Melech?" Kelly wanted Leana to finish what she was telling them.

"He shot his father," she blurted out. Skepticism consumed Anderson.

"Why would he do that, ma'am?" Anderson pulled his notebook out.

"His father raped me." Leana looked down at her hands. "He was so angry. I've never seen him like that before."

"What exactly was Mr. Buckley angry about?" Anderson needed the blanks filled in.

"I don't understand the question." Leana did not want to give them the wrong answer.

"Sweetie," Tracy interjected herself into the questioning. "What exactly provoked your husband to shoot his father?"

"Oh." Leana wiped her eyes with the Kleenex she had been holding on to. "The rape."

"I see." Not looking up from the notepad, Anderson kept asking questions, "Did you tell your husband what his father had done or did he walk in on the two of you having sex." Kelly was focused on Leana's demeanor while answering.

"Um…" Leana looked up at Tracy.

"It's okay," her words were soothing.

"Melech walked in on us having sex." The tears came back like clockwork. "They argued…"

"Where exactly were you when your husband shot his father?" Kelly added.

"I ran to the bathroom."

"Hmm, okay," Anderson looked into Leana's eyes. "And today? How did you end up in the middle of the street with the gentlemen?"

"Levi wanted me to stay away from, Halina. They were trying to kidnap me." You could see the difference in Leana's body language, which tensed up at the mention of Levi's name.

"Did you have a gun with you at the time?"

"No…no sir, I didn't." Leana knew Levi took her little beauty away from her. If he got arrested with the gun in his possession, she was not going to take credit for it.

"I see. Why do you think Levi and his associates were trying to kidnap you?" Kelly was still unsure of his involvement with the case.

"Um…he hates me, maybe." Leana's eye twitched. "He would do anything to protect, Melech. I just wanted Halina to know what her husband did to me."

"How would he have known?" Kelly swiftly spoke.

"Huh?"

"How would Mr. Levi know what happened between you and your father-in-law or that you were at their home?"

"I don't know." Leana held her hands in her lap. "Melech must have told him."

"That's interesting." Anderson scratched his head with his pen. "Your father was under the impression you were missing." Anderson glanced at Leana once again. "What gave him that impression?"

"I don't know." Leana shrugged.

"How long after the encounter with, Mr. Buckley, did you leave a message on your father's phone?"

"I'm not exactly sure."

"Where have you been all this time?" Leana's story was not adding up in Kelly's mind.

"I...I've been at the Ritz."

"So, you called your father, not the police, then checked into another hotel, instead of going to the hospital?" Kelly drilled her.

"No." She shook her head. "I already had that room. I've been there since my husband, and I split up."

"I don't understand, Mrs. Buckley? If you already had a room downtown, why were you in another one by the airport?" Anderson questioned.

"Because Melech went crazy on me, Kaden was hiding me until he could calm Melech down."

"Your father-in-law was hiding you from his own son?" This made no sense to Anderson.

"Don't you get it, Melech has a bad temper." The tears fell like a leaky faucet. "And Levi does all his bidding."

"How did your husband know how to find you, if his father was protecting you from him?" Anderson needed to put Melech in the hotel room.

"I...I'm not sure." Leana ripped the Kleenex into small pieces. Maybe he tracked my phone." Kelly and Anderson looked at one another.

"Do you have your phone on you right now?" Kelly asked, knowing it was at Melech's house.

"I don't know where my belongings are."

"That's all for now, Mrs. Buckley. If we need anything else, how can we get in touch with you? Where are you staying now?" Anderson asked.

"I'm still at the Ritz."

"Not your fathers?" Kelly inquired.

"No, I want to be alone," she whispered. The two detectives walked out of the room when Anderson turned around, going back into the room.

"One last thing." He got Leana's attention away from Tracy. "Why did you and your husband split up?"

"We wanted different things." Her head shook back and forth, a telling sign for Anderson. He distinctly remembered Leana's father telling him she fell in love with someone else.

"What was that all about?" Kelly hung up his phone.

"I wanted to see if Mrs. Buckley would tell me why she and the husband split up."

"Did she?"

"What do you think?" Anderson looked at his partner. "None of her story is clicking for me."

"That was the hospital." Kelly held up his phone. "It appears senior Buckley is in surgery again."

"Complications?"

"Blunt force trauma to the back of the head that was apparently missed," Kelly informed him.

"How on earth?"

"Youngster is looking better and better for this."

"You can't be serious?" Anderson was in disbelief. "You aren't buying that story she just sold us."

"Only the part that hubby walked in while she was having sex with the old man. Notice the word rape was not used?"

"Oh, I picked up on that. Hearing Mr. Buckley was struck in the back of the head really makes me look at her. That's a clear sign of anger. What was she doing across town in a hotel room if it wasn't for a good time? And the phone. What's the actual story on that?"

"I can see the Buckley boy losing control and his little counterpart helping him cover it up. You saw the shape he was in when we got to the house. Wonder boy lied about Buckley even being there. Fits what she said about him being the fixer."

"You also saw the surprise in the man's face when we told him about his father."

"Excuse me." Tracy's blond curls came bouncing down the corridor, matching the clicks of her expensive shoes.

"Yes," they said in unison.

"I rarely do this," Tracy started. "Every woman deals with trauma differently. This young lady is a little…"

"Off…" Anderson helped Tracy find the words she was looking for.

"Yes." She shook her head. "It may be shock setting in, or she doesn't want to remember what happened to her." Tracy paused. "It's just her story changed several times since I've been with her. I wish she came in sooner for the rape kit, you know." Tracy pulled her glasses from her head. "There is something up with this Levi character because she gets extremely agitated when she speaks about him. Leana may be covering something up about him. It could have been him who assaulted her and now she is afraid to tell anyone transferring the blame onto her father-in-law. I'm not really sure because she doesn't trust me yet."

"Why would she put this on her husband then?" Anderson did not understand the reasoning behind it.

"That's your job to figure out." Tracy patted him on the chest. "Start with fear," she said, walking past the pair.

"Told you." Anderson pointed at Kelly.

"Let's turn the heat up on this family," Kelly was not amused any longer. "Have them pick up the son for questioning. Make sure everyone thinks he's being charged with his father's murder."

"What's that going to accomplish?"

"That, Levi is a loose cannon, he'll slip up. The mother may finally tell us something and this girl will get comfortable. Put an unmarked car on her and go pay her father a visit again. He's the only one who seems to be honest."

"On it."

CHAPTER FOURTEEN

Mr. Buckley was back in ICU after his surgery. The doctors were optimistic about the way he was progressing, even though they put him in an induced coma. His wife, son, and Levi were still at the hospital standing by his side.

"Baby," Halina touched the back of Melech's head. "Why don't you take a break? You know your father won't be awake for a while."

"Yeah, I think I will. I want to shower, then stop by the Lounge."

"I'll stay here with, mom's," Levi let him know.

"That place will be fine," she patted Melech's hand.

"You say that now, but it pays our bills." Melech kissed his mother on the cheek, getting up to leave.

"I've been on the horn with, Rylee. She's got us covered, man." Levi would not let them fail while Melech was dealing with his father. "I trust her."

"I do too. I just want to show my face."

"I get it. I slid through yesterday. Everyone is worried about you," Levi let him know.

"Yeah, right! You are the beloved one. I just write their checks."

"C'mon, man," Levi was exhausted with the comparisons. "Those folks love yo' pretty ass."

"This coming from, Mr. Green eyes," Melech jabbed.

"Ah, really, suave'. What keeps 'em going is your chocolate dipped ass, Morris Chestnut."

"Really?"

"Oh, my goodness, if you two don't stop!" Halina had watched the two go back and forth for years; each thinking one had something the other didn't. "You are both very handsome men. You are both special. Go get yourself cleaned up, baby. Levi is here with me. I'll be fine."

"Yes, mother." Melech bent over kissing her once again, hitting Levi in the back of the head as he walked past him.

"Really?" Levi held both hands in the air.

"I'm happy to see the two of you got past your differences." Halina patted Levi's leg.

"I wasn't going to let him hate me, ma. I made a mistake."

"I know, son. I think you had some help with that slip-up. You're getting older. I need you to get smarter, Levi."

"I know, ma." Levi always valued Halina's opinion of him. He loved his mother; he just did not respect her the way he did, Halina. Working hard to make sure Levi had what was needed in his life, his mother did that. Making sure Levi was better than his father? That was another story. She was embedded in the hood and did not try to keep Levi out of it. Allowing her husbands' homeboys to take Levi under their wings was perfectly fine with his mother. Someone needed to teach him how to be a man with his father incarcerated was how she saw it. Halina, on the other hand, always tried to remove the street mentality from Levi. He did not think he would have finished high school if it were not for the Buckley's. Levi knew he would not be a legitimate business owner if it were not for Melech and his father. Standing by them during their time of need came naturally.

Melech did not know how relieved he would be to see his home. Putting the key in the front door, he realized it was already unlocked. Slowly Melech entered the house; his first mind went to Levi probably forgot to lock up. Looking around downstairs, everything appeared to be in its proper place. Melech went to his room to retrieve his gun from his safe before he went on a thorough search of his home. Unlocking the safe, it shocked Melech to see it was empty. Pulling his phone out of his pocket, Melech called Levi.

"Did you take my heat?" he asked as soon as Levi answered his phone.

"No. Why?"

"It's gone."

"It's what?" Levi was worried.

"Gone!"

"Hold up." The burner Q had given him rang. It was a number Levi had not seen before.

"Eh, bro. I don't think this chick is supposed to be up in this house. I didn't know who I was sittin' on," a panicked voice rang into Levi's ear. He knew this call was going to be a problem if anyone was listening.

"Who is this?"

"It don't matter. I'm on this clucker, and she just went into your partners' crib."

"Dammit!" Levi switched phones. "Leek?" he said into his phone. "Melech!" There was no answer. "Mom, I need to go check on Melech."

"Is everything alright?"

"I think so."

"Be safe, baby."

"I will." Levi rushed out of the hospital.

♥♥♥

"Mr. Stone." Anderson knocked at his front door. It took several minutes for him to finally open it.

"Yes." Chester appeared to be sleeping.

"May I have a word with you?"

"Sure." Chester opened the front door, allowing Anderson access to his house. "What do you need?" He rubbed his eyes.

"Have you spoken to your daughter?"

"No, not yet." He looked around for his glasses. Anderson observed a pillow and blanket on the couch. "Is she okay?" He reached on the small table next to the sofa that housed a lamp and a spot for his glasses. Putting them on, Chester was able to look at the detective. "Where is she?"

"Your daughter has not reached out to you at all, sir?" Anderson found this odd, considering she allegedly experienced something traumatic just days ago.

"No...no, I haven't seen her." Chester knew that Leana had been in his house. He did not want to tell anyone until he spoke to his daughter.

"We met with her at the hospital yesterday. I was hoping she was here with you." Anderson knew that Leana told him she would be staying at the Ritz. This visit was to gather more information from her father.

"Is she still there? I need to get over there."

"I don't think so, sir." Anderson did not want to outright lie to the man. He was not sure if they had released Leana yet. "She was not admitted. Your daughter appeared to be okay. She was there for some testing."

"Oh, okay." Chester felt better.

"Can you give me some insight into her relationship with her father-in-law?"

"There's not much to tell."

"Are you sure, sir? Think really hard?" Anderson pushed.

"No." Chester was still in denial over the relationship Leana had with Kaden. He could not bring himself to believe his daughter had a personal relationship with her father-in-law. It was too disturbing for Chester to conceive.

"You mentioned that your daughter fell in love with someone else."

"Oh, that was nothing." Chester diverted his eyes.

"Who was your daughter being silly about?" Anderson used Chester's exact words.

"That little trouble-maker Levi. The three of them spent way too much time together. Melech should have known better. You can't turn a blind eye to a boy that let the streets raise him." Chester still blamed Levi for his daughter's indiscretions that ruined her marriage with Melech. "I know Kaden tried to step up and help that kid, but he was already in high school. You know by then a kid is lost to the streets. I wouldn't have let my daughter keep that kind of company."

"I see." This was a turn Anderson was not expecting. "So, Levi and your daughter were close?"

"Yes, yes." Chester shook his head disapprovingly. "Like, brother and sister. I think that's maybe why she got a small crush on him. They just all spent too much time together. Leana will realize how silly it was, and she and Melech will work through the whole thing in time."

"You're telling me the three were really close?"

"Um, hmm, yes. Ate dinner together almost every night," Chester volunteered.

"Were the three sexual?" Anderson was curious.

"What are you saying about my daughter?" Chester didn't like what the detective was saying about his little girl. "She was not raised that way! I think you should leave now."

"Sir, it was not an insult. I was trying to figure out the relationship. Your daughter did not describe it the way you just did." Feeling alarmed, Chester realized he needed to stop giving this cop information. Halina told him he was telling them information that was going to get his daughter in trouble.

"You should listen to what Leana has to say, not me. Since she got married, I see little of her."

"Hmm, I see." Anderson wrote a few things down before heading to the door. "One last thing, Mr. Stone, was your daughter sleeping with her husband's father?" Anderson wanted to know if Chester would overreact to the statement.

"Get out! Get out now! That man hurt my daughter!"

"Has Mr. Buckley ever been known to be a violent man?" Anderson asked.

"Now!" Chester held the door open for him.

"You have a great day, sir." Anderson stepped onto the porch. "Have your daughter give us a call." Anderson was pleased he information he obtained. Levi was closer to Leana than she let on. The hatred for him was coming from somewhere. Anderson was going to find out where. It was time to take a ride out to the Ritz. He called Kelly to let him know what he found out.

♥♥♥

"Hey, Leek."

"What are you doing here?" Melech turned to see Leana in their bedroom doorway.

"I needed to see you." He saw the knife in her hand.

"For what?"

"Leek, where did it all go wrong?" Leana walked closer to him.

"Let me see. For me, it all started with the letter you left behind."

"I know, Leek. That was a mistake." She scratched her head with the knife. "I really, really love you."

"How can you say that when you slept with my best friend, Leana?" Melech needed to know the answer to that question.

"Baby, you don't understand that was all him." Leana hung her head. "I know you won't believe me because you take Levi's side on everything."

"No! Hell no, Leana! If you told me, Levi stepped to you I would have put him out of our lives for good."

"Really?" Leana found some hope in his words.

"How could you question that? At what point did I not prove my love to you?" Melech did not understand how she would even question his loyalties to her.

"Always." Tears came to her eyes. "You always treated me like a princess." Leana stood, looking at him.

"Then, why?"

"I don't know." It was the most honest Leana had been.

"That's not going to work, Leana. You through all this away for Levi? You broke my heart for him!" he shouted at her.

"I know. I know, and it was the biggest mistake I ever made. I still love you, Leek."

"No...no, you don't," Melech whispered. "You can't possibly love me."

"I do, though, Leek." Leana went to Melech, wrapping her arms around him. Melech could feel the tip of the knife on his back. "You are my everything. I need you to forgive me."

"No!" He pushed Leana off of him. "You slept with my best friend and my father." Anger took over him.

"Baby, no!"

"Leana don't lie. My father would never rape you." Melech grabbed Leana by both arms, shaking her. "He's not that kind of man."

"He took advantage, Leek. He saw I was hurting over you, …and…he…I was so sad." Leana fell into his chest. "I just wanted you back." Melech did not know what to do with her being so vulnerable at this moment. He could tell she needed affection, Melech did not know how to give it to her. Pulling Leana off of him, Melech looked into her eyes, seeing the emptiness in them.

"Leana, you have to live with the mistakes you made. I don't know what else to tell you."

"That you still love me, Melech," she pleaded with him.

"I really don't," he lied. Melech would love Leana for a lifetime; he could just never be with her ever again.

"Sorry, you feel that way, Leek." She put her head on his chest.

"Awww…" Melech felt the steel enter the side of his stomach. Grabbing the knife, his knees hit the floor before rolling onto his side.

"I made a fucking mistake, Melech." Leana kicked him over. "You could have forgiven me if you truly loved me. You forgave Levi with no problems," she sneered, circling him. "Yes, I slept with your friend. The two of you are interchangeable; he's just a little more exciting than you. I got bored with your perfect life and I needed excitement." She hit herself in the head. "You were the perfect man, Melech. Don't bring your friend around so much when he's the life of the party. Your daddy didn't teach you that?" she was smug. "You could have just taken me back, and we could have been happy together, but noooo, you're too arrogant for that." Leana stood over him. "I love you, but now I have to do what's best for me." She reached down to pull the knife out.

"Oh, damn!" Leana turned to the woman's voice. Melech was stunned to see the figure enter his room.

"What are you doing in my house?" Leana asked her.

"Umm…" she didn't know how to answer the question. She never wanted to come inside Melech's house. Her job was to just follow Leana. This was not worth the grand she was paid.

"You made a big mistake," Leana told her.

"Hey, look. I don't want any problems."

"As you see." Leana looked around the room. "You just walked into a big one."

"Ooh…wee…yeah. It's not good." She stood, assessing the situation. Leana went for the knife sticking out of Melech. Before she could pull it out, Leana was lying next to her estranged, bloody husband.

"Are you alright?" she asked Melech. He shook his head, no.

"What the fuck?" Levi said, rushing into the room. "What the hell are you doing here?"

"Q asked me to follow this chick when she got released from the hospital. Shit, didn't seem right, so I came in. Melech was on the ground with a knife in his abdomen. I had to do something." Mona explained.

"You shot her?" Levi saw the gun in her hand.

"Are you serious? No. I hit the dumb bitch in the head when she turned her back on me."

"Hood chicks," Levi chucked.

"Don't start."

"Excuse me," Melech got their attention. "I'm in pain here, bleeding out."

"Oh, shit, my bad." Mona attended to the knife wound. "Actually, you're lucky. She didn't get deep enough for you to bleed out." Mona did not remove the knife. She covered the wound with towels she found in Melech's bathroom. "Let me call an ambulance for you."

"Wait, how you gonna explain your being here and crackin' her ass with a gun?" Levi asked.

"Damn, I can't lose my license over this." Mona wanted to smack Q with her gun.

"Go, I got it," Levi told her.

"You sure?"

"Yeah, don't touch shit." Mona held up her hands, showing Levi that she had on gloves.

"I should have known." He winked at her.

"I'll hit Q up, let him know what went down. Make sure you keep those towels on that wound and let the paramedics remove the knife."

"Got it." Mona slipped out as quietly as she came into Melech's house.

Getting Melech off the floor and into his bed, Levi made sure his friend was alright. Stepping into the bathroom, he called 9-1-1. Levi gave all the information needed to get them to the house. He heard Melech calling his name. Rushing back into the room, he saw Melech trying to get out of the bed.

"She's trying to leave." Melech pointed towards the door.

"Lay back down. I got it." Levi got Melech back in the bed then went after Leana. As he ran out the front door, Levi saw her Mercedes speeding down the street as the ambulance pulled up. "Fuck!" Levi yelled with disgust. She had gotten away from him again. "He's upstairs." He gave instructions to the paramedics, still gazing down the street. How Leana kept escaping his grasp was driving Levi insane.

Detectives Kelly and Anderson got the call that Melech's estranged wife had stabbed him. They walked briskly into the Emergency Department at Centinela Medical Center, side by side.

"I'm telling you, kid, this case gets better and better every day," Kelly was jovial.

"Are you taking pleasure in this family's misfortune?"

"Never. I'm just saying this case just keeps going and going. The case started off with a gunshot victim and has evolved into a reality show." Anderson did not bother to respond to his partner. He could not imagine Kelly sitting down with a TV dinner watching the Kardashians. "You take the mother." Kelly tapped Anderson. "That woman scares me."

"I finally found your weakness," he chuckled.

"What?"

"A strong black woman." Anderson responded.

"My second wife was black, I'll have you know." Kelly defended himself.

"Was she strong?" Anderson teased.

"Just ask the damn questions!" Kelly ordered him.

"Hello, Mrs. Buckley," Anderson greeted her.

"What now?" her icy tone made Anderson uncomfortable as well.

"We are here to check on your son. How is he doing?" Anderson was kind.

"Alive, no thanks to his wife. She has put both my husband and son in the hospital. What are you people doing about that?" she sternly asked them.

"We have patrol cars en route to her hotel as we speak ma'am," Kelly informed her. "If she did this…"

"If!" Halina cut him off. "Don't you dare insinuate, there is an *if* in all of this."

"That's not what I'm saying, Mrs. Buckley. As you know, we have to question everyone before we can accuse anyone of a crime."

"Is that so, because on her word, you believe my husband is a rapist."

"That's not accurate, Mrs. Buckley," Anderson interjected. "If we went on your daughter-in-law's word alone, there would be a guard on your husband until we could formally charge him."

"Did you just say that to me?" Halina was fuming.

"He didn't mean it like that," Kelly tried to clean up Anderson's blunder. "We're exploring all the evidence, ma'am. We want to find out who did this to your husband and prosecute them."

"Leana, did this to my husband and my son." she countered what he had to say.

"You may be right, and we will get to the bottom of it, I assure you." Kelly reassured her.

"I'll believe it when I see it." Halina walked away from them.

"I think I'm in love." Kelly accidentally said out loud.

"Don't let me catch you pulling, Mr. B's plug." Levi walked up behind them, startling both detectives with his comment.

"We are professionals". Anderson quickly replied.

"I'm not so sure about that. Leana has a way of twisting men around her fingers. Both of you seem like suckers to me."

"You are just the person I wanted to talk to." Anderson uttered, trying to maintain his disdain for Levi.

"Poof, here I am." sarcasm filled his tone.

"The young Mrs. Buckley, what's your relationship with her?" Anderson inquired.

"She's my boy's wife. Why?"

"There seems to be conflicting statements about your association with her." Anderson informed him.

"Depending on who you talk to, I can see that."

"What's your take on it." Anderson wanted to know Levi's view on the situation.

"Figure it out. Isn't that what you get paid for?" Levi taunted him. "What I will give you is Leana isn't what she seems. I thought she really loved my boy. We were all wrong."

"Let us help, your friend," Anderson hissed. "She is telling us several things that don't put him in a good light, and she's also implicated you."

"Typical." Levi shrugged it off. "Leana was a good girl in Melech's eyes, so, hey, she was in with me. I had Melech's back. He loved that girl and as his friend, I accepted her into the fold and treated Leana the way my boy expected me too. Turns out, she's a whore. That's all you're getting from me. Do your job," he scolded both of them. "I walked into the room with Leana standing over Leek with a knife in his gut."

"Why was she gone when the paramedics arrived?" Anderson inquired.

"The broad bounced while I was trying to save his life. At that moment, Leek was more important than she was."

"Question," Anderson needed to know. "Some statements were made that the three of you were like a throuple, and others say that you hated her. You wanted Mrs. Buckley out of Mr. Buckley's life."

"The only person that could have told you I had a problem with her is, Leana. We were all very close until she lost her mind. That throuple nonsense, you made up. Black folks don't do weirdo shit like that."

"Why do you think she doesn't like you?"

"She bumped her head somewhere along the line and started doing crazy shit."

"Like what?" Anderson was hoping Levi would continue to be forthcoming.

"Mr. B would never rape that girl. Start with that. I'm not doing your job for you."

"You know, if this family would stop holding on to secrets, we could solve this so much faster," Anderson retorted.

"Check this out, bro. All you're gonna do is twist up anything we say. The fact you think the three of us had some weird Utah relationship already proves that."

"Listen, Mr. Johnson," Anderson stopped Levi in his tracks. "We are just running with what is being told to us. What we are getting at this point is your friend in there is the one who shot his father." Anderson knew he was compromising the case. "If you don't talk, he's going to take the fall for this."

"Melech would never, let me repeat this to your simple ass, he would *Never,* ever hurt his father. Whoever blew that bullshit up your ass is 51/50."

"You, Kevin Hart, now?" Kelly snickered. "His jokes aren't that funny, either."

"Was it you?" Anderson asked accusatory.

"If I shot the old man, he'd be dead, and you wouldn't find his body." The words were alarming to both detectives.

"Who was it then?" Kelly wanted his take on the case.

"I think you already know that." Levi tried to walk away from them.

"Johnson," Anderson could not let Levi leave with those words. Levi turned back to look at them. "Was it you, looking out for your friend?"

Levi shrugged his shoulders. "I'm not this sloppy. Plus, I don't hate the old man enough to devastate, my boy. What's a woman scorned to do? That chick is a *"Black Widow"*. Do your job, homie. Ain't that what they pay you the big bucks for?" They watched Levi disappear before they could speak another word.

"I told you, the wife did all of this." Anderson watched Levi vanish before his eyes.

"What If this boy stabbed his best friend to throw us off?"

"Nope, not at all. The wife has not been consistent in anything she's told us. Stone said the three were very close, yet his daughter told us that man did not like her. It's the other way around. Trust me, that man was involved with Mrs. Buckley in more than a friendly matter."

"You think she really stabbed her husband?" Kelly was still not convinced someone as small as Leana could take on a man of Melech's stature.

"I'd bet my life on it," Anderson said, still looking in the direction Levi vanished in.

"Why would she shoot the father-in-law?" Kelly searched for a reasonable answer.

"To set up her husband."

"Then why stab her husband?" Kelly was not following Anderson's way of thinking.

"That is what we need to figure out." Anderson turned his attention to Kelly.

"We know she wasn't raped. That relationship between her and the father-in-law was consensual. You think Buckley turned her advances down?"

"That could drive almost anyone to murder, especially if you gave up everything for nothing." Anderson knew of several cases involving violence from women that could not handle a man refusing to give them what they wanted. Leana appeared to be losing everything she wanted in life, and she more than fit the profile.

♥♥♥

"How you feeling, bro?" Levi asked, walking into Melech's room.

"Sore as hell." He held the wound on his stomach. "I wanted to strangle Le's ass when I felt that knife slide into me."

"How you let her get that close to you?" Levi was curious.

"She started crying when I told her there was no way I could forgive her for being with you and my dad, she played possum on me. How she thought everything could go back to normal is beyond me."

"Easy. It's not like you haven't done it before."

"C'mon, Levi, that was different. Dude was all the way in New York. Long distance relationships don't last. Especially childhood shit."

"Maybe not, but she took you fo' a buster after that. My dude, you been a blow pop since Le met you."

"What the hell does that mean?"

"A sucka. How many licks does it take to get to the middle of yo' dumb ass?"

"She should have known me better." Melech may have bent over backwards to make Leana happy when he thought he held her heart. He could care less about her feelings after he read her letter.

"You didn't get weak at all while she was trying to pry her way back in?" Levi knew Melech did.

"Not at all. She tried hugging me, and all I could envision was Leana with you and my dad. I can't deny my feelings to you because you know when I'm lying." They knew each other too well. When Levi kept defending Leana, Melech knew in his heart it was more to it than Leana being his friend as well. Instead of confronting Levi, he told Levi to pick a side. Melech should have listened to his inner voice. "My feelings for her vanished when she did. When she hugged me, I felt nothing for her, man. Well, maybe regret. I really should have listened to you when you told me I was moving too fast." In retrospect, Levi saw what he couldn't. "I don't know why, Leana thought we were going to all sit down to Sunday dinner after all of this? My mother would kill me."

"Mom will slaughter all of y'all."

"You too," Melech reminded him.

"Not me. We have a bond," Levi bragged.

"You're living in la-la land." Melech could not believe Levi still thought he was the golden child. "My mother is disappointed in all of us."

"You might be right on that one."

"I hate that I brought Leana into our lives," a sadness filled Melech's words.

"It's not your fault, bro. She even had moms take her under her wing. The girl was good."

"Do you think she ever loved me?" Melech thought about what Leana said before she stabbed him.

"I do," Levi recalled his encounter with Leana when she poured out her undying love for him. It was something he would never tell his best friend. Levi did not know if her words were from the heart. If they were, he was not going to dig the knife Leana stabbed Melech with any deeper.

"Le tried to apologize for everything she's done. She really tried to tell me I was the one she really loved. Her true colors appeared and Le flipped the script when she realized I wouldn't take her back. I never saw the ugly side of her until then. She pretty much told me I was a bore." Melech sighed nervously. "Le blamed me for bringing you around."

"I don't get it."

"Don't bring a gun to a knife fight," Melech gave an analogy. "The Knife will always be the weapon of choice."

"Don't listen to anything, Le has to say, bro. Her dim-witted ass blamed me for being crazy after throwing your father in my face when I told her your pops would never rape her."

"I'm trying to figure out what Chester put in her head when she was little to do these things." Melech thought Leana's father raised Leana well.

"It's not his fault. The girl did not have a mother to give her the tender side she needed, but that old man parted the red sea like Moses for Le."

"I don't believe that, Levi. Leana went from her high school boyfriend to me, you, and then my father. What makes a woman do that?"

"One looking for a bigger payday," Levi advised him. "Chester could only give his daughter so much. Leana is in search for the best things in life."

"If that were true, why go from me to you. I get my dad." Melech was not trying to dismiss Levi's worth. Melech just knew financially, he was more stable than Levi. Kaden was doing better than both of them put together.

"She broke into my place and stole money from me." Levi did not take Melech's comments personal. His family was working to gain generational wealth. Kaden earned more money than his father. He went to college and learned how to double up honestly. All Kaden wanted was for Melech to be more prosperous than he was.

"Say what?" Melech was astonished at this revelation.

"She knows I keep lots of cash on hand."

"I have to admit it hit me hard when, Leana told me you were more exciting than I am," Melech confessed.

"Well, she told me pops was better in bed. Le's mission is to make you feel less than a man. If you're not her father, I don't think you mean much to her."

"That's not true, Leana could not wait to get away from him. Hate to say it. She had little respect for Chester even after he gave her everything when her mother died."

"Really?" Levi found this odd. When they spoke about Chester, Leana made him out to be the greatest man she ever met. "She only had good things to say about him to me."

"Levi, it was a job to make Le go visit him. I spent more time with Chester than Leana did. It was the reason my parents started inviting him to Sunday dinner."

"Do you think he did something to Leana?" Levi questioned.

"Never. Le felt her father was a weak man. The sad part is that Chester catered to Leana's every whim. Something every father should do. She admired my father for how strong he was. We both know how selfish Kaden can be. The only person he puts above himself is my mother."

"You're too much like her father. You did the same thing, Leek." Levi let him know. "You picked up where Chester left off. Each and every disagreement, you let Leana have her way. Any and everything she wanted, you gave it to her. That's not me. It's the only reason she set her eyes on me. Not that I was a better man than you. It was my, *'I don't give a shit'* personality." This was the most insightful thing Melech had heard since he read Leana's letter.

"I'm starting to get a better understanding of why Leana did what she did. I don't understand my father, though."

"Money." Levi blatantly told him. "Who has money to set on fire and still be able to live a glorious life?" Leana knew how to maneuver up financially. "Your pops is whipped when it comes to moms."

"That he is," Melech chuckled. "I learned how to treat a woman by the way he is with my mom. He may be harsh with me, but not with her. That was the love I was looking for."

"You'll find it, bro."

"Hiii," Mona poked her head into Melech's room.

"Hey." Melech lit up.

"I don't know if I should light your cute ass up or hug you," Levi joked with her.

"Just love me, baby." Mona entered the room. "How are you feeling?" she turned her attention to Melech.

"A lot better, thanks to you." Melech's stomach started feeling queasier with her presence. "You keep saving the Buckley men."

"It's just what I do." Mona played with her pretend bob. While she was at work, she wore her hair tied back in a neat bun.

"What am I missing?" Levi asked.

"She's my dad's nurse."

"Oh, I see."

"How do you know each other?" Melech remembered the discussion the two had while he had a knife in his stomach.

"We met at Fatburger."

"Oh…" The disappointment came over Melech. He had a small crush on Mona.

"My girl was all up on him, but he wasn't studying her," Mona corrected Levi.

"Man, she got a dude that ain't my thing." Melech looked over at Levi. "Don't start," he warned him.

"I have to go check on my patients. I just wanted to pop in on you before I started my shift." Mona's attention went back to Melech.

"Thanks to you, I'm still alive," he flirted with her.

"You give me way too much credit."

"No, I don't. You are going to have to tell me how you ended up at my house?" Mona got uncomfortable.

"I'm not a stalker or anything," she tried to explain.

"I'll fill him in," Levi interjected.

"Don't tell him nothing crazy," Mona scolded Levi. "I'll come to see you when I get a break," she told Melech.

"You can't handle that one," Levi told Melech once Mona was out the room.

"I'm grown."

"Are you now?" Levi snickered. "She's all hood, you know?"

"How do you know her?" Melech was probing because he had taken a liking to Mona. If Levi had any type of liaison with her in the past, he would have to bow out gracefully.

"She told you. I met her at Fatburger with one of her friends pushin' up on me," Levi was flippant.

"So, you never?"

"Nah, she was giving Misfit the eye, but you know he got a girl," Levi let him know.

"What does that mean with Misfit?"

"He talks a good game. His ass is booed up. Misfit didn't even get Mona's number."

"What's her deal with, Q? How'd she know to be at my house?" Melech adjusted his position in the hospital bed.

"Q told me he had a girl sittin' on Leana at the hospital. I had no clue who she was till I walked up in yo' house."

"What made you come to the house?" Melech was still trying to figure out if Levi heard the conversation between him and Leana.

"She hit me up while I was talking to you. When I got back to you, and you didn't answer, I rushed over to your crib."

"Damn. Man, Mona saved my dad's life then came to my rescue." Melech scratched his scruffy beard.

"Awe…she's your superwoman," Levi joked with him.

"Yeah, sort of." Melech had to admit. "I'm lying there listening to this psycho ranting and raving over me all the while I was thinking if I pull the knife out, was I going to bleed to death."

"I was wondering how you let a little knife stop you from not slapping the hell out of that little ass girl."

"C'mon on man, Leana caught me off guard when she stabbed me. I would have taken that shit from her when she walked into the room. I thought she was trying to make a statement."

"She made one all right." Levi poked Melech where his stitches were, causing Melech to slap his hand away, and grab his side in pain. "I don't get how you didn't pull that muthafucca out of you, though. The homie snatched a knife out of his arm, thinking he was going to use the shit." Levi's entire body shook in disgust. "His shit started bleeding like in one of those scary movies. That nigga hit the ground jerking and shit."

"When Leana went to grab it, I held on to her tiny ass wrist. That's when I saw Mona crack her over the head with the gun." Melech described to Levi what happened. "I realized quickly she wasn't the sweet nurse that helped me with my dad."

"Shit, finding out Mona was a nurse was shocking to me. I thought she was just another dope boy's girl," Levi relayed the irony to Melech. "Her friend is though, keeps trying to get me caught up."

"What…" Levi always blamed others for the insanity he brought into his life. Somehow, he found himself in trouble with a woman more often than not.

"Her friend is Payback's girl. I keep running into her, and she's always throwing that shit at me my boy."

"Don't touch it," Melech warned him.

"I ain't scared of that nigga, I just ain't feeling her. Plus, Misfit said she was trouble."

"The cockiness," Melech insulted his friend.

"Which one of you?" Halina came into the room.

"Him." They both said, pointing at the other.

"How's my boy doing?" she gave Melech a kiss. "And here you come to the rescue once again." Halina hugged Levi.

"Don't pump his head up any bigger than what it is already, mom," Melech warned her.

"You just hatin' cause she loves me." Levi hugged Halina again.

"Oh, my goodness." Melech huffed. "How's dad doing," he asked his mother.

"Still out. I came over to check on you."

"I'm fine, mom," he comforted her, reaching for her hand.

"Does anyone know where Leana is?" Melech glanced at both of them.

"Those cops said they sent someone to her hotel to pick her up," Halina informed them.

"What hotel?" Levi looked at her, puzzled. Q did not tell him about any hotel.

"I don't know. I assumed Leana went back to Chester since I haven't heard from him."

"You don't think she's done something to him?" Melech was worried for Leana's father. "I mean, she has come for me, dad, and tried to get close to you mom."

"Plus, she broke into my house," Levi added.

"That's her father," Halina questioned. She knew Leana was not acting like her normal self. Still she could not see Leana harming her own father.

"That girl ain't thinking straight, ma. What if he says the wrong thing to her?" Levi spoke the truth to everyone.

"I'll send Q over to check on him. The old man can't stand me."

"I don't care for him any longer," Halina admitted.

"He's a little rough around the edges, ma, but he's straight."

"If you say so." She put her arms over her chest.

Anderson sat across from Kelly, watching him drink his black coffee. This case had them both worlds apart on a theory of who did what. This was not the first time they did not agree on a case. Kelly was set in his ways, and Anderson was used to it. He did not want to see anyone else hurt before they arrested someone.

"Hey, guys," officer Diaz pranced over to their desk.

"Well, hello, stranger," Anderson greeted her.

"Haven't seen you in a while." Kelly sat up, smiling at her. Diaz was a good cop, in his opinion. She had helped them out with a few cases.

"After losing my partner, I need to take a little time off before I break in a new one," she informed them.

"How's that going?" Anderson asked her.

"It's going. Hopefully, I make detective soon."

"You will. You're a smart one, kid." Kelly let her know. "If you need anything, let me know."

"I'm actually here because I have some information for you."

"Really now?" She piqued Kelly's interest.

"Did you wonder why they let those three guys go without even questioning them on the Buckley case you are working on?" Diaz asked them.

"What three guys?" Anderson inquired.

"Hmm, no one told you they brought in three suspects after the incident out at the mother's house?"

"No!" Kelly angrily put his coffee down.

"Interesting. You didn't hear this from me." She pointed at both of them.

"Of course," Anderson affirmed his loyalty.

"I overheard this hothead talking down in the break room. Apparently, this idiot had an altercation with that wife and didn't complete his paperwork. From what I picked up on, he and his partner responded to a disturbance call at the house of one of the guys they let go. Supercop, must have done something wrong if there's no paper trail, and they let them walk. If that wife yelled she was being kidnapped when we showed up." Diaz tilted her head forward, raising her eyes into her eyelids. "With several people outside watching. Why weren't they at least questioned? I talked to another respondent who went into the house and spoke to the mother. She claims the wife was in her house when she arrived with a gun."

"We got that report, nothing in it stated they brought anyone in. It just stated that Mrs. Buckley was transported to the ED," Kelly informed her.

"She said, Levi was there as well," Anderson enlightened Kelly. "We just thought nothing of it because he's the one who brought Mrs. Buckley back to the hospital."

"We need to find that disturbance call."

"I'll get on it. The young Mrs. Buckley's disdain for Levi goes deeper than what she has been telling us."

"Those two cops made this case so much harder, keeping this from us." Anderson was angry at their actions. Dropping the ball on the paperwork was one thing. Not informing them made their conduct unforgivable. Anderson was going to make sure he let them know as soon as he found out who they were.

"Thanks, Diaz. You really shed some light on this case." Kelly was grateful she came forward.

"We'll keep your name out of it," Anderson assured her.

"Thanks, guys. I hope you get this case closed. I hear it's a crazy one. Both Buckley men and the wife ended up in the hospital."

"We don't want anyone dying on us." Anderson was honest with his statement. They still had no word on Kaden since he came out of surgery. He did not want this case to turn into murder.

CHAPTER FIFTEEN

Candy stood on the porch, knocking on Chester's front door. Q knew he would not open it for him. It was taking longer than he expected it should take. Just as Q was about to exit his car, the door barely opened.

"Yes," Chester said through a sliver of his door.

"Sir, are you okay?" Candy asked him.

"Yes, what do you need?" he asked her.

"My car broke down, and my cell phone is dead." Candy raised her phone in the air. "Can I use your phone, please?"

"I'm sleeping, can you go next door?"

"That's just it, sir." Candy politely smiled at Chester. "Neither one of your neighbors are home."

"Hold on." Chester closed his door. After several minutes he came back barely opening the door handing Candy his cell phone.

"Sir," Candy spoke again.

"Yes?"

"This phone is dead also," she informed him.

"Is it?" Chester took the phone back, looking at his dead phone.

"You don't look well, mister. Are you sure everything is okay?" Candy was troubled. Chester had a dullness to his skin tone with dark rings under his eyes. She could tell that he had not been taking care of his hygiene just by looking at his uncombed hair and overgrown beard. The man looked as if he had been on a drunken bender. She was getting leery about going inside his house.

"I'm fine, young lady. Hold on, let me get my house phone." Chester walked away from the door. Candy motioned to Q, then followed him into the house. Candy wanted him close by, just in case Chester was dangerous.

Candy watched the elderly man search around the dark room for his phone. She noticed a blanket on the couch with a dim light flickering on a table next to it. There was a half-eaten sandwich sitting on the coffee table with a glass of liquid next to it.

"Sir." Candy startled him.

"What are you doing in my house?" Chester chastised Candy.

"When is the last time you ate?" Candy could tell the food on the table was days old.

"Last night," he said, handing her the phone. "I had a headache, laid down to take a nap." Chester sat in the armchair next to the couch. He was feeling unusually tired.

"How long have you been sleeping?" It was not a few hours the way he thought it was.

"Um…not long." Chester scratched his chest. Hearing a noise, Candy looked down his hallway.

"Are you here alone?" Candy was trying to take stock of what she walked into.

"Yes," Chester quickly answered her. Seeing the bat against the wall by Chester's kitchen, she grabbed it, and walked down the hallway. She had an uneasy feeling. Slowly opening the first door she came to, Candy looked around and noticed boxes everywhere. She could tell they had frantically been gone through.

"What are you doing here?" She saw a chocolate young woman wrapped in a towel, curly hair in a sloppy knot on top of her head, with a few strands hanging loosely around her face.

"The man that lives here let me in to use the phone." Candy explained. "He told me he was here alone."

"My dad is senile," Leana told her.

"That's your dad?" Candy pointed the bat behind her. "What's wrong with him? When is the last time you fed him?" she was angry at Chester's appearance. Candy would never allow her father to be in that condition.

"He's grown and been taking care of himself for years!" Leana snapped at Candy. "Besides, I just got here, and my father is none of your business," Leana realized she was explaining herself to a complete stranger. "Did you make your call, because you can get out?" Leana demanded.

"Or I can call the authorities on you!" she threatened Leana.

"Is that right?" She pushed past Candy, pulling a gun out of one of her boxes next to the closet, pointing it at her.

"Girl." Candy swung the bat, hitting Leana in the head, sending her crashing into the boxes. "Next time take the safety off, you dumb bitch." Candy picked up the Glock 9, spit on Leana, and walked out the room bumping into Q. "The hoe whipped this shit out on me." She handed him the nine.

"Who?" Q looked around.

"Her dumb ass is in there." She pointed the bat at the door. "I cracked her ass."

"Well, damn."

"Don't call me for shit like this again, Q."

"How much money yo' man owe me?" He reminded her.

"Fuck him and you," she hissed. Going to assist Chester, Candy wanted to make sure he was okay so she could go home.

Q wiped down the house and got Chester and the bat securely in the car with them. Q wasn't going to take any chances in case Candy left any prints on it. Omar went in the house to deal with Leana.

♥ ♥ ♥

"Hey, you." Mona popped her head into Melech's room. An instant smile came over his face.

"Well, isn't this a nice surprise?"

"I told you I was going to come back to see you." Mona stood next to his bed. "How are you feeling?"

"A whole lot better now that you're here."

"You are just saying that because I broke into your house and spared you from a knife fight," Mona teased him.

"About that," Melech did not know how much Mona heard during the confrontation with Leana.

"Your wife is a furious woman." Mona did not want to relive the ugly words Leana hurled at him. She thought Melech was a nice guy. The type of man you would like to share your day with. Mona knew getting involved with a man whose wife put a knife in his gut was bad news.

"She really doesn't have a reason to be so angry with me," his gentle words were off putting to Mona. Melech had to do something to make this woman so vicious. The words this Leana blurted out rang loud in Mona's head, *'You were the perfect man, Melech. Don't bring your friend around so much when he's the life of the party. Your daddy didn't teach you that?'* She saw how close Melech was with Levi. It made Mona wonder if Melech was the type of man to put his friend before his woman? Meeting him that day, Mona could tell right away Levi loved himself first. She was not sure if Melech had the same mentality. *'You could have just taken me back, and we could have been happy together, but noooo, you're too arrogant for that.'* Leana's words were heartbreaking. You could tell she loved Melech in her own twisted way. Mona wanted to know what Leana did that was so unforgivable. She was aware they gave the rape kit to Leanna in the ED. Mona was not sure if Melech knew why Leana was there.

"My ex-wife did unforgivable things. I'm grateful you showed up when you did." Melech held on to her hand.

"Women aren't crazy. Men need to be as forgiving as women are." She thought about it for a second. "Well, that's not actually true, unless they sleep wit' your daddy or enemy," she laughed at her own joke. Seeing the look on Melech's face, Mona could tell she hit a nerve with him. *Did Melech's wife sleep with his father,* she thought to herself. "I just wanted to come see you and let you know they are going to bring your father out of his coma later today." Mona rubbed his hand. "He is really doing a lot better."

"All thanks to you," he gave Mona her due credit.

"It's all in a day's work." She patted her fake bob hair for effect.

"I like you," Melech revealed without thinking. Mona blushed through her caramel flushed tone.

"You think you do 'cause I've helped you out here and there," she bashfully responded.

"I'm not some teenage boy, Mona. I know the difference." Melech's confidence caught her full attention. "Women seem to be looking for something, you know, what can you do for me. I keep seeing you give, asking for nothing in return. It looks good on you."

"When you get divorce papers, Mr. Honest, come talk to me. This girl doesn't do married men."

"I'm separated," Melech argued.

"Which always leaves the door open for y'all to get back together," Mona explained to him.

"Did you not see the cold silver ice sticking out my side?" Melech pointed to his twelve stitches in his stomach.

"Some men enjoy homicidal women," she giggled.

"Not this man!"

♥♥♥

"You." Anderson approached officer Mann, "Need to be fired," he seethed.

"Get out my face!" the Ken doll look-a-like officer slapped Anderson's finger out of his face.

"Do you know your incompetence hindered my case?" Anderson yelled at him.

"Eh, man, you need to calm down." Monroe stood between the two men. Anderson looked at the man who looked like he should be shouting from the top of a raggedy car shouting, *King Kong, ain't got nothin' on me!'*

"You, his partner?" Anderson inquired.

"Yes."

"The two of you sat on information pertinent to my case because you don't know how to conduct yourself in the field."

"What case?" Mann looked him up and down.

"Buckley." Anderson held the 9-1-1 transcripts up in the air. "You made a service call out to the Johnson house?"

"Yeah, what about it?" Mann's arrogance suffocated the locker room.

"We needed to know the connection between the woman and Johnson, you've been sitting on it this whole time. Then you released key players in the case."

"We didn't release anyone!" Mann defended himself.

"No, but your actions kept us from getting Johnson in an interrogation room. A kidnapping charge could've got us some answers."

"Okay, okay." Monroe stopped their disagreement. "We dropped the ball. What do you need to know?"

"Why was Mrs. Buckley at the Johnson house?" Anderson directed the question to Monroe.

"She was causing a disturbance at his house. Johnson would not let her in," Monroe gave him the information.

"Why was she there?"

"Probably because he dumped the wildcat," Mann was going to give Anderson his assessment. "The woman is insane."

"It looked like a lover's spat. Johnson didn't tell us much, and the young lady had been drinking," Monroe explained. "We took her to a Hotel downtown. It was not reported because we weren't trying to add to her stress. We could tell she was distraught and a woman of means."

"Sounds like one of you went overboard?" He pointed the paperwork back and forth at the two of them. "You better hope no one else ends up in the hospital, or I'll report both of you for misconduct." Anderson stormed off.

"What crawled up your pantyhose?" Kelly asked as Anderson sat at his desk.

"I got the 9-1-1 call." He tossed the transcripts onto Kelly's desk. "Several calls were made because a loud woman was yelling, screaming, and kicking on a door. I confronted the Bozos."

"Who?"

"Mann and Monroe responded. It was definitely the wife and Johnson."

"I see."

"They confirm she had been drinking and was out of control. They also admitted the two appeared to be in a domestic dispute."

"As in a lover's quarrel?"

"Yes."

"Which means they had something going on too." Kelly liked where this was going.

"It looks like she was having relations with the best friend and the father-in-law," Anderson confirmed.

"Don't see why the father got shot instead of her," the tasteless statement did not sit well with Anderson when it came out.

♥ ♥ ♥

Mona felt her phone buzzing in her pocket. When she pulled it out, the screen had a cryptic message.

I gotta package for you. ED parking lot.

The message came from an unknown number. Hesitantly, Mona walked out to the parking lot only to see Q sitting in a car she'd never seen before with a gray-haired old man.

"What the hell, Q" she fussed at him.

"I'm sorry, but I can't walk up there with this old guy."

"You want me to?" Mona questioned him.

"This is, Melech's father-in-law," Q pleaded with her. "Your girl Candy found him."

"You're getting us way too deep in this mess, Q."

"Who paid for your schoolin', then you boned out on my ass, Mona? He shouted at her.

"You know why I left, Q, so don't keep throwing that shit in my face."

"My bad Just get the old man in there. Something's wrong with this dude. We couldn't just leave him, and Candy don't want no heat comin' her way."

"Only because I can see he needs help. Not cause of nothin' else."

"I know, I said my bad, Mona. Stop trippin'," Q snapped at her. He knew that he had cheated on Mona one too many times. It was just a matter of time before she left him. Paying for her to go to school was his way of trying to make it up to her. Mona was a good girl trying to make a life for her and her little girl.

"Mister." Mona woke up, Chester. "Are you okay? I need you to come with me." Mona helped him out of the car.

"Where am I? Chester asked, looking around.

"A friend brought you to the hospital. I found you sitting here." Mona tried to protect Q's identity. "Are you feeling weak at all?"

"Just a little sleepy, dear," Chester informed her.

"Let's get you inside so someone can check you out, okay."

"Yes, sure." Chester walked in with Mona. She walked up to a nurse in the ED she trusted.

"Hey, Liv. I found this gentleman outside while I was on break. He's not looking too hot. Can you check him out for me?"

"Why?" Liv asked.

"Because he's someone's father."

"Yeah, I got him." Liv rolled her eyes, putting Chester in a wheelchair. "You owe me, girl. What you cookin' tonight?" she said over her shoulder. "I'll be over there with my little one and make sure you got wine on deck. This gonna take me into overtime."

"Yeah, yeah. I'll see you tonight, crazy." Mona knew Liv was going to come over regardless if she dumped Chester on her or not. She was always hoping Q would pop up or one of Candy's men friends was over checking on her. Liv was looking for a man to pay her bills in the worst way.

Mona did not like being so heavily involved in Melech's world. Especially, when she found herself attracted to him. After making her rounds, she went to the ICU to see if she could find Levi. She needed to let him know that Leana's father was in the ED. She found him sitting with Halina, right where she hoped he would be. Mona did not want another strange encounter in front of Melech. She checked on Kaden, then gave Levi a look to follow her.

"I'm going to go check on, Leek. You going to be okay," he checked with Halina before he walked out of the private room.

"Yes, of course, baby," she warmly told him. "That boy is probably driving everyone crazy by now."

"You know you spoiled him," Levi teased.

"Yes, I did," Halina, admitted. "I'll be fine. Go." Levi left out to find Mona. She was standing right outside the door, waiting for him.

"Hey," she said, startling him.

"Girl!" Levi held his hands up to her throat as if he was about to choke her. "Don't do that!"

Slapping his hands away, Mona let him know, "I just took Melech's wife's dad into the ED. He looked pretty bad."

"Bad like what, and how do you even know him?" Levi was mystified by this information.

"Your boy keeps putting me in the middle of nonsense," she spat. "Just by looking at him, I'd say he was dehydrated. Q said he couldn't stay awake. I don't know him. Do you think he'd try to take his own life?"

"Not at all, but his daughter would," Levi informed her.

"Is she that awful? He's her father."

"Trust me, the girl has lost her fuckin' mind somewhere along the way. She didn't use to be like this. I don't really know what happened to her."

"People don't just change overnight, Levi. Something traumatic happens to them, or they've been crazy for a long time," she educated him.

"Trust me, I've known Leana for a long time. She didn't use to be like this."

"Are you sure? Maybe you missed some signals because she's a beautiful girl." Levi stopped to think did he miss signs Leana had put out that her beauty covered up. Leana always seemed to have a happy-go-lucky disposition with him, a little too flirty at times. Melech was the only one who dealt with her ill-tempered nature. He seemed to like the spontaneous nature. Levi was just now seeing how malicious Leana could be.

"Rejection is what made that girl crazy. That's it, that's all,"

"I don't know, Levi. When I walked in the way she was ranting and raving at Melech, it really wasn't directed at him. It was weird. I'm no psychologist, but I'm just telling you there is something definitely off with that one."

"I guess." Levi shrugged. "How's the old man doing?"

"I don't know I had to get back to work."

"I'll go check on him." Levi left Mona standing there. He knew Leana was crazy. He just didn't want to contribute it to any psychobabble.

After Anderson hung up with Diaz he was filled with intrigue. "Hey, we need to get out to the front of the station," he told Kelly.

"What's going on?"

"I don't know. Diaz said it was something we need to see." They both headed out to the front quickly. Diaz had never stirred them wrong.

Breaking their way through the crowd, they made their way to a 2016 all black Mercedes E class with Leana sitting in the driver seat handcuffed to the steering wheel with a custom-made Louis Vuitton Glock seated in the passenger seat. Leana was only wearing a towel as her mangled hair sat with a halfhearted bun on the top of her head while wild curls escaped, falling into her face and the nape of her back. Leana was still passed out. She had no idea she was parked at the last place she ever wanted to be, the police station.

"Back up!" Kelly order.

"Get this area taped off before they destroy the crime scene," Anderson instructed the officer's standing by like every other bystander. "Who put her here?" Anderson questioned Kelly.

"Could be anyone."

"There has to be evidence in this car. I'll get CSI down here to see what they can find," Kelly let him know.

"You won't find anything," Kelly was cynical.

"There are no perfect crimes. Even if the perpetrator wore gloves, he left something behind."

"Youngster, there is a perfect crime. You must know by now some criminals are too smart to leave anything incriminating."

"They always forget evidence doesn't always come in the form of blood or skin left behind," Anderson wanted to take this time to enlighten his partner.

"None of that matters when you have a cop on the payroll."

"Say what now?" Anderson wasn't naïve; he was hoping he would never have to work with a cop that did not have ethics or morals. Kelly had an old school nature about him that made him easier to tolerate. Diaz's partner had been killed off duty with known drug dealers. The department could not determine if she was a dirty cop, but it did not stop the rumor mill from spinning throughout their station.

"I got you covered," Kelly wanted to ease his partner's mind. "Someone hand-delivered, the young Mrs. Buckley for a reason. Get an ambulance out here for her. They left her alive, which means they think she has some answers for us. Let's get to the hospital. See what her husband and friend have been up to today."

Levi wanted to make sure everything was alright with Chester before he told Halina what was going on. He did not want to add more to her stress level with Kaden still in a coma and Melech getting stabbed.

"Hey, I'm looking for a Chester Stone," he told the nurse behind the counter, tapping her fake nails on the phony wood countertop.

"Who are you?" She put her hand on her hip, tilting her head to the side.

"A friend of the family."

"Yeah, well, you have to be family…"

"Listen, sweetie." Levi put his arm on the counter, gazing at her in his charming way. "The old man's daughter is in the wind. He doesn't have no one to check on him right now. You not gonna leave the poor dude out there like that, are you?"

"So, you a do-gooder?" Liv lost the cold princess act, giving Levi the once over.

"I'm good at a lot of things, sweetheart." He winked his eye at her.

"I'll let you see him only because I'm the one taking care of him," Liv explained. "They found him wandering around out front, poor guy."

"What's wrong with him?" Levi followed behind the woman who was as tall as a model.

"The doctor is running test on him right now. All I know is we got him on an IV drip, he was extremely dehydrated."

"Wow, I know he's been worried about his daughter," Levi confessed to Liv.

"You think that's who left him out front?" she asked.

"Who knows, she's been off her rocker lately."

"That's too bad. Mr. Stone seems like everyone's papa." Levi chuckled.

"He's not that old, girl."

"Really?" Liv shrugged as she opened the curtain for Levi to visit with Chester. "Hey, there, Mr. Stone. Someone is here to see you."

"What's up, old man?" Levi stood over Chester. "I hear you were wandering around out front. You straight?"

"I think so. How did I get here?"

"He doesn't remember how he got here," Liv whispered to Levi.

"What's the last thing you remember?" Levi questioned Chester.

"Letting a young girl use my phone."

"Maybe that's who brought you here," Liv told him.

"Sh...she asked me." Chester swallowed hard, stammering over his words.

"What did she ask you, Mr. Stone?" Levi asked.

"The last time I ate."

"Huh?" Levi glanced at him. "You let a strange chick in your house, and she asked, what you ate?"

"Uh, huh, that's what I remember."

"That doesn't sound right, old man." Levi was trying not to get irritated with Chester. "Are you sure that wasn't Leana?" Chester rubbed his eyes, trying to remember what took place at his house. Visions of Leana were bouncing around his memory, but he was sure his daughter wasn't at the front door.

"I...I...don't think so, Levi. The girl heard a noise." Chester suddenly remembered.

"Are you protecting, Leana, Chester?" Levi persisted. "When's the last time you saw her?" Chester laid back on his pillow, shutting his eyes.

"I'm tired, Levi."

"Let him rest; he may remember something later," Liv uttered, pulling Levi by the elbow.

"Yeah, alright. I'll come back down here a little later." Levi allowed Liv to escort him out of the room.

"Can you let me know when the test comes back on him?" Levi was sure Leana was in the house with him. There was no way Chester was going to tell anyone where his daughter was now.

"I get off a couple of hours ago. I only stayed to make sure Mr. Stone got settled in before I head out."

"Can you tell one of the other nurses to hit my phone? No one else is gonna check on him."

"Sure, but you owe me," Liv teased. "You're gonna have to pay up one day." She went over to another nurse. Levi watched them talk and giggle, then point at him. Liv motioned for Levi to come over to where they were standing.

"Hello." He greeted them. "Levi." He said, reaching his hand out to the nurse.

"Give her your number so she can put it in your uncle's chart," Liv winked at him.

"Oh, yeah, sure." Levi pulled a card out of his wallet. "I will be upstairs," he let them know. "My best friend and his father are both here."

"You're not having an enjoyable week, are you?" Liv perceived from the statement.

"Not even close."

"Let me have my girl pick up my son, she owes me. I'll stick around and make sure Mr. Stone is good before I take off," Liv told him.

"You don't have to do that," Levi insisted.

"Your good." Liv took Levi's card from the nurse. "Go to your friend, I'll let you know if anything changes."

"Thanks." Levi touched her hand, giving her a warm smile. Liv looked at his card after Levi walked away.

"Nice." She noticed Levi owned a hookah lounge. "Really thought he was a drug dealer." Amusing herself, Liv went to check on Chester again. The sweeter she was to him, the better impression she would make on Levi.

CHAPTER SIXTEEN

"We're here to see Mrs. Buckley," Kelly informed the nurse passing by him. She pointed to the nurse's station without answering him. "I love how helpful these nurses can be."

"Maybe it's just you," Anderson taunted him. "Hello, miss. Can you tell us which room Mrs. Buckley is in? They brought her in by ambulance," he politely asked.

"Yes, I'll show you. Come with me." Anderson shot his partner a devilish smile.

"Thank you," Kelly told her after she opened the door for him.

"No problem."

"You're not the only one who can be nice."

"I know you can be nice," Anderson told him. "For about five minutes. What was your longest marriage?"

"Have you ever been married, youngster?"

"Too busy working, my friend." Anderson opened the curtain that was providing Leana a little sense of privacy, and noticed she was sleeping. "Mrs. Buckley," He tried waking her up.

"Is she sedated?" Kelly thought out loud.

"How would I know? I walked in with you," Anderson protested.

"Mrs. Buckley," Kelly spoke loudly. Slowly fluttering her eyes, Leana saw the two detectives at her bedside.

"What?" she asked, keeping her eyes closed?

"Do you know how you got to the station?" Kelly asked her.

"No, someone hit me in the head," Leana replied.

"Someone?" Anderson interjected. "Do you know who?"

"No."

"Was it your husband?" Kelly questioned her.

"I can't remember," she was getting frustrated with the third degree. It was making her head hurt more than it was before they walked into her room. "Maybe, he hates me."

"Do you remember stabbing, Mr. Buckley?" Kelly inquired.

"What?" Leana opened her eyes.

"They brought your husband in the other day with a knife wound," Anderson explained.

"He attacked me. It was self-defense." Leana stated.

"Your husband attacked you in his house, is that where you got the head injury?" Anderson asked.

"Yes." She held on to the tender spot on the back of her head, feeling the stitches. *That bitch* Leana thought to herself. She had no idea who the woman was that hit her with the bat. "Levi hit me in the head. I was just trying to save myself." She knew the likelihood of ever seeing the woman who broke into her father's house was very slim. This was her chance to take Levi down right alongside Melech.

"I thought you could not remember who hit you?" Kelly challenged her.

"It, um…it just came back to me."

"Why would your husband attack you, Mrs. Buckley?" Anderson pulled his pad out.

"He's angry with me."

"Why?" That was not an answer.

"Because we're separated," Leana snapped at Kelly.

"You never told us why you and Mr. Buckley separated." Anderson flipped through his notes.

"Is that a question?" Leana was not sure if the statement required an answer.

"Did it have anything to do with your personal relationship with Mr. Johnson?" Anderson glanced up from the pages on his notepad to Leana's face.

"My what?"

"Why did you leave your husband, Mrs. Buckley, was it for Mr. Johnson or your father-in-law?"

"I got attacked yet again, and this is what you're asking me," Leana was irate. "When are you going to arrest my husband for what he did to Kaden?" She grabbed her head; the yelling brought a defining ringing to her head.

"Ma'am, please calm down," Anderson tried soothing Leana. "We are still working on that case. Right now, we are trying to gather information on what lead you to stab your husband."

"He attacked me, I already told you that."

"We need more than that, Mrs. Buckley. We need a step-by-step account of what happened that led up to the moment you stabbed your husband."

"And how Mr. Johnson hit you in the head, and what did he use?" Kelly added.

"I have a terrible headache. Can we do this later?" she asked.

"It's best to get the answers while they are still fresh in your head, ma'am. It's already been almost twenty-four hours." Anderson did not want to give Leana a chance to make up a story. He did not believe a word she said since their first interview.

"What do you need to know?"

"Why were you in your husband's house? Last time we spoke, you were staying at the Ritz." Kelly stated.

"Melech invited me over?"

"He called you?" They were working on getting a search warrant for Melech's house after discovering Leana's cell phone signal was coming from there.

"Um, no. I saw Melech in the parking lot at the hospital."

"Really?"

"Why were you here?" Kelly wanted to know.

"I wanted to know how Kaden was doing."

"Okay. Mrs. Buckley how did you end up at the house, and why did you stab your husband?" Kelly was losing patience with Leana.

"He told me to come by so we can talk. When I got there, he was in the bedroom we used to share. Melech was in the closet where he keeps his gun talking on the phone. After arguing, he shook me, and threw me to the ground. I didn't know what he was going to do to me. He tried to grab me, so I stabbed him."

"Where does Mr. Johnson fit into all of this?"

"I was trying to leave when Levi hit me in the head with a gun."

"Mrs. Buckley?"

"Yes?"

"Where did you get the knife from?" Anderson inquired.

"Do you carry a kitchen knife in your purse?" Kelly sarcastically added. Leana did not take the time to think about the knife; her head was really throbbing.

"No," she hissed at Kelly. "I overheard him on the phone with Levi when I first got there. Melech told him he would kill me if I said the wrong thing, so I went down to the kitchen."

"Was he on the phone with Mr. Johnson or is he the one who hit you in the head."

"Both."

"Okay, Mrs. Buckley. We will be in touch with you soon." Anderson headed out of the room with Kelly right behind him.

"I say we go and talk to twiddle dee and twiddle dumb before we leave and get their take on the story the lovely Mrs. Buckley just told us," Kelly told his partner.

"You know she's lying."

"From the second, she opened her mouth. Why can't we just arrest her?"

"In due time." The two went to talk to Melech and Levi.

Liv pulled Levi's card out of her pocket to call him. She had stayed after work three extra hours just to take care of Chester.

"Levi," he said into his phone.

"Hey, it's Liv."

"What's up, girl?"

"The test results came back for Mr. Stone. It looks like he had an excessive amount of Temazepam in his system. Do you think he was trying to kill himself?"

"Chester? Never!"

"Well, they put a psych hold on him because they cannot find a prescription for that medication in his records," Liv informed him.

"Word? That's crazy," Levi told her. "The old man was worried about his daughter but trying to kill himself over the dumb shit she's been doing, nah."

"I just wanted to let you know what's going on with him before I head out of here. I need to get home to my son."

"I really appreciate all you've done today."

"It really isn't a problem. How's your friend doing?" Liv asked him.

"A lot better, thanks."

"This is my cell phone. Lock it in just in case you need anything."

"I will definitely do that, ma," Levi flirtatiously said into his phone.

"Now, who are you flirting with?" Melech asked.

"That's the nurse I told you was lookin' out for Chester. She said he had Temazepam in his system."

"The sleeping pill?"

"Is that what it is?" Levi asked.

"Yes, Leana takes those."

"Well, there you have it." Levi shrugged his shoulder. "They got the old man on suicide watch. She was trying to kill her old man."

"Leana wouldn't do that."

"I don't know why you keep seeing good in that girl." Levi did not understand how Melech kept defending Leana.

"Excuse me." Anderson knocked on the door, letting himself in. "Can we have a few words with you?"

"Do I have a choice?" Melech moaned.

"Not really." Kelly barged into the room. "We just spoke to your wife."

"You what?" Levi was overcome. "You arrested her?"

"No, she's in the ED at the moment." Anderson let them know.

"So, you're gonna let her walk?" Levi hissed.

"That depends on what you tell us," Anderson informed him. "What happened the other night when you got stabbed, Mr. Buckley?"

"That crazy girl stabbed him." Levi pointed at Melech.

"Why was Leana in your house?" Anderson asked, ignoring Levi.

"I have no idea. When I got there, my door was unlocked. I went to get my gun and as soon I realized it was missing, I called, Levi. I turned around, and there she stood."

"Did you say your gun was missing?" Kelly asked.

"Yes, I keep it locked in the safe right next to my wife's. Hers was missing as well." That just came to Melech's mind.

"What provoked the stabbing?" Anderson questioned.

"Leana got upset because I didn't want to take her back. She gave me a hug begging for forgiveness the next thing I knew I was on the ground with a blade in my stomach."

"When did you intervene, Mr. Johnson? You are the one who hit her with a gun causing, Mrs. Buckley to get stitches?"

"Excuse me?" Levi knew for sure Mona did not leave Leana bleeding when she hit her.

"That's why she's here," Anderson informed them. He verified with the nurse the two had been at the hospital all day, so neither one of them brought Leana to the station. He was not ready to give them that piece of information yet.

"That's not from me. I never touched that girl." Levi held his hands up. I called for an ambulance, and she ran for the hills.

"So, you never came into contact with Mrs. Buckley?" Anderson needed clarification.

"No."

"Did you see your wife at the hospital, Mr. Buckley?" Kelley questioned.

"When. Today?"

"The day she stabbed you?"

"Before she stabbed me, I have not seen my wife since I put her out of my house."

"When was that?"

"The day before she shot my father."

"I see." Anderson pulled his notepad out again.

"The knife?" Kelly asked. "When did she get the knife?"

"It was in her hand when she walked into my room."

"Alright, thank you for your time," Anderson told them.

"You gonna arrest her now? Shit she shot Mr. B and stabbed, Leek here."

"We can't prove she shot Mr. Buckley just yet," Kelly informed them.

"If she didn't do it, then who?"

"Him." Kelly pointed at Melech, who started laughing at the comment.

"You cannot be serious?"

"Your wife was earnest with the statement she gave."

"And she's so honest!" Levi protested.

"We'll keep you updated," Anderson informed them. Hearing that Melech's gun was missing confirmed it for him. Kelly was still moving in the wrong direction.

When they got into the elevator, Anderson spoke again. "When are we going to arrest, Mrs. Buckley?"

"I'm on it, youngster. I have a patrol on the way to pick her up as we speak."

"Thank you." Anderson gave praying hands. "It's about time. You know she took his gun. That's premeditation on the father."

"I'm still not convinced she shot Mr. Buckley."

"Kelly, the woman, stabbed her husband and has been sleeping with the man's father and best friend."

"That makes her a terrible person, not a killer."

"I sent a car for her because she lied about the stabbing. What if Mrs. Buckley stabbed her husband because he shot her lover?"

"Kelly, you're really grasping at shooting stars."

"Listen, the husband walks in on the two, loses his mind, and shoots his father. Young Mrs. Buckley gets so upset she goes to confront the mother-in-law to tell her what a horrible son she has, but Mr. Johnson stops her. The girl is out here alone and desperate. What does she do? Seeks revenge on her husband because Mr. Buckley made her lose everything."

"That would sound like a perfect case, but you left out a key component, Johnson. She went to his house in the middle of the night, causing a ruckus, and she had a sexual relationship with him as well. Let's not forget, Mrs. Buckley did not leave her husband for her father-in-law. She left him for his best friend."

"That shows some reasonable doubt in my theory," Kelly confirmed Anderson's assessment.

"And in front of a jury, Mrs. Buckley walks with what you want to present to the DA," Anderson warned him.

"So, what's your take on it?"

"Easy, just from listening to her father, Mrs. Buckley left her husband for Johnson. He was not with her plan, so she turned to the father-in-law. I think he wasn't willing to leave his wife. After two rejections, the young lady snapped, and Mr. Buckley just happened to be at the wrong place at the wrong time. I think Mrs. Buckley went to tell her mother-in-law for some sympathy with the rape story, when she encountered Johnson. I believe everything young Buckley said about the stabbing. Having lost it all, he was her last chance at getting her old life back. When Buckley did not bite, she stabbed him the same way the girl shot the father-in-law."

"You keep forgetting she has had her own set of injuries through each incident." Kelly reminded him.

"We don't know if they are defensive wounds or not. They may have come from mutual attacks."

"Let's get back to the office to go over the statements and medical reports again. Something has to give and soon."

♥♥♥

Looking out of Melech's hospital room door, making sure the detectives were gone, Levi turned back to his friend. "What did I tell you?" He pointed at him. "They were gonna come straight for you. You should have kept yo' mouth shut without your lawyer here."

"I have nothing to hide. I didn't shoot my father. We were together that night."

"Yeah, they gonna try to say we're covering for each other," Levi warned Melech.

"Paranoid much?"

"Yes, and you should be too," Levi scolded him. "Leana is trying to put that hot one your dad took on you. She already claims yo' pops raped her. You look like the crazed husband."

"But my dad would never rape, Leana," Melech defended his father.

"Bet they found his dead children all up inside of her."

"What is wrong with you?" Melech shook his head.

"Even if they don't buy her rape claims, them cops ain't dumb as they look. All they have to say is you tried to kill the old man out of jealousy. Leana stabbing you could be revenge for what you did to your, dad."

"Yeah, okay, I get what you're saying." Melech thought about what Levi was telling him. "And she's claiming you cracked her in the head down to the white meat."

"Crazy thing is, she knows someone else was there that could blow her lies up."

"Leana's isn't thinking about the lies at this point, she's making them up as she goes along," Melech told him.

"Still wondering what plans she had for, moms. Glad I got there before something terrible happened."

"You and me both," Melech confirmed Levi's feelings.

"I'm going to go down and check on the old man. If she's in this hospital somewhere, your dad ain't safe, and neither is hers."

"I'm going to try to sneak out this room and check on my dad. My mother has to be exhausted by now."

"I'll meet you over there."

♥♥♥

Sitting at his desk, Kelly noticed an envelope from CSI. "We've got mail." He showed the envelope to Anderson.

"What new surprises will we find out today?"

"Let's take a gander." Kelly pulled the papers out of the envelope, reading the content. Anderson watched him with anticipation.

"Come one, man. Read it out loud," Anderson demanded.

"Oh." Kelly gave him a smirk. "It looks like they found fluids on our lovely, Mrs. Buckley."

"We knew that was going to happen."

"That's just it partner, it was on the inside of her jeans, and it does not match what was found at the hotel."

"Are you serious?" Anderson was not expecting that. "Johnson!" he snapped his fingers, then pointing at Kelley.

"If it were only that simple."

"Her husband?" Anderson asked.

"Nope. The two samples we got from young Buckley's house does not match either."

"How many men did this girl have?"

"I can't tell you. What I do know is there were no signs of trauma, so we know the girl wasn't raped," Kelly informed him, "Except for bruising around her neck. The way she's bouncing around these men, I wouldn't doubt that Mrs. Buckley likes it a little rough now and again."

"You and your assumptions." Anderson objected to every word Kelly spewed. "If Mrs. Buckley was a man, would you have the same take on her? You would applaud her conquests."

"That's where you're wrong." Kelly stood his ground. "Everyone she touches seems to get hurt. That's nothing to give a round of applause to. She like eats her mates after she has a good time with them."

"A Black Widow."

"What?" Kelly asked.

"They say black widows kill after mating. I don't know if it's fact or fiction. No one really knows if they kill every spider they mate with," Anderson explained to him.

"Okay, Mr. Facts, no one cares about." Annoyed with Kelly, Anderson grabbed the papers from him.

"Hey, maybe that's why she hasn't attacked, baby gangster, yet. She's tried to hurt everyone else thus far."

"Or he just hasn't told us." Anderson did not look up from the report. You know he's from, Rolling 60s. He's only going to tell us what he wants us to know."

"How do you know that?"

"I traced him back to Crenshaw high school. He did not grow up like the Buckley kid. I got his mother's address, it's smack dead in the heart of that gang's neighborhood. His father has been in jail for over a decade and a notorious member of the gang."

"You're just now telling me this?" Kelly did not like his partner keeping things from him.

"We got the call the Buckley woman was out front, I didn't get a chance."

"So, who's this, Childs person?" Anderson glanced over at Kelly.

"That's what we need to find out. Apparently, that's the last person she had physical contact with."

"What's the ETA on her getting here?"

"Let me find out."

♥ ♥ ♥

"What's up, old man?" Levi asked Chester, walking into his shared room.

"What did you tell these people?" he whispered, not wanting the person in the next bed to hear him.

"What are you talking about?" Levi was clueless.

"They're trying to say I overdosed on sleeping pills," Chester explained.

"The nurse told me that dumb shit." Levi dismissed the suicide aspect of it all. "Chester, when is the last time you saw Leana?"

"Levi don't start that again. You don't have her best interest at heart."

"Did you know the medicine they found in your system is the same sleeping pill she takes?" Levi informed him.

"How would you know?" Chester was grateful Levi was checking on him. Without Leana, he was feeling lonely, but he still did not trust him.

"Melech just told me."

"What does that prove?" Chester grumbled.

"Considering it's your crazy daughter, she wanted to keep yo' ass quiet after she showed up on your doorstep."

"Leana would not kill me!" Chester was tiring of defending his daughter.

"Maybe...maybe not. Your daughter didn't want you opening up that gigantic trap of yours. Did Leana tell you she stabbed Melech?" Levi asked.

"No..." Chester was unsure of where Leana's mind was at. "Is he alright?"

"Thank goodness that fool does a thousand sit up's a day, and Leana isn't strong enough to do any serious harm. My boy should be out of here tomorrow."

"That's good to hear."

"Be glad you're alive to hear it!" he fussed at Chester. "Whoever got you to the hospital saved your life."

"About that," Chester was remembering some details of the days' events. "The young girl came to the house to use the phone, saying her car broke down. She was more interested in what I ate and who was in the house."

"What did she look like?" Levi was sure it was Leana in his haze Chester may have been confused, precisely the effect Leana was looking for.

"A pretty girl with a long ponytail." *Candy?* Levi thought to himself. *Of course, she's friends with Mona.* That's why Mona was the one to bring back the details of Chester being in the ED.

"I know you don't want to hear this old man, but if Leana pops up in here call the nurse for security," Levi warned him. "She's dangerous. I don't know what her motives are or what she told yo' ass, but you damn sure lucky ponytail showed up when she did. Now your daughter got you lookin' like a senile old muthafucka that doesn't like life."

"I don't think, Leana would…"

"Well, she just did, Chester!" Levi cut him off."

"She shot Mr. B, stabbed Melech, broke into the Buckley house to confront Mrs. B. Why? Your daughter thought it was a good idea to tell her who Kaden really is, all while packin' her heat. Leana also broke into my crib, tossed it like the fucken FBI, then stole forty large from me. That girl is capable of shit none of us ever suspected."

"Levi, Leana's just hurt," he tried to give some insight to his daughter. "Leana hasn't taken to losing things well since her mother passed away."

"You know what, Chester, she should have thought about that before she left Melech and slept with his father."

"Didn't she sleep with you also?" Chester asked.

"That was mistake number one." Venom filled his words. "Leana lost the best thing that ever happened to her for a man like me. Think about that." Chester could not respond. Knowing Levi was right about his daughter did not make him feel good about the person his daughter had become. After Leana's mother died, simply denying her of anything caused a significant meltdown in their home. Chester learned to oblige his daughters every whim. After seeing how things have unfolded, overcompensating Leana may have been the wrong thing to do.

Leana poked her head out of the ED room that housed three different beds. She had no plans on sticking around waiting for another social worker to come in and shrink her head after everything she had been through. Leana thought Tracy was a nice lady. She asked too many questions and told too many stories about her friend and what the woman went through when she was abducted. It was all la, la, la in Leana's head as she nodded and let the tears fall. The only problem was Leana was not listening to Tracy. Leana gave odd answers to Tracy's questions. She thought Tracy was the worst psychiatrist she'd ever met. She did not have to make excuses for the inconsistencies in her stories; Tracy did it for her. Leana had the same degree Tracy did, hers was from UCLA and Tracy went to Loyola. This made Leana feel superior to Tracy in some strange way. What Leana did not know is that Tracy was not as idiotic as Leana believed her to be. Tracy did not want to accept that any woman would lie when it came to sexual assault, but she knew in the pit of her gut; this was not the case with Leana. Leana refused to share with the detectives any of the details she shared with Tracy in confidence. Tracy made it a point to let them know it would be wise to keep digging into Leana's story. Something was not adding up.

Leana watched Levi enter a room close to the one she was in. She quickly slipped back into hers, closing the door behind her. *He must know I'm here.* Her mind was spinning in a million different directions. *Damn detectives.* Leana searched the room for her purse. It was nowhere to be found. She needed her phone to make a call to get out of the hospital.

"Excuse me, sir," she spoke to the young man sitting next to the little boy in the next bed. "Is it possible I could use your phone? I came in an ambulance, and they did not bring my purse in with me," Leana was modest with her tone. "I just need to get myself home. It's a local call."

"Yeah, no problem." He handed Leana his phone, turning his attention back to his son. Leana went back behind her curtain, whispering, not wanting to be heard or seen should Levi pop his head into the room.

"Thank you, sir." Leana handed him back his phone.

"Are you okay?" he finally paid attention to Leana as she peeked out the door once again.

"My ex is looking for me," Leana answered without looking back. "He's the one who put me in here. I can't let him find me."

"That's terrible, what are you a hundred pounds?" he asked. "How can someone hurt such a small thing like you?"

"I'm one-twenty, and he doesn't really care. Hurting me seems to be his favorite pastime these days." Leana closed the door. She looked around for clothes to put on; they did not bring those to the hospital either. "Man!"

"What?"

"I have no clothes. Someone must have taken them." Tears filled Leana's eyes.

"Here." He took his jacket off, handing it to her.

"I can't." Leana shook her head, wrapping her arms around her body.

"Take it. It's fine, hun. You go meet your friend and be safe. Just promise you won't go back to that guy."

"Never," Leana reassured him. "Thank you."

"Be safe…" he did not know her name.

"Le," she told him. "I don't know how to thank you." Leana gave him a hug. "I hope your son gets better."

"Me too." He gave Leana a weary smile. Checking to see if Levi was near, Leana slowly stepped out of the room wearing the extremely large leather coat. Quickly rushing past the room, she saw Levi going into, Leana could hear his voice yelling at someone. Her heart was racing as she tried to get out of sight before he came out of the room, Leana bumped right into what she thought was a security guard.

"Sorry...sorry!" she said, holding her hand up, rushing past him. Once she made it out to the parking lot, Leana's heart settled down, and breathing became a lot easier until a horn scared her. A familiar face pulled up next to Leana.

"You called?" Climbing into the car, Leana was able to relax, if only for the moment.

"You always come through for me." Leana gave him a hug and tender kiss on his thick lips.

"For how many years now? Luca touched her face with his knuckles. "No matter how many times you hurt me."

"Baby, I told you I was leaving, Melech, and I did, right?"

"Took you long enough. You never should have never married, that man."

"Luca, you left me here by myself," Leana held him by the back of the head, pulling Luca into her. "You know I have issues with abandonment."

"I know, babe." Luca kissed her forehead. "I made a mistake. I didn't realize how much you needed me." Leana pleaded with Luca to stay home and attend school with her. He had the choice between USC and NYU, Luca wanted to spread his wings to see new things. His four years ended up turning into eight. "I wasn't here to protect you, but I am now. Melech and his family won't hurt you again. I promise." He lifted her chin with his finger. "You hear me?"

"Yes." Leana sat back in Luca's Lexus truck, feeling everything was looking up for her. Melech and Levi were going to jail. Hopefully, Kaden would die, and she could start a whole new life with Luca.

*** To Be Continued ***

CONTACT INFORMATION

DD Hairston

Email: ddhairston@gmail.com

Website: https://www.ddhairston100.com/

Instagram: dd_hairston

Facebook: DD Hairston

YouTube: **DDHairston 1oo**

Amazon: https://www.amazon.com/~/e/B0872GVH9M

Love Lee Unlimited

Email: beinglovelee@gmail.com

Instagram: ItsMeLoveLee

Facebook: Love Lee

Books By DD Hairston

Other Love Lee Author's

B.L. Burton

Manufactured by Amazon.ca
Bolton, ON